Praise for the Dark Alchemy Prequels to
Nine of Stars

DARK ALCHEMY

"This fun adventure in modern-day Wyoming introduces Petra Dee, a geologist looking for her missing father and trying to make peace with her past. Bickle (*Rogue Oracle*) adds a dash of romance to the charming adventure, wrapped up with a perfect ending."

Publishers Weekly (★starred review★)

"If *Dark Alchemy* was a movie, it'd pass the Bechdel Test and more than passes equity tests . . . . *Dark Alchemy* was a compelling read with a satisfying conclusion promising more Petra Dee stories set around Temperance. I'm hooked."

Dark Matter Zine

"Mix in some Native lore, great characterizations, a gift for bringing a setting to life, and a plot that eschews any hint of the tiredness of too much contemporary fantasy, and *Dark Alchemy*'s a winner on all fronts for this reader. Bickle writes with an individual clarity and style, leaving the reader to appreciate a dark sense of wonder that's all her own. Highly recommended."

Charles de Lint,
Fantasy & Science Fiction

"*Dark Alchemy* reads like a stand-alone work, but Petra is such a likable protagonist and the slightly off-balance world in which the town of Temperance exists is so well drawn that it's hard not to hope we'll see more of Petra's adventures. There are elements here that easily could have shaded into standard tropes, but Bickle is skilled enough to put her own spin on them, and she has a clear, clean sense of plotting that gives the novel a wonderful pace and sense of completeness. More, please."

RT BOOK *reviews* (4 ½ ★)

MERCURY RETROGRADE

"This wonderfully unusual Weird West novel combines the best of contemporary fantasy with metaphysical magic and mayhem, and even a bit of romance. Bickle has a knack for creating atmosphere, and she fills the fast-paced narrative with vivid scenes of wonder and a poignant story of death and rebirth. Fans of the first book will be enthralled, and new readers will easily fall into the quirky, dusty land that Petra and her unusual friends inhabit."

Publishers Weekly (★starred review★)

"Petra's adventures in a magic-choked version of Yellowstone continue to balance nicely with a sense of fun, well-done and subtle world-building and characterization, plus some serious stakes. The ramifications of *Dark Alchemy* are definitely felt—and in fact there are some interesting consequences readers might not have seen coming—and our protagonist is competent, resourceful and tough without becoming unrealistically formidable. The series feels like it's building splendidly, and there's certainly room for expansion."

RT BOOK*reviews* (4 ½ ★)

"Bickle's world and characters are enjoyably complex, sinking the reader happily into this contemporary fantasy landscape."

Omnivoracious

Also by Laura Bickle

NINE OF STARS

A WILDLANDS NOVEL

LAURA BICKLE

HARPER Voyager

An Imprint of HarperCollins Publishers

This is a work of fiction. Names, characters, places, and incidents are products of the author's imagination or are used fictitiously and are not to be construed as real. Any resemblance to actual events, locales, organizations, or persons, living or dead, is entirely coincidental.

Cover and interior spot art by Shutterstock.

NINE OF STARS. Copyright © 2017 by Laura Bickle. All rights reserved. Printed in the United States of America. No part of this book may be used or reproduced in any manner whatsoever without written permission except in the case of brief quotations embodied in critical articles and reviews. For information, address HarperCollins Publishers, 195 Broadway, New York, NY 10007.

First Harper Voyager mass market printing: January 2017

ISBN 978-0-06-243766-2

HARPER Voyager and) are trademarks of HCP LLC.

17 18 19 20 21   QGM   10 9 8 7 6 5 4 3 2 1

For my husband, Jason,
who understands winter.

NINE
OF STARS

CHAPTER 1

Falling Stars

Winter was always the cruelest season.

It had been true since the very beginning of the pack's collective memory. When the air turned sharp and crisped the leaves, the brutal cold was coming. The Nine Stars pack migrated away from their home in the summer valley, where the grasses were warm and teeming with newly born food. With the shadows of Canada geese flickering over them, the wolves of the pack followed herds of pronghorn to the gentler climate of the meadows. As the cold deepened, they culled the weak prey.

Winter was the wolves' glory.

Their coats grew shaggy and the fat thickened around their ribs as they worked the ragged edges of winter. Food in this territory had always been plentiful. As long as they stayed within the invisible boundaries of what men had deemed the park, laced with blacktop roads and fences, they were free. The ancestors of the Nine Stars pack would likely have considered this a gilded cage. Their ancestors were, after all, not quite wolves. But the Nine Stars pack had worn the skins of wolves for so long, they had forgotten what it was like to walk upright. They had grown both fat and feral, concerned with little more than seeing that their pups were fed and that men were avoided.

Until last winter. Last winter had been brutal, even by wolf standards. The pronghorn had fallen ill. The Nine Stars pack could smell it—their blood was all wrong. The prey began to bleed from their mouths and fell to the ice with steaming blue tongues. Humans had descended on them, shooting the infected and taking away the bodies.

Ever wary of men, the wolves had backed away. There was little food that winter; they subsisted on what they could steal from the otters and eagles. They lost two of the adults, and all three pups born that year, to starvation.

This winter there would be no such starving. Ghost, the alpha male, and Dancing Shadow, the alpha female, had decided to find a new winter range. Humans weren't much risk in this place. Nine, the omega, hadn't smelled any at all, not since they left the warm summer valley. The human roads were covered with snow and no lights or noisy machines had been seen in weeks. Nine suspected that the humans were as fearful of winter as most other creatures.

Nine was the omega, and she had no say in any of this. She simply followed, the last in line, nosing along behind the clumsy pups. There were only nine adults left, and four pups who had been born in spring. They were nearly as tall and lanky as the adults, but inexperienced in the ways of winter. Snow was still fascinating to the pups, and they blundered and rolled in the powder, play-fighting. It would become less of a novelty when it reached beyond the backs of their parents, but the small drifts were exciting now.

This was new terrain to Nine. She had heard tales of the northwest, that there was steaming colored water there that reeked of sulfur, where buffalo brined themselves in its warmth. Mountains so tall that one could lick the moon. She wasn't sure if these were pack stories or if they came from her own experience. She'd lost sense of her age and time. She only lived in the moment, suspended in the changing seasons of the wheel of the year.

But she was certain that this new place had to have better pickings than last winter, or she would not survive. Nine was skinnier than the others; her fur sank into the spaces between her ribs. As the omega, she ate last. She dreamed of a place plentiful enough that there would be more left for her than just the marrow.

They were climbing at night, over the rippling foothills of a mountain, when Ghost caught the scent of an elk up ahead. He made a soft yip, and Dancing Shadow slowed with the other mother, Starling, the pups ranging behind them in a tangle of skinny legs. They paused in the shadow of a stand of pines. The pups were old enough to try to tussle with an elk, but Dancing Shadow was an overprotective matriarch. They could watch, and learn. After losing all the pups last year, she would abide no risks to them.

Nine followed Ghost and the others, trotting across solitary hoof tracks that had not been scrubbed clean by the wind. Elk were formidable in herds, but a lone one might be an easy supper. Her mouth watered in anticipation.

Lightning nipped at her flank, and Nine growled halfheartedly, baring her teeth. Lightning was always harassing her to move faster, to plunge forward. Nine, frankly, didn't have the instincts that Lightning did. She hesitated. Which was why she was the omega.

There. Ahead. The full moonlight picked out a shadow. A massive rack of antlers splayed out over a dark figure on the ground.

He was down. Alone. He was food. Nine's heart soared.

Lightning was first, as always. He plunged into the snow, pale white fur a blur against his perfectly winter-camouflaged body. Nine ran as fast as she could, but Lighting was still faster. He was even faster than Ghost and the other, bigger males. It was a great point of pride for him to take the first chunk from prey, then offer it to Ghost. And they were all suffused in the heady thrill of the hunt.

Nine's nose wrinkled. The wind had changed and something smelled off. She had not smelled anything like it, not in her recent recollection. She reached back, deep into her ancestral memory . . .

She skidded to a stop and barked a warning.

But the others didn't hear her, or didn't care. Likely, they dismissed her as being too timid.

Lightning had reached the antlered shadow on the ground. He leapt upon the elk with teeth bared, snarling, reaching for its throat before it had a chance to try and get up.

But it was no elk. Human arms reached out of a black cloak winging open on the snow. Had a human hunter already claimed this prize? Would the man fight for the stag?

No. He *was* the stag. He walked upright on massive hooves. Antlers grew on either side of his head and he tossed them the way an angry elk would, at Lightning. A spur caught the wolf under the ribs, and the man-shaped creature flung the wolf away. Lightning shrieked as he hit the ground.

Nine crouched down, paws digging into the snow. Whatever this was, it was not human. Was it an old god of men, awake and angry? She glanced at Ghost for guidance. Ghost advanced upon the man, his white ruff raised, growling, with teeth bared. Nine and the others followed suit. If blood had been drawn, the pack would not allow this to go unpunished.

The Stag rose up to his full height. He was taller than any man should be, gathering night around him. His cloak was made of pelts—pelts of wolves, she realized. If she concentrated, she could smell the fear that still clung to them. His long-fingered claws glittered around bone knives.

He lowered his head, and his eyes glowed behind a mask of bone.

"You will pay for what you did," he growled, in a voice rusted black with hate.

Nine's instinct was to flee. People scared her, enough that she would go miles out of her way to avoid them. They were terrible, with their guns and cars and traps, killing things that they would not even bother to eat. She would rather face an angry bison than a man on any day. And this was not even a man. This was something more. This creature smelled like sour magic, like rotten carrion too spoiled for vultures to touch. Every instinct in her urged her to *run*.

And in another time, another place, the pack might have run. But the Stag had hurt Lightning, flinging the pale wolf into a snowdrift. The wolf bounced and flipped like a salmon plucked out of the river and flung to earth by a bear, red spotting his hide.

This was not something that Ghost would permit. The alpha wolf lunged for the Stag, and the other wolves in the pack followed suit, kicking up snow. There was, after all, only one of him. And the wolves of Nine Stars acted as one.

The Stag spun in the powder, his fur cloak scraping bare earth. Ghost's teeth clamped down on his arm, but the Stag shook him off with a mighty thrash, sending Ghost sliding across the ground with a yelp. Bent Arrow and Falling Stone leaped on his back, sending the Stag reeling, clawing and snarling.

Nine dove in low, her paws digging into the frozen earth, nipping at his knees. Her stomach wrenched, tasting fear and the stink of magic on his skin. But she held on as the Stag crashed to earth. She worked her jaws back and forth, expecting to taste a gush of hot blood.

But there was no blood. Nothing—it was like biting a sapless stick.

Yelps of pain rattled across the snow. Lightning had rejoined the fray, slamming his white paws into the Stag's chest.

The Stag lowered his head, the cage of sharp antlers aimed at Lighting.

Nine tried to hold fast but was kicked away with a blow that drove the breath from her lungs. She landed in the snow, whimpering, in enough time to see the Stag pin Lightning to the ground, goring him.

Ghost howled, tearing at the Stag's cloak. But it was no use. The antlers had pinned the squirming wolf to the ground. A great red stain spread out from Lightning's hide to the snow.

He was done for. They knew it. They could see it in the way his eyes rolled back, showing the whites, in his cry and the way red foam leaked from his mouth.

The Stag lashed his head from side to side, flinging Lightning's body away. He turned to face the rest of the wolves, stinking and bloodless.

Ghost gave three yips: a retreat.

The wolves limped to his side, loping over the bloodied drifts. Nine struggled to her feet, wheezing, and tried to follow as best she could.

She looked back over her shoulder. The Stag had picked up Lightning's body by the scruff of his neck and brought his knife to the wolf's throat. A trickle of steam leaked into the darkness as the blade slid through the carcass.

She couldn't look anymore. Limping, she ran.

She didn't understand what she'd seen, but she

knew instinctively that this thing that was shaped like a man and fought like a beast would be the end of them all.

THERE WERE SEVEN stages of grief and seven stages of alchemy. To Petra Dee, this was no coincidence.

She sat in a chair in a doctor's office, staring out the window. Her hands were folded in her lap, underneath her battered leather coat. She'd made some effort to look respectable today, wearing dark jeans and the cleanest pair of boots she had. Her blond hair was pulled back in a ponytail. She didn't own an iron or an ironing board, so her white dress shirt was a bit rumpled. She had tried to hide that fact by rolling her sleeves up, maybe making it a fashion statement, but the effort only served to show the scars on her arms: a burned handprint, slashes, and a pale speckle from corrosive acid. The doctor had asked about these during her exam, probably fishing for some evidence that she'd cut herself. Petra had simply said that she'd had a colorful life, but her voice had quivered when she said it. If she'd told him that the handprint had been the last touch of a lover who died in a fire, he'd have referred her to grief counseling. If she had confessed that the slashes were from an attack by a drug lord, he'd write her a prescription for a few weeks of Klonopin. And if she dared tell him that the speckle was from the blood of a basilisk she'd taken to the spirit world . . . well. He'd have the looney bin on speed-dial and be offering her a new white jacket with fancy hardware.

She reached up to rub her thumb over the back of the gold pendant at her throat. It had been a gift from her father, a self-proclaimed alchemist. It depicted a green lion devouring the sun, a powerful alchemical symbol of transformation. In the last weeks, she'd developed the nervous habit of rubbing it like a worry stone. It seemed to have no more power than that, no matter how much she willed it to be different.

Petra had seen magic before, things she couldn't easily explain. But her scientist's mind was still trying. She was that, before all else. She was a geologist, a scientist. She worked with her hands in the dirt and her eye in a microscope. She believed in laws and rules and the miracle of deductive reasoning.

But she was also the daughter of an alchemist. She had seen amazing things, felt shocking wonder and bewildering pain that left physical scars behind. But grief touched her most deeply now, as she gazed outside the window.

A man in a parka was rolling a black body bag on a gurney across a freshly shoveled sidewalk. A nondescript van, filthy with a coating of blackened road salt, had pulled up to the back entrance, and a man in a snowsuit came out to load the body into the back. Apparently, hearses didn't have four-wheel drive.

There were seven stages of grief, weren't there? She seemed to remember that from a college psychology class. Shock, denial, anger, bargaining, guilt, depression, and acceptance. Was that the right number? She felt as if she'd jumped straight into guilt and had been swimming through it without coming up for air. In the last few months, she felt she'd managed to screw up her own life and the lives of everyone around her. Go directly to guilt in the game of life. Do not pass go. Do not collect two hundred dollars. Did the stages have to be worked through sequentially for a healthy psyche? She couldn't remember. Probably.

Alchemy seemed to be more or less sequential: calcination, dissolution, separation, conjunction, fermentation, distillation . . . and . . . coagulation? Was that the last one? Her brow knit. She'd have to ask her father. He'd give her a right proper lecture about it, and then warn her about the perils of skipping around . . . if he didn't fall asleep in his oatmeal midway through. Petra had never worked alchemy herself, but she understood enough to know that in some idealized world that didn't exist, the processes should be worked in sequence, and *Ta-da!*— gold or eternal life to the winner. Player's choice.

The door opened, and Petra turned.

A thin man in a white doctor's coat held a folder

with her name on it. "Good morning, Ms. Dee." He reached over to shake her hand. His hand was cold as lunch meat.

"Good morning, Dr. Hoffer." Petra had picked him out on the Internet. He seemed about as qualified as she was going to find in this neck of the woods, and he took her insurance.

Dr. Hoffer slid behind his scarred wooden desk and opened her file. "I wanted to talk with you about your test results in person."

"Of course." It was never good when a doctor wanted to see you in person. Never. But Petra had been hoping that this guy was just old-fashioned. For chrissakes, he still kept paper records and had a corded phone on his desk. She twisted her fingers together in her lap.

"How have you been since I last saw you? Anything unusual?"

She shook her head. "Nope." *Other than the complete insanity that my life seems to be? Should I tell you about my dad's latest crackpot theory about the composition of the universe, that ether is a real thing that can be created in a bottle? Maybe you want to hear about where I lost my shoes on my last trip to the spirit world? How about the underground world beneath the Tree of Life, where the undead sleep? Yeah. No.*

He opened the folder. "Your blood work shows some significant abnormalities. Your white blood cell count is elevated, as was noted by the ER in your last visit. You have enlarged lymph nodes, and you'll remember we did a needle biopsy of your right axillary lymph node, to see if there's sign of infection."

Petra resisted the urge to rub under her arm; it still hurt like a sonofabitch, even more than a tetanus shot. "And?"

"I'm afraid that it looks as if you have leukemia."

She sat back in her chair, silent. Fuck. No candy-coating that.

The doctor continued. "Based on your history of exposure to chemicals in the petrochemical industry, it's likely that you have acute myeloid leukemia. Exposure to benzene is a risk factor in such a diagnosis."

She nodded. She'd been up to her neck in petroleum for years before she came to the quiet-seeming town of Temperance, Wyoming. "Okay. So . . . how advanced is it? What's the treatment? How do I fit that around my work schedule?" Her brain was already trying to leapfrog ahead to the next stage.

"I'm going to send you to the university for treatment. They will want to do a bone marrow biopsy. The results will determine the course of treatment. They'll probably discuss chemotherapy with you. That can last weeks or months, depending on a number of factors."

Her hand slipped up to her neck, and her thumb

rubbed the back of her pendant. "Will this be on an outpatient basis? Or will I be hospitalized for the treatment?"

"We're really getting ahead of ourselves." Dr. Hoffer closed the file folder. "The important thing is that we get a handle on the extent of the problem, and then work to find the optimal course of action."

She gave a sharp nod. That sounded eminently rational.

"I'll go get a referral set up for you. Please take your time." He awkwardly slid a box of tissues across the desk to her, though her eyes were dry.

"Thank you very much."

The doctor patted her on the shoulder ineffectually on the way out. He closed the door, and Petra stared out the window at the empty sidewalk. Soft shock settled over her, like snow, and she recognized it for what it was, this muffled reaction. Stage one of grief.

And it occurred to her that perhaps this was the one process she was finally doing in order.

PETRA RETURNED HOME in late afternoon. The sky spat intermittent snowflakes, and a white sun peered through the blanket of grey clouds overhead. She had no memory of the actual drive to her Airstream trailer at the edge of town, which bothered her. She stopped her 1970s-vintage Ford

Bronco before the trailer and shut off the ignition, listening to the engine settle.

She glanced at the referral paperwork and informational brochures she'd been given. In a flash of anger, she stuffed the papers in the glove box and slammed it shut as hard as she could. She stared at the closed glove box. Something about stuffing that diagnosis into a small space and slamming the door on it seemed to take away its power, like it didn't really exist. She tried not to think about it sitting there in cold darkness, festering with her car insurance paperwork, registration, and bits of used-up pens.

She jumped down from the truck and shut the door quietly. Crossing the snow to the front door of the trailer, she saw her footprints from earlier in the morning, coming back to meet her in a slushy loop.

As she opened the front door to the trailer, an avalanche of grey fur fell over her, licking her face. Petra squirmed through the door and shut it behind her as her coyote companion wriggled with joy at seeing her.

"Hi, Sig. Sweet fellow, you."

She sank to the linoleum floor, letting the keys fall and wrapping both arms around Sig's neck. His heart thumped against her cheek, and tears slipped between her cheek and his fur.

Sig whined and leaned close against her.

"Yeah. It didn't go well. And it may not go well from here on out." She lifted her hands to the sides of his head. Her nose was drippy and she snuffled ungracefully. "I want you to know that I'll make sure that you're taken care of. No matter what, okay?"

Sig pressed his head into her chest. She stroked his soft ears with her fingers, tracing the gold flecks of his coat and the edge of his collar. She would do right by him.

She scrubbed her face with her palm, took a deep breath, and climbed to her feet. The trailer was empty, and she was grateful for the solitude. But a cup of coffee sat on the kitchen table. She placed her hand around the cup. It was lukewarm. She lifted it, drained it, and peered out the window over the sink.

A man stood out in the snowy field, alone, unmoving. She watched him. A trio of ravens walked across the field, muttering to themselves, seeming to ignore him.

After some time, she put the cup in the sink and walked out the door. Sig came with her, tangling around her legs, ears twitching. Her boots crunched down the steps and followed the tracks around the trailer, out to the field.

The ravens spied her immediately and took wing, cawing.

The man in the field watched them go, his amber

eyes swallowing up their flight patterns in the grey sky. Petra stepped up beside him, her hands in her pockets.

"Any luck yet?" she asked him.

"No." Gabriel shook his head. "They won't speak to me."

Sig snorted through the ravens' tracks on the ground. Petra spied bits of things strewn in the snow meant to lure them in: gum wrappers, cat food kibble, and bottle caps. Sig fell upon the bits of kibble in delight, picking through the shiny bits of metal for the treats.

Petra's mouth flattened. Gabe had been trying to connect with the ravens, spending hours in silence in the field every day until she'd come out to lead him in. He was lost, somewhere on the land, missing the sky. Once upon a time, he'd been one of them.

As a Hanged Man, he'd been nearly invincible and immortal, living in Temperance at the margins of the living world for more than a hundred fifty years. He'd split his time between land and sky, shifting effortlessly from earthbound flesh to weightless feathers. "You miss them," she blurted, unnecessarily.

"I miss them," he said.

She reached for his hand. It felt cold and lifeless in hers.

He nodded wordlessly. The Hanged Men had

always worked at the nearby Rutherford Ranch, but Sal Rutherford had been the cruelest master his bloodline had ever produced. When the Hanged Men finally rebelled against his domination over magic he didn't understand, Sal had burned the Alchemical Tree of Life, the Lunaria, in revenge. Sal had gotten what was coming to him, but the damage was done.

"I destroyed all of it." Gabe was pale.

"You should come in. You'll get frostbite." It felt as if she was reminding him that he was human. She didn't do it to be cruel; she hoped he knew that. With the death of the tree, Gabe had become mortal, powerless, and all the men he'd lived and fought and worked with were now dead. He was the last of them. Petra couldn't imagine what that felt like. She led him away, through the field and back to the trailer.

His brow wrinkled, as if he just remembered that she'd been gone. "How was . . . your trip?"

She squinted out at the white afternoon sun, trying to break through the clouds. "It was fine. Roads weren't bad. Got behind a plow, and hung back a half mile."

"That's good." His eyes were still scraping the sky, hunting for ravens.

"Yeah."

She couldn't bring herself to tell him. Not yet.

CHAPTER 2

The Vanishing of Sal Rutherford

A crime had been committed. He could feel it in his bones. He knew that something awful had happened to an equally awful person.

He just couldn't prove it.

Owen had been poring over Sal Rutherford's ranch with a fine-tooth comb these last several weeks. Sal, the fat old bastard, had vanished. Normally, the disappearance of a pitch-perfect asshole would not bother Owen in the slightest. Assholes vanished every day, and that was not a bad thing for public order. But Sal was his cousin, and he was supposed to do *something* about it. As the county sheriff, Owen knew he'd look pretty damn ineffectual if he couldn't keep track of his own relatives.

Owen jammed his hands into his uniform coat

pockets as he gazed over Sal's snowy field. He still thought of it as Sal's field. If Sal had met a bad end, then all this land would become his, instead. It was vast—hundreds of acres of cattle, grass, and hills that had been in the family for a hundred fifty years. He wasn't sure how he felt about that. Maybe in a larger jurisdiction this would be one of those things that would be considered a conflict of interest, and he'd punt the investigation over to someone from a nearby city or to the state for the sake of appearances. There sure was enough muttering behind his back about Sal's impressive collection of enemies, but there was no one else to take over in this place where cows outnumbered people.

Owen reached into his pocket for a cigarette, lit it, and squinted at the field. Cows milled through the snow, oblivious to Sal's absence. Sal's house, too, had been pretty much in order. There'd been no signs of a tussle, and a good dousing of Luminol had shown there were no scrubbed-up puddles of blood hidden under the rugs. Sal's truck had been parked in the driveway with a full tank of gas and a curious smell of something burnt on the upholstery. Whatever had happened to Sal, it hadn't been at the house.

And it wasn't as if Sal had gone on a spontaneous trip. The old bastard wasn't well. Last time Owen had seen him, liver cancer was eating him alive. He was pretty much confined to a wheel-

chair, except for a few bouts of drunken lurching
around with his cane. Sal's motorized wheelchair
was here, in the house, and the scooter was parked
in the garage, fully charged.

Sal's closets had seemed undisturbed. Dusty
suitcases remained in the corners, and his drawers
hadn't been emptied of socks. If he was heading
to Florida to relax, he would have at least packed
his sunglasses. The only things Owen couldn't find
were his keys and his wallet.

The one weird thing that Owen had found was
a burned tree in the back forty of Sal's property. It
might just be coincidence, but he came back here,
again and again, to stare at the blackened timber.
The tree had fought through the fire, a new sapling growing from the roots. Owen's men had
found traces of gasoline. Someone had deliberately
burned it. Maybe this was something simple, like
the old tree had been harboring a nest of yellow
jackets. Maybe the ranch hands had waited until it
got cold outside and the bees grew sluggish enough
to burn it, and the fire got a bit out of control.

But it bothered him.

And the ranch hands bothered him. Sal had
more than a dozen men that did his bidding.
Creepy guys. Owen and his deputies avoided them
as much as possible. They were Sal's private goon
squad, and Owen turned a blind eye to their activi-
ties in his official capacity as sheriff.

But that was the weird thing. Sal was gone, and so were all the ranch hands. Nobody had seen them, anywhere. All the vehicles were accounted for on the property. Owen had to scramble to hire some temp workers to make sure the cattle got fed and watered.

So. It wasn't just one disappearance. This was a mass vanishing. Maybe Sal had taken his men and gone to do some dirty business somewhere and would return, smug and full of himself, tomorrow. Maybe the ranch hands had had enough of Sal, killed him, hid his body, and split. Owen was thinking that was more likely. Sal had never developed any people skills.

"Sheriff, what's your twenty?" a voice crackled over the radio receiver clipped to his collar.

Owen keyed it. "Rutherford back forty. What's up?"

"You wanted an APB put out for all the ranch hands and Sal. We got one put out for Sal, but . . . we're having problems with the rest."

"What do you mean?"

"There's not a whole lot of information on these guys. We found pictures of a couple of 'em on the surveillance camera at the post office. Got some descriptions from the hardware store owner, and he's working with a sketch artist."

"What about names?"

"We searched to see if anyone besides Sal has a valid driver's license that lists the Rutherford

Ranch as a home address. We got a bunch of names that were dead ends, with no corresponding records, but there are photos. One of which looks an awful lot like the surveillance video. We checked the registrations of all the vehicles on the property, and they all go back to Sal."

"Payroll records?"

"None. No checks cashed through the bank or written by Sal."

Owen rubbed the dark beard on his chin. "Howsabout you get someone over here to dust for prints in the barn and the house. Run those through CODIS and see if we get any hits. I want to know who these guys are."

"Roger that, Sheriff."

Owen clicked off the radio and stared at the tree. He was expecting that at least half of 'em would come back with priors. Most ranch hands drifted around, working for cash under the table, not looking for a helluva lot of scrutiny. But these guys . . . it was like they were ghosts.

He took a drag on his cigarette. He'd figure it out. People just didn't vanish into thin air, especially in small towns.

"Do you think Sal's dead?"

Owen looked up. A little girl sat on the lowest burned branch of the tree. She was about nine, her blond hair stringy wet and green with algae. She was dressed in jeans and a pink T-shirt with glitter

that had worn off, and a hoodie covered in a car-
toon cat print. Only one sneaker dangled from her
right foot. She looked him right in the eye as she
spoke, the way a good hallucination should.

Owen tossed his cigarette away in the snow. No
one was around to hear him. "Probably," he admitted.

"Why?"

"Sal's the kind of guy who deserves to get mur-
dered," he blurted. He regretted it as soon as the
words escaped his mouth. But it was true.

The girl lowered her eyes. "Did I?"

"No." He was able to say that with true conviction.

NOT THAT HE knew many details about the girl's
death. On his first day as a sheriff's deputy, Owen
had responded to a call from a hunter who said
he'd found what looked like a human head in the
bottom of a well. The hunter had hiked three miles
to the nearest spot where he could get cell recep-
tion, and was waiting by the side of the road for
Owen to show up.

Owen had answered the call by himself. That
wasn't the way things were supposed to go. Rook-
ies were supposed to be supervised at all times by
a more senior deputy, and Owen sure as hell made
sure that policy was followed when he became
sheriff. Newbs could get hurt or get somebody else

hurt. But on this day, Owen's dad, the sheriff at the time, had sent him on a run to go pick up coffee filters.

Yeah, coffee filters. Super-duper official business. A harmless enough errand.

Nonetheless, Owen was psyched to go on a run by himself. Even if it was for fucking coffee filters. His uniform was freshly starched. His badge was shiny, and he was full of a sense of his own destiny. And when the local store was out of coffee filters, he went to the feed store to check to see if they had any. They did. He also picked up a pound of the fancy ground stuff to make a good impression on his coworkers, and a root beer for himself. He caught the eye of the checkout girl, tipped his hat and made her blush. She was a cute blond girl with blue eyes and a tattoo of a daisy on her wrist. Sharella. He got her number and whistled to himself when he walked out to the leaf-strewn parking lot.

Everything was right with the world, dammit.

The autumn sky was a cloudless blue, and Indian summer had drenched the land in sunshine. He rolled down the windows on the cruiser, took the chance to gun the engine on a straightaway to feel how fast the car would go. He'd pegged a hundred thirty, felt the wind whipping through the cruiser and getting caught in the cage behind his seat. He let out a whoop of sheer joy and dangled his left hand out of the window to feel the wind rush through his splayed fingers.

He almost missed the radio. Cindy, the dispatcher, was trying to raise some noise.

". . . Delta Five, what's your twenty?"

Owen took his foot off the gas, cranked the windows up, cleared his throat, and keyed the dash radio. Dammit. He'd taken too long, and now they were checking up on him. "Base, this is Delta Five. I'm at Harbinger and Route 12."

"Got a call from a civilian at Stout's Run. Please check in on him for a 10-17 before you return to base." The dispatcher made a half-chortle that got cut off by the radio key.

"Roger, that."

Owen reached in his pocket for his cheat sheet of radio codes. A 10-17 was "meet complainant." Stout's Run was way back in the boonies. There was literally no one out there but moose. This was feeling like a prank. He sighed, pretty sure there was no way to avoid being hazed as the new kid on the block, regardless of who his father was. Hell, his dad was probably in on it.

Owen turned down the gravel road at Stout's Run. The road was bordered by quaking aspen with brilliant yellow leaves. A man in a quilted flannel coat was standing beside the road in a bright orange hunter's cap. He had a gun slung over his shoulder. Owen recognized him—Larry

Marten was a known person to the law. His dad had reeled him in many times for public intoxication and DUIs. Larry had never hurt anybody, not even when he was found asleep behind the wheel of his car in the middle of the highway last June. He'd stopped for a deer, he said, but apparently didn't bother to start back up again. Larry was famous for telling stories—he'd seen Bigfoot three times and Jesus twice.

"Larry," Owen said, climbing out of the cruiser. "You need a ride somewhere?"

Larry had his arms crossed over his chest, and the man's craggy face was pale. "I saw somethin' back there, somethin' I need to show you."

"Okay. Like what? Bigfoot or something?"

Larry shook his head. "Uh-uh. Something bad."

Owen reached back for his radio and gave his position, all according to the book. Larry wouldn't tell him what was up, and Cindy was irritated. Owen decided to just follow the guy, look at the Bigfoot tracks, and then drop Larry back off at his home.

He followed Larry into the forest. The old coot walked noiselessly, but there was an odd silence about the forest. No birds gossiped overhead, and no squirrels bickered in the underbrush.

"So, you gonna tell me what you seen?" Owen asked, wanting to fill the silence.

"I was out here, lookin' for squirrel," Larry said. "Fell asleep."

"You been drinking?"

"Nope."

"You know you can't be carrying a firearm under the influence, Larry." Owen didn't figure on making Larry his first arrest. That was kind of pathetic, really aiming for the low-hanging fruit.

"I swear I'm sober. Right hand to God." Larry raised his hand.

Owen did a field sobriety test on him. The man could follow his finger with his eyes, walk a straight line, and recite the alphabet forward and backward.

"So, what did you see?" Owen wanted to know, feeling impatient.

"I woke up after my nap, got thirsty. I went to this well. Over there." He pointed to a worn circle of stones, partially obscured by a drift of golden leaves. A broken tripod perched above it, from which a piece of nylon rope, bleached white by the weather, dangled.

"Ohhkayy," Owen said slowly.

"And somethin' came up in the bucket. It looked like a human head."

Inwardly, Owen rolled his eyes. He was being pranked, he knew it. "Halloween was two weeks ago, Larry."

"I ain't lyin'. Go look."

Owen circled around the opposite side of the well. He wasn't taking any chances that Larry might push him in. He reached out for the fuzzy rope and yanked back.

A plastic bucket banged hollowly against the side of the well. The bucket lurched up over the edge and landed on Owen's shoe, spilling out black muck.

And a skull rolled out into the leaves. It was smallish, about the size of a cantaloupe, with strands of blond hair clinging to a bit of leathery flesh at the brow.

Owen stepped back, heart and guts slamming into his throat. "Jesusfuckingchrist."

"See? I told ya."

Owen turned away, keyed his radio. "Base, this is Delta Five. Come in." He fumbled in his shirt pocket for his card of codes. There wasn't a fucking code for what he wanted. There was one for animal carcasses, but nothing for *Fuck! I found a human body!*

"Delta Five, this is Base."

"Base, I've got a 10-78 . . . uh, 10-79." According to the card in his shaking hand: *Need assistance. Notify coroner.*

"Delta Five, you need assistance with . . . a 10-79? Confirm, please." Cindy clearly thought he'd lost his card or his marbles.

"10-78," he repeated. "10-79."

"Roger that. Hold your position."

"10-4."

He released the radio key, took ten paces away, and vomited into the shrubbery. The vomit obliterated some of the black goo on his shoe, for which he was thankful. After emptying the contents of his stomach, he took a deep breath and turned back to the well.

Larry was just standing there, staring at the skull, looking shocked.

"You should back away from that," Owen said, without much conviction.

Larry stayed rooted in place.

Owen didn't push the issue. He made himself peer into the well, shine his flashlight down into the darkness. He could see nothing but black water reflecting the noonday sun.

Within an hour, the whole place was crawling with cops. Owen returned to the cruiser, where he filled out every form he could find, in longhand, on the dashboard.

The passenger door opened and Owen's father slid into the passenger seat. He put his hat on the dash and rubbed his brow.

"Helluva first day," he said.

"Yeah," Owen agreed.

"You did good," his dad said.

"Yeah." Owen wasn't convinced. Mostly because that was the only time his dad had ever told him that.

He drank himself into oblivion that night. He stopped at the drive-through liquor store on his way home, filled his trunk, and drank so much when he got home that he passed out on in his own bathtub, fully dressed. He wasn't sure what he'd been thinking, but he awoke in his clothes in a pool of tepid water, staring up at the buzzing fluorescent light with the world's worst headache. It was quite probable that he'd pissed himself. A lot.

Something moved behind the shower curtain.

Owen splashed in the water, reaching for a gun belt that wasn't there. He knocked over his shampoo bottle and soaked the floor.

A little girl stood on his soggy bathmat, peering in at him.

"Hello," she said.

"Gah!" Owen said. "What . . . what are you doing here?"

"I'm not sure." She screwed up her face and stared into the bath. "I think I came home with you."

"Where are your parents?" Owen panted.

"I don't know."

And the little girl faded right in front of him, like a photograph bleeding ink into water.

"Shit. Shit. Shit." Owen clambered out of the bathtub. He'd clearly been hallucinating. Water rained from his clothes onto the tile floor, and he reached down to drain the tub. He stripped off his waterlogged clothes and wrapped himself in a robe. He ripped open the medicine cabinet and stuffed his face with aspirin.

He promised never to drink that much again. But he failed.

Five days later, the coroner got back to the office with her report. The body had belonged to a nine-year-old little girl. Anna Jean Sawarski. She had blond hair and blue eyes, and her school picture looked just like the girl who appeared in Owen's bathroom. She'd been missing for seven months.

Owen had insisted on going along with his father to break the news to her parents. There was shrieking and howling and wailing to Jesus. The couple got divorced right afterward, and then the dad killed the mom in a murder-suicide in the parking lot of a waffle shop at two A.M. The patrons said they were arguing about whose fault it was that Anna was dead.

The other night had been hallucinatory coincidence, he thought. He had fully dried out after his bender and even made himself sit through a church service. He went directly home, didn't watch the news, and went to bed.

He awoke in darkness, under that prickly blanket of feeling that someone was watching him.

He opened his eyes. The blond girl was leaning over, peering at him. He bit his tongue, and could feel it. He wasn't dreaming.

"Hi," she said.

"Are you Anna?" he whispered.

"Yeah." She had a piece of hair tangled in her fingers, picking at the mold on the ends.

"Why aren't you in . . . in heaven?" He struggled to sit upright. He clicked on the lamp, and the girl remained standing there, in her pink hoodie, jeans, and one sneaker.

"I don't know." She shrugged. "I just know that I'm here and not in that cold place."

Owen was never able to solve her death. Any usable evidence had rotted away, and the coroner couldn't even give a good cause of death, declaring it "undetermined." The bucket and the rope still sat in a banker's box in Owen's office. The case haunted him. And so did Anna, literally. At first, she appeared only at night. Then, during the day. And then she'd disappear for a week. Some days, he was convinced that she was just a projection of his own guilt about not being able to solve the crime. Other days, he was convinced that she really was a ghost. He wasn't sure which possibility baked his noodle more.

But he threw out the pair of boots that he'd vomited on. And Sharella's number from the feed store. She was blond and had blue eyes, and Owen couldn't stomach the possibility of dating a blond girl who might someday, if the stars aligned right, give him a blond child who looked like Anna.

ANNA HAD HAUNTED Owen for ten years now. He was used to it, he guessed.

Anna swung down from the tree. "Do you care?" she asked.

"Do I care about what?"

"Do you care if Sal's dead?" Anna was nothing if not direct.

Owen shrugged. "I don't like him."

"Did you kill him?"

Owen was sure that was the question on the lips of everyone behind his back. He had the most to gain from Sal's death, as the next in line to inherit the Rutherford Ranch. The cousins tolerated each other publicly, and Owen did his best to sweep Sal's messes under the rug whenever he could. But there was no love lost between them.

"Nope." Owen looked up at the sky. "But I'm sure gonna find the sonofabitch who did. And when I do . . . I'll shake his hand before I ship him off to the electric chair."

CHAPTER 3

The View from Above

Petra hadn't yet gotten used to the sound of Gabe breathing.

Well, it wasn't exactly breathing. It was more like snoring.

Moonlight reflected off the snow through the Airstream's window blinds, rendering night as bright as a cloudy morning. She glanced at Gabe sleeping beside her on the futon. From a century and a half of sleeping in the glowing embrace of the Alchemical Tree of Life, he was clearly accustomed to sleeping with the lights on, and bright moonlight didn't faze him. He'd somehow figured out a way to snore softly with his mouth closed. It was intermittent and shouldn't have been too terribly annoying, but she found it disconcerting. He had a pulse now, one that she could hear if she turned her head the right way against his shoulder. She wasn't sure whether to be happy for him now that he was mortal, or worried about him. Maybe it was because it seemed to her that he hadn't yet decided for himself if becoming human was a good thing.

Sig did *not* think this was a good thing. He sat on Petra's stomach and stared at Gabe as he snored, eyes shining in the dark. He cocked his head and looked at Petra, as if to say, *This is all your fault.*

Petra sighed, trying to shift her bladder out from under Sig's back foot. Gabe had chivalrously offered to sleep on the floor when he'd come to stay. Perhaps she should have let him do that. Sig certainly seemed to think so; he resented the loss of his sprawling area on the futon, and had expressed that displeasure by sleeping on Gabe's chest with his ass in the man's face more than once.

She wondered if Gabe dreamed. Wondering about his internal workings kept her from thinking about her own problems, which she was determined not to face. Not yet. Not today.

She watched the light grow less sharp as the moon set, and eventually slipped out of bed to shower and get ready for work. Sig rolled over to her side of the futon with a dramatic *harrumph,* but got up when she'd dressed and was ready to leave.

She leaned over Gabe to kiss him. She knew she

needed to explain to him what was happening. It seemed they were in a moment of stasis in their lives right now, and she knew that it couldn't last.

His lips curved in a smile as she kissed him. She resolved to tell him about the diagnosis when she got home from work. For now . . . he'd been through a lot, and it was worth so much to see him peacefully sleeping. Letting him sleep, Petra slipped out into the cold winter with Sig.

She pushed the snow off the Bronco with a broom and climbed into the truck to start it. She let it warm up for several minutes, watching the stars fade through the windshield. Sig snuggled into his fleece blanket on the cold bench seat, rolling about as if to make the point that he was pleased to finally have room to stretch out.

The engine chattered sluggishly, and she tooled down the gravel road that led into Temperance, the nearby town. There were no other cars on the road at this hour, and the one main street was dark. The only light emanated from the single stoplight set permanently on flashing red, and Bear's Gas 'n Go convenience store. She stopped at Bear's to fill up the Bronco. She meant to get a coffee for herself but decided to buy orange juice and a yogurt cup, instead. She also picked up a bottle of multivitamins. The only kind Bear had in stock were the animal-shaped ones for kids, but she figured they were good enough. Her body was going to be going through hell soon, and she needed to get a head start on getting healthy.

Bear gave her a lifted eyebrow. It was intimidating, coming from a big, bearded man who could have been a lumberjack in a previous life. "You aren't dieting, are you?"

"No." To assuage his concerns, she picked a sandwich out of the case that she intended to feed to Sig. She made a face at the coyote, who had delicately plucked a stick of beef jerky off a low-hanging display.

"You don't need to lose any weight." The burly man stabbed the keys on the register. "You wouldn't believe the girls that come in here, looking like Popsicle sticks, refusing to let a carb pass their lips, but smoking like chimneys." He pointed at her. "You are not allowed to get on that bandwagon, young lady."

Petra lifted her hands. "No worries. You know I can be trusted to do the right thing with a hoagie."

"I'm watching you." Bear slid an oatmeal chocolate chip muffin across the counter at her.

She took a bite to be polite and it melted in her mouth in warm, chocolate lava. It couldn't have been more than fifteen minutes out of the oven. "Oh my fucking God, Bear . . . when did you start with *these* bits of heaven?"

He crossed his arms over his chest, a grin spreading above his beard. "I've been experimenting with doing a breakfast spread since I started watching those cooking shows on the Food Channel. You're my first guinea pig for the muffins."

"You must make these." She nearly leaned over the counter to threaten him.

"Come early. They roll outta the oven around five. I'll set another aside for you tomorrow."

"Deal." She reached over the counter to shake his hand.

The muffin had disappeared by the time she got back to the Bronco. It felt like warm, gooey love in her stomach, like optimism. She opened the vitamin bottle and dumped the first one into her hand. The candy-flavored purple bear-shaped vitamin made her feel like she was eight years old again at her mom's kitchen counter.

"Maybe today will be a better day than yesterday," she chirped at Sig, who had crawled under his plaid blanket, exposing only his tail. His tail wagged, which was a good sign. She opened his sandwich and delivered it under the blanket. The tail continued to wag, while chewing sounds emanated from Sig's nest.

The sun was beginning to lighten the horizon by the time they got back on the road, headed to Yellowstone National Park. Snow had smudged the borders of the road, pushing across in waves. Petra glanced at the snow markers beside the shoulder, which recorded wintertime snow levels by colorful marks on poles. She wasn't looking forward to four feet of it.

The old dinosaur of a truck plunged forward, winding into the park with sure traction on brand-new snow tires. Just in case, she had chains rattling around in the back, a shovel, and a bag of kitty litter. She hoped she wouldn't need them, but better safe than sorry. Winter so far had been relatively mild for this part of the country, but she didn't expect it to last.

The summer and fall had seen the roads packed with tourists. This time of winter, the park felt abandoned. She passed no traffic on the road in, and the only sign of human habitation she saw was a couple of snowmobilers in a distant white field. The economy had taken a nosedive lately, but she expected to see more winter-sports enthusiasts than were here. Lodgepole pines bent under the weight of snow, nodding at each other in what looked like a conspiracy of trees. A herd of bison meandered through a valley, and a lone tourist was taking pictures of them with a telephoto lens.

She stopped off at the Tower Falls Ranger Station, her home base, to gather her paperwork for the day. There were only two ranger vehicles parked outside today, covered in a blanket of snow. The old log structure looked like something out of a Cur-

rier and Ives china pattern, a spot of darkness in
the white, with smoke churning from the chimney.

She hoped to get in and out, to pick up some of
her geology gear without talking to anyone. Her
friend, Ranger Mike Hollander, worked here, but
she wasn't much up for company. But when she
opened the door, he was sitting at the counter with
another ranger, the two of them squinting at an up-
turned plastic cup on the counter.

"Morning, gentlemen." Petra stomped snow off
her boots on the mat inside the door, as Sig trotted
around her legs to find his water dish in the back
conference room.

"Morning, sunshine." Mike wagged his fingers
in a wave and continued to stare at the cup.

"It's a little early for beer pong, isn't it?"

The men made noncommittal noises and didn't
look up from the cup. Petra had noticed that things
got weird late in the season here, when tourists
were few and far between. Most rangers used the
time to catch up on paperwork, futz around with
neglected indoor projects, develop education pro-
grams, and the like. But there were always moments of sheer boredom. Last time she'd popped
in, she'd interrupted a game of chess played on
the floor with pine cones and pop cans on squares
made of legal paper. She wasn't sure what the rules
were for ranger-chess, but there was a moat of
potato chips and something that looked like a por-

cupine made of sticks that seemed to have the ability to knock pine cones off the playing field with a rubber-band catapult.

The cup slowly moved across the counter.

"I was *not* shitting you," Mike confirmed to the other ranger.

Petra peered over Mike's shoulder. "What the hell is that?"

"It fell out of the ceiling." Mike pointed upward to the rafters.

Petra squinted. She had a hard time imagining that termites got big enough to move cups on their own.

The other ranger lifted the cup, while Mike laced his fingers like a cage over the critter beneath.

"It's a bat," Petra exclaimed. A tiny one, not much bigger than Mike's thumb. It was light golden brown, and had a pair of large crested ears.

"Yep." Mike scooped it up, and the bat crawled around his fingers. "It's a Townsend's big-eared bat."

The other ranger, a mustachioed fellow named Sam, inspected its wings gently. "I don't think it's hurt itself. No sign of white-nose disease that I can see. Do you wanna swab him anyway?"

"Is that the fungal disease that kills bats?" Petra asked.

"Yeah. We've had a lot of problems with that out here."

"It seems small . . . is it full-grown?"

"Yep. He should be hibernating this time of year, but maybe he rolled over a bit too far in his sleep." Mike rubbed the back of the bat's head with a pinky finger. The bat squinted. Petra couldn't tell if it was an expression of happiness or displeasure.

"What are you gonna do with him?"

"Well . . . much as I'd like to keep him down here as a pet, we're gonna go find a ladder and tuck him back into bed," Mike said.

Petra grinned. It was nice to see that some part of the world was still running as it should. She left the two men cooing over the bat to ditch her bags and gather her gear. Sig had nearly drained his water dish in the conference room, and she topped it off for him while she collected her forms and plastic vials for geological samples. When Sig had slurped down his fill, he trotted out to the main room behind her.

Mike was crawling up on an extension ladder held by the second park ranger. The bat peered out of his shirt pocket as he ascended.

"I'm off, fellas," Petra said, adjusting her pack over her shoulder.

"Where you off to?" Mike asked.

"Northwest. Sampling near Mammoth Springs and the terrace." She rattled her bottles. "This is probably the only time to get there that the place isn't completely overrun by tourists."

"You know that the roads are closed up that

way, right?" The northwest part of the park was off-limits to the public every winter, owing to the snow and hazardous conditions.

"I brought chains. Science, man. It's gotta get done."

"You should be all right going to Mammoth. Road's always open between here and the north entrance. But stay on the paved roads and keep in touch."

"Will do. See you fellas later."

Mike sometimes got irritatingly protective, but he had a bat to fuss over now. He climbed up to the rafters and was poking around for a good nook into which to install the bat. "Whaddaya think, buddy? Here? Or here? The furnace duct is over here . . ."

"Little dude needs a name, you know," Sam suggested from the bottom of the ladder.

"You're right. I think he looks like a Norbert . . ."

Petra grinned and ducked out of the station. Life was going on as usual, and that cheered her.

She cranked the Bronco's engine and arranged Sig's blanket for maximum heat-vent exposure. As she wound her way through the park, she passed a tour of snow coaches, looking like vans on tank treads, churning away. A handful of skiers and snowmobiles dotted the landscape, which was mostly silent. Petra expected that her work would depend on snowmobiles later in the winter. If . . .

She would not finish that thought. She turned on the radio and sang with it, to Sig's irritation, as they drove to Mammoth Hot Springs.

The boardwalks around the terraced springs were closed. She parked as close as she could at the Upper Terrace. After rummaging around through her gear, she decided that the snow wasn't yet deep enough to warrant snowshoes. Her winter boots were knee-high with gaiters, and she thought she could gather her samples without too much trouble. She grabbed her cleats, hip waders, and her sample bag. Sig climbed out of the truck and rolled around in the fresh powder, shaking it off like a dog in a bath. Winter didn't seem to bother him, but he'd spent most of the fall growing a luxuriously thick coat. Petra dreaded spring, when she expected he'd blow it all out in the trailer.

The Mammoth Springs complex was full of motion and color, even in the dead of winter. On a terraced hill of travertine, hot water gurgled from more than twenty miles underground. Snow faded immediately upon contact with the warm, moist air in this area, never touching the ground. Petra checked her footing as she hiked to the lip of Canary Spring, which had taken on a vibrant yellow color. The cyanobacteria in the water were full of life, contributing to the ever-changing color. The shapes of the terraces were forever in flux, owing to the reaction of limestone and carbonic acid, depositing travertine. She filled her sample bottles, warning Sig that if he took a dip, he'd be regretting it on the rest of the trip, after burning himself and then drying off in the bitter cold. Sig seemed content to stay on firm land, digging for rodents beneath the snow-crusted boardwalk.

She continued on to New Blue Spring. The surrounding new stone was rusty, but a blue pool stretched in the middle, the color of the sky on a perfect summer's day. Petra hadn't seen blue sky for weeks, but she could imagine it, looking at that spot of color. She waded out with her hip waders as far as she dared, scraping samples into her bottles.

This wasn't terribly challenging work for a geologist, but minding her footing and figuring out the logistics of the sample distances was enough to keep her mind occupied. Still, in the back of her head, she didn't know what she'd do without something to occupy her thoughts during treatment. Without something to do, except stare at the television in a treatment room . . . she was certain she'd go batshit within a day. Maybe she could write a paper, or ask USGS for a paperwork assignment coding data. She was pretty sure she'd signed up for disability insurance when she took the job, and the money would be welcome. She hadn't been in the job long enough to have much leave banked. She'd need to be at the university for weeks at a time, and she'd likely be too exhausted after treatments to do much but push paper.

She mulled her options as she went off trail, walking up toward Minerva Terrace. The dove-grey stone had split into a steaming series of terraces that looked like the surface of another planet, alien and gorgeous. She poked around the perimeter while Sig meandered in the snow. He'd found some rabbit tracks and was busily amusing himself with trying to figure out where the rabbit had gone to ground. She frowned, wondering how she'd take care of Sig while undergoing treatment. Maybe he could stay home with Gabe, or he could go to her friend Maria's. Both of which would necessitate difficult conversations. And . . . no matter how much Sig acted like a dog, there wasn't any boarding facility or veterinarian's office that would take a coyote.

Sig yipped, and she turned, thinking he'd found the rabbit. But he was halfway across a snowfield, trotting northwest.

"Sig!" she called, but he didn't turn. Not that the coyote always came when called, but something had clearly captured his interest.

Slinging her sample bag over her shoulder, she struck out after him. His furry feet skimmed across the crust of snow, while her boots plunged through. She waded through the broken snow and the crust of ice that had formed on top, wondering what the hell he'd found.

Sig had clambered up a hill to the edge of a pine forest. It was the highest point for miles around. He parked his ass down on the snow and looked up. Petra struggled to catch up, winded as she reached him.

"What the hell—" she began, but broke off as she followed his gaze. "Oh."

The skin of an animal had been strung thirty feet up in the pine tree. As she squinted, she could see that it was a wolf hide, a white one, suspended and filled out with a bristling mass of sticks like a malformed puppet. It was a display, something clearly meant to be seen.

Tears bristled in her eyes. That poor creature. At her feet, Sig whined and thumped his tail on the ground.

She reached for her radio. Whatever had happened here, Mike was not gonna be happy about this.

CHAPTER 4

Free Advice Isn't Free

He dreamed of flying, as he did every night.

Gabe dreamed that he was soaring in a summer sky, surrounded by ravens. His consciousness had been poured into many of those light bodies. He could see from many vantage points and many eyes, skimming above the earth, feeling the sun on his wings. It was one of the few true joys he'd experienced as a Hanged Man. When he was in the sky, he felt as if he were still a part of nature. He often wondered what would happen if he'd decided to stay in raven form—could he live forever as a bird, even a flock of them? Would he forget what it was like to be human, and eventually fade into the teeming life of the backcountry?

He knew that he'd forgotten a great deal about what it was like to be human.

Gabe had grown accustomed to sleeping in the underground embrace of the Tree of Life, the Lunaria, over the last hundred fifty years. He'd dreamed in the artificial sunshine dripping from the tree, listening to the crackle of the Lunaria remaking his bones and knitting his flesh as it restored his injuries. He'd sometimes hear the murmur of the thoughts of the other Hanged Men intruding upon his sleep. It was like sleeping in a hive, a buzzing dream within a dream worming tunnels in his psyche.

That was all gone, now. The Lunaria had been burned to the ground, replaced by a tiny sapling with no power. The Hanged Men were gone. He was the sole survivor. In the darkness and silence of night, he couldn't fully apprehend the transformation that had stripped his cells of magic and rendered him human.

Human. Gabe had wished for this, many times over the years. But the price had been too high.

He had been responsible for Sal's death, just as much as any of the Hanged Men. More so, as their leader. He'd let them string Sal up and snuff him out in a shimmering rage, after Sal had burned the Lunaria. He regretted none of that. Sal was a terrible man, and he deserved death, many times over, many times more horribly than he had actually suffered.

But the Hanged Men deserved better than the sad end they'd gotten. It had been Gabe's decisions that led to Sal burning the tree. Gabe had underestimated Sal's blind stupidity, and it had come crashing down on all of them. They'd gone to sleep one last time under the burned roots of the tree, and Gabe had been the only one to wake up. He was the last man standing, and that was the most unjust thing of all.

Out here, in the snow-swept field behind Petra's trailer, the ravens, once his familiars, ignored him. Despite the strings of pop can tabs, caches of coins, buttons and wads of aluminum foil he'd gathered to attract their attention, they treated him as if he didn't exist. As they swept up into the sky after stealing a bit of cat food from the ground—never from his hand—Gabe would close his eyes and imagine what it was like to fly. No matter how hard he tried, he couldn't so much as sprout a feather from his ordinary flesh. He was forever earthbound now, and he knew it in the marrow of his heavy bones.

He'd awoken this morning to find Petra gone. She had been giving him space to process this transformation, he knew. She'd silently put plates of food before him and brought him books to read.

When he'd fled from the Rutherford Ranch, he'd taken his few earthly possessions with him: a coat, a hat, and some battered boots. It had been a long time since he'd had things that might have the possibility of gathering dust. The books she'd brought him were paperback thrillers from the gas station and a box of dusty classics from the pawnshop. She clearly had no idea what he liked to read, and he didn't really either. He found that he was most enjoying a science fiction tale about a man marooned on a planet with three suns, a world with no night.

There was another book he was working through, examining it as closely as if it were the Emerald Tablet of alchemy itself. It was a children's picture book, *The Velveteen Rabbit*. It had been at the bottom of the box of dirty books, and he'd initially flipped through it to see the pictures. But something about it drew him—the simple line drawings and the contemplation of what it meant to be real. The toy rabbit became real because of the love of a boy, hopping away into the forest on real feet to be with the other real rabbits.

It seemed facile, the transformative power of love. Gabe knew that Petra loved him, and he loved her right back, as much as he remembered how to. But he doubted that even her love could make him real. Whatever "real" was anyway.

What was real was the fact that he was irrevocably human. He'd spent weeks staring at the ravens in the sky and wallowing in the guilt of loss. His life had changed. And all that remained for him to do was to put one foot in front of the other, to figure out what to do with the forty or so years of natural life that remained to him.

He struck off down the gravel road leading toward town, his hat pulled low and his hands stuffed in his pockets against the cold. He could feel it seeping into his bones now, an ache that he'd long forgotten. He would have to deal with it, like the grief, and get on with things.

And the first thing in that order of business was to find some work. He couldn't putter around Petra's backyard, chasing birds, for the next four decades. He knew ranches and horses; there had to be someone around who had need of a guy who would work uncomplainingly under the table. He was conscious of the fact that he had no references and hadn't paid taxes since the 1900s. His last legitimate work had been as a Pinkerton agent, solving occult cases. There wasn't much demand for that kind of work, he was quite certain. But cheap manual labor was cheap labor, and it would always be in demand.

He headed instinctively to Temperance's social hub, the Compostela.

By the time he reached the slushy main street of Temperance, there were a few trucks parked before the bar that had formerly been a church.

The stained-glass windows were dim in the winter gloom, paint peeling away on the gothic arches under the force of a winter wind that could skin the hide off a buffalo.

Gabe ducked inside, his toes and fingers numb. A dusting of snow slid off his hat to the scarred wood floor. The pews that had been converted to booths were steeped in darkness, where a few old-timers sat and muttered.

Gabe made his way to the bar, a polished surface of what had once been a single massive tree. He could remember that tree when it was cut, seeing it dragged down the street to be made into an altar. He slid into a bar stool at the end, his back to the wall, and waited for the bartender to approach. He reached into his back pocket for his wallet, which contained a residue of cash that Sal had given him for an errand months ago.

The bartender arrived, dressed in a black shirt buttoned up to his neck. He had been here for many years, much longer than one would have thought by simply looking at him. The blond man was of indeterminate age, but he seemed to have hovered around his fifties for as long as Gabe had been paying attention.

"Didn't expect you around here," the bartender remarked.

"Been busy."

The bartender made a noncommittal noise,

poured him a dark beer from the tap, and passed it
to him. Gabe tasted it and examined the glass carefully. "New brew?"

"Nah. It's your usual."

Everything tasted different now. Sharper. A
little more bitter. Gabe took a long draught of it,
trying to figure out how to savor the sensation. The
bartender seemed to watch him closely.

"You've changed."

Gabe froze. Was it that obvious?

"Things are slow," Gabe said nonchalantly.
"Wondered if you heard of anyone with work?"

"Not lately. Is your boss outta town?"

Gabe rubbed a bit of foam from the corner of his
mouth with his thumb, eyes narrowed. "Dunno
where he is."

"Folks are looking for him." The bartender had
lowered his voice and leaned forward. The guy
was never what Gabe would call exactly trustworthy, but he knew that he had no love for Sal Rutherford, so that was something. And he was discreet.
Likely had to be—when Gabe had been a Hanged
Man, he'd been able to sense a low-key miasma of
magic about him. Just a glimmer, like the shimmer
of heat mirages on pavement in summer. Try as he
might, now, as a human, he couldn't detect such a
thing. Frustrating. He hadn't realized how much
he'd taken that extra sense for granted.

"Folks?" he echoed.

"Folks like Sheriff Owen. He's been circling around town like a buzzard, asking questions and shitting in nests."

Ah, great. Gabe maintained a neutral mask of expression on his face as he drank. He hoped that laying low for a couple of weeks would chill law enforcement into looking for other things . . . especially since Owen Rutherford stood to control everything Sal once had. If Sal was gone, that was good news for Owen. A rational guy wouldn't spend a whole lot of time looking that kind of outrageous fortune in the mouth. But, in Gabe's mind, Owen was completely batshit. No telling if he was counting his newfound money and doing a pro forma investigation . . . or if he was out for vengeance.

"I'm sure Owen will find him soon," he said. Hopefully, not until spring next year, but "soon" was a relative concept in Gabe's long life. He reached for his wallet and tossed some bills on the bar.

"You want some advice?" The bartender's eyes gleamed in the half-darkness.

"Is it free?"

"Always."

"Shoot."

"You'd better get out of town while the getting's good."

Gabe nodded and drained his glass. He tipped his hat. "Thank you, sir."

The bartender nodded and turned away to stack glasses.

His hat low over his brow, Gabe sidled out of the bar. He waited on the street corner while a car passed through the one streetlight in Temperance. He scanned up and down the road. The sheriff's deputies rarely came to Temperance; they stayed in the county seat an hour away, where they kept their cars spotlessly clean behind a fence. He weighed the bartender's warning against what he knew of the deputies' own laziness.

His gaze paused on a nearby telephone pole, and his breath quickened. He took two quick steps to it and scanned a sign, printed on eight-by-eleven-inch copy paper.

WANTED FOR QUESTIONING: GABRIEL MANGET
HAVE YOU SEEN THIS MAN? CONTACT THE SHERIFF'S OFFICE.
DO NOT CONFRONT—ASSUMED ARMED AND DANGEROUS.

Below the lettering was an artist's rendering of a face that looked a helluva lot like Gabe and a grainy copy of his driver's license photograph.

"Shit." He snatched the flyer down, stuffed it in his pocket, and walked briskly away.

"WELL, IT'S NOT poachers."

Mike examined the wolf's skin, turning it over in gloved hands. Rangers had come with tree spikes, marked the area off for evidence, and cut the wolf down. Petra squatted beside Mike in the snow, looking over his shoulder at the skin. It had been stretched over a skeleton of sticks and a thin stuffing of leaves, like a child's effort at taxidermy.

"What makes you say that?" she asked, her stomach turning.

"Poachers would have taken the skin—that's worth good money. Especially an unusual color of fur, like this." Mike ran gloved fingers over the edges of the skin and the white fur twitching in the cold breeze. "But this is someone who knows how to field dress a carcass."

"Was it shot?"

"I don't see any shot in it, but we'll know for sure when we take apart this . . . whatever it is." Mike peered at the nestlike structure inside the wolf. "It's a fresh kill—not yet cured."

Petra could tell that much. The interior of the skin looked wet and pink. The chill had kept the skin from smelling too badly, but she was stymied. "Who would have done this?"

"Wolves sometimes go missing on the edge of Yellowstone and ranch land. I tried to get Sal Rutherford charged a few years back with luring a couple of wolves out and shooting them. He claimed they were harassing his cattle, and they well might have been. There's not much love for wolves outside of the park. But this wolf is squarely within park land, and most ranchers who want wolves dead dispose of them quietly, without this much . . . pomp and circumstance."

"Was this wolf tracked by any scientists?" Petra wanted to know. She knew that many packs were tracked by radio collars and their movements closely monitored. There was give and take with the wolves in Yellowstone; their movements and habits could change anything. She'd seen a documentary in which wolf predation on ungulates caused increases in river shore vegetation, which ultimately changed the flow of rivers. They were pretty powerful creatures.

"I don't know for sure if this one was being watched," Mike said. "I'll have to get this back to the station and see if it matches a description of any that were being studied."

"Would it be microchipped? Like for dogs and cats?"

"Yeah. If a wolf has been trapped here before for scientific purposes, it should have one. It's likely that a chip would have been lost in the skinning. But I'm guessing this one will be relatively easy to identify. This coat is unique." His hand brushed the soft fur, and a line of sadness had settled over his shoulders.

Petra sat with him a moment, blinking back

tears. It was a terrible waste. And she couldn't fathom the reason. "If it wasn't poachers or ranchers . . . who could have done this?"

Mike turned the carcass around. Where the eyes should have been, there were blank holes, and Petra and Mike were staring into knots of twigs. "If I had to guess? One sick motherfucker."

Petra sat back on her heels. Mike rarely swore. "I know you'll get him," she said.

"Yeah." He stood up and brushed the snow from his pants, his eyes distant. "I'm gonna."

The rangers bundled the wolf's skin and wooden skeleton in a plastic tarp for evidence. Mike took pictures of the tree and the surrounding area. Fresh snow had fallen and there were no footprints but their own. Petra returned with the rangers back to the Tower Falls Ranger Station, writing out her statement in the warmth of the conference room, with one hand wrapped around a cup of hot chocolate. Sig lay at her feet, his tail tickling the back of her socks. But no matter how precise her lettering was, she couldn't shake the image of the wolf's sightless eyes from her mind.

She glanced down at Sig. "I should get you chipped, too. Just in case."

He looked up at her, his eyebrows twitching.

"It won't hurt. Just a needle. I promise."

He hadn't been fond of the battery of shots and worming medicine he'd been given when it became clear that he was going to be a companion animal, sleeping in her bed and eating cold cuts from her fridge. She couldn't really call him a pet—there was still that streak of wildness in him that she'd seen today, when he went running across the snow to the strange display of the wolf. He had a nose for the invisible, that was certain, and a curiosity that matched her own.

But today's scene had been weird. The question that bugged her was . . . how weird? Was it just some sicko looking to reproduce an art project he'd seen on Pinterest? Or was there more to it?

"We got a tentative ID on the wolf." Mike leaned in the doorway.

"Oh, yeah?"

"He's wolf A26, from a pack called Nine Stars."

"That's a very . . . nonpoetic name for a wolf belonging to a poetic pack."

"It's an old pack—the eggheads have been tracking them off and on since the 1970s. That was the name the Arapaho gave them, and the researchers kept that. A26 was caught in 2000—he's been around for a while. He's one of only three wolves in that pack that have ever been tagged. The first one ditched her radio collar, so they've been chipping them as a backup."

"This sucks. What will you do now?"

"We'll comb through A26's fur and remains for evidence. Look for baits, poison, and traps in the area, consult with the wolf researchers to see if they have any insight. I'll put out my feelers and see if there's any chatter about a weirdo with a thing for wolves, see if anyone's selling anything similar on the Internet. I'll check with other parks to see if they've seen anything like this."

"What will happen to A26?" Petra had always been scrupulous about burying pets that died. She had buried every goldfish she'd ever owned, and it bothered her to imagine that the white wolf was going to stay in an evidence bag forever. It bordered on superstition, but still . . . it bothered her.

"Until we're done processing him and close the case, he'll be chilling in our freezer. I promise we'll take good care of him."

"I know you will."

The phone rang up front, and Mike retreated to answer it. Petra sat at the conference table and stared down at Sig.

"This is weird, isn't it?" she asked him.

Sig huffed.

"How weird?" She spiraled a pen through her fingers. A year ago she might have been able to look at this situation as a regrettable crime scene. Something that an unhinged mind might have created, under the influence of mental illness or drugs. But since she'd come to Temperance she'd encountered magic that defied all explanation . . .

The pen stilled. What if this was magic, some

ruined bit of leftover ritual, or a threat? The wolf had been deconstructed and reconstructed with an incredible amount of care and deliberation, as if there were some unseen purpose. Was it crazy for her to think there could be something unearthly here?

Maybe.

But it would be crazy not to find out for sure. Wouldn't it?

She headed for the door. Sig lifted one eyebrow and followed her. She glanced left and right down the hallway; Mike was still on the phone.

Mike said that the wolf was in the freezer. She paused beside the break room. No way the carcass could fit into the top freezer compartment of the refrigerator here, jammed around the rangers' stock of rocky road ice cream. She turned right into the utility room, flipping on the light and closing the door behind Sig's fluffy tail.

This room was cold, and she wished she'd taken her coat with her. Metal utility racks held boxes of file folders, evidence bags, and bits of random equipment. Fire suits and axes hung on pegs, while the shelves contained a rack of antlers, canoe paddles, life jackets, first aid kits, bottled water—all the bits and pieces of the many duties of a ranger. She stepped around a stack of coloring books, and sucked in her breath, startled, at a lump of fur in the corner of the floor.

Is that a . . .

It was a bear. Just not a live one. She reached down and held it up. It was an empty Smokey the Bear suit, made of fake fur and green felt. Petra chortled to herself, imagining Mike or one of the other rangers having to don it for safety talks.

She turned the corner around a battered file cabinet to find a freezer chest pressed up against the wall, the compressor humming.

Taking a deep breath, she opened the lid. There were frost-covered plastic and paper bags here, some suggestions of wings and antlers. Everything was neatly labeled and stacked. She looked past them, peeling back a piece of tarp, down at the face of the wolf skin, stretched by sticks. Sig stood up on his hind legs to peer in at the hapless creature.

"Are you magic?" she muttered at it.

Only one way to be certain. She dug into a pocket of her pants for an artifact Sig had found for her months before: the Venificus Locus. The golden compass, surrounded by alchemical symbols, glittered in her hand. Gabe had told her it was a magic locator, created by Temperance's first alchemist, Lascaris. It wasn't a terribly precise tool—it could tell her whether magic was present, and in what direction. Depending on its agitation, she could sometimes get a sense of how powerful it was. But it couldn't tell her whether what it sensed was good or evil, or where it had come from.

And the worst bit about the gruesome little

device was that it ran on blood. Petra reached into her other pocket for her pocketknife, unfolded the blade, and poked it at her palm. Her fingers were growing calluses from consulting the device; she'd even tried it on Gabe, at his request. The Locus had confirmed there was nothing magical about Gabe now, that he was ordinary. He'd worn a wooden expression when she told him, but she knew that the knowledge of his ordinariness ached.

Petra hoped the same for the wolf. A bead of blood welled up, and she dribbled it into a groove circumscribing the edge of the compass. The blood droplet seemed to pause a moment in that track, as if considering. The Locus ran on ordinary, nonmagical blood. Distantly, she wondered if there would be a time when her own blood would become too fucked-up to run it, on chemo and such.

She held her breath, focusing on the compass. If there was no magic here, the blood would simply soak into the gold. And she would have evidence of the continuing sickness of the garden-variety criminals of humankind.

But the blood droplet wobbled, holding tension, and began to slide around the circle of the compass. She held the compass at arm's length, over the wolf's skin. The blood paused, then raced around it as if circling a Help Wanted ad in a newspaper.

"Fuck," she growled.

Sig's ears perked up, and he turned his head

toward the door. Petra jammed the compass into the front pocket of her hoodie as the door opened.

"What are you doing in here?" Mike stood in the doorway, looking in puzzlement between her and the coyote and the open freezer door.

Petra looked him in the eye. "I wanted . . . to see the wolf. I feel bad for him." That was true. She was terrible at lying, so it was best if she stuck close to the truth.

Mike crossed his arms over his chest. "Yeah. I know. But you can't be in here, poking around evidence."

"Okay. I'm sorry." Inside her hoodie pocket, she closed her fingers over the cut in her palm to staunch the bleeding before it got all over the fleece. "I shouldn't have done that."

Mike crossed the floor and closed the freezer lid. "I know you mean well, and it's hard for civilians to see this stuff."

She looked down, and her gaze fell on the Smokey the Bear costume. "Almost as hard as it is seeing the body of the dead Smokey the Bear in here. You guys got Hoffa's body back here, too?"

Mike snorted. "Stick around for the fire safety program in spring. You are now officially in the pool to draw lots for who gets to wear the costume and pose with the ankle-biters."

"Awesome." She rolled her eyes and followed him out of the room.

"Look," he said, serious now. "I know that seeing that wolf is gonna stick with you for a long time. You wouldn't be a decent human being if it didn't. But we're gonna do everything we can to find the culprit."

"I know," she said, feeling her brow wrinkle at his determination. "Just be extra careful with this one, okay?"

He nodded and snapped off a Boy Scout salute. "Scout's honor."

"That's the best I can ask for. But . . ." She opened her mouth to say more, to utter a warning . . .

But the other ranger on duty, Sam, was yelling from the hallway: "Heads up, Mike—we got a call about some stranded skiers drunk driving a snow tank down near the Canyon. They hit a bridge and managed to set the tank on fire. Some rocket scientist brought marshmallows, and there are bears circling. Bears that are not hibernating."

Mike shut his eyes and slapped his forehead. "Jesus. I know exactly the morons that are involved in this." He wheeled and sprinted from the room, yelling: "Lock up behind you, will ya, Petra?"

"Sure. Uh . . . good luck, guys," she said lamely. "Go get 'em."

There was the clink and rummage of equipment and the squawk of radios before the slam of doors. "Fucking bastards."

A DUI with a snow tank and bears sounded

decidedly unsupernatural. And the Canyon was south of here, far away from the area that Petra had found the wolf skin. The current situation with the skiers sounded much more urgent, and would likely keep Mike tied up for a while. Given the amount of paperwork involved, it could be for days. Which was a good thing. It gave her time to figure out what to do.

Her fingers tightened around the blood-slick Locus, and she could feel the droplets of blood bubbling against her palm, like hydrogen peroxide on a wound.

Whatever had killed the wolf was magic. Not to be fucked with. She wanted to tell Mike, to warn him there was something weird out there. But there was no way she could go down that rabbit hole of crazy with him and make him believe, not without jeopardizing Gabe and his secrets. Not yet, anyway.

CHAPTER 5

The Alchemist in His Natural Habitat

The alchemist of Phoenix Village had set up a small lab to explore his art: bits of tin foil, straws, six packets of salt, a stone with a hole in the middle, a book of matches, a mirror, and various pills scavenged from the floor. Only a few of those pills were covered in lint, and he had recently found a roll of copper pennies to add to his collection. He usually kept his laboratory in his bedside drawer, but whenever it was discovered, the night nurses cleaned out the contraband, and he had to start all over again.

Petra had heard all about these great injustices—first, from the staff, and then from him. She listened and made sympathetic noises to both parties but refused to take a side.

He was ranting about this today, rolling around the floor between the bathroom and the empty nightstand in his wheelchair, when his daughter came to his room.

". . . And it's not like those things are easy to find. Especially that stone!" He shook his fist at the ceiling, to whatever gods might be listening, but it was probably just the duty nurse doing the rounds on the second floor who stomped down a couple of times on the ceiling to get him to quiet down.

"Hey, Dad," Petra said. She stood in the doorway, her coat folded over her arm, shifting her weight from foot to foot. She wasn't sure if he was having a lucid moment or not. Those were hit or miss. About half the time she visited him, he was in the here-and-now. The rest of the time, he'd be muttering about some strange event in the past that involved gnomes stealing his slippers.

Her father's face broke into a craggy smile. "Hello, darling!" He cocked his head, taking in her face. "What's wrong?"

She sighed. Good. He was mostly with it today. She closed the door behind her and went to sit at the edge of his bed. He wheeled up beside her. "It's late for you to be here."

Petra glanced at his alarm clock. It was six-thirty, already long dark. Visiting hours were over by seven, so she decided to cut to the chase: "Dad, I need to ask you about something weird I saw today at work. I wondered if . . . it could be related to his work. Lascaris."

She told him about the wolf she found and how the Locus reacted to it. He nodded vigorously, running his fingers over his stubbly scalp. They'd shaved his head when he'd been in a catatonic state. Now that he had bouts of lucidity, he'd insisted that they stop, and he rubbed his own plush grey scalp as if it could make his brain work better. He seemed to soak in all the details, asking about the direction of the sun and what kind of sticks were used. She wasn't able to answer all of his questions, but he sat back in his chair, deep in thought, scratching a spindly knee through his sweatpants.

"It sounds like some kind of separation process," he said at last. "A shell with its guts removed and stuffed with something else. All magic is an attempt to control something else—whether it's other people, luck, spirits, or the weather. And it sure sounds like someone is trying to control your wolves through magical means. Whoever made it is literally trying to get underneath its skin, to separate the shell from the body."

"I don't understand," she said, brow wrinkling.

"And it's probably a good thing that you don't." He reached out to take her hand. "Now. How are you holding up?"

She blinked at him. It was like . . . it was like he *knew*. "What do you know, Dad?"

He covered her hand with his other one. "I know that you're not well. I see it."

She squinted at her reflection in the highly waxed floor. To her eye, she looked no different. Tired, maybe. But not sick.

She told him, just the bare-bones facts: "I went to the doctor. There was some weirdness in my blood last time I was in the ER. They ran some tests and, well . . . it's leukemia. I'm going to see a specialist next week to see what the treatment options are."

He listened attentively without moving, processing what she was saying with glistening eyes. "I'm sorry, dear."

Her lip quivered. "Yeah, well . . ." She looked away. "I don't know what to do."

"I'll tell you what not to do," he said. "Don't go chasing alchemical cures, like I did, feathers of phoenixes and elixirs of eternal life. Go to the damn doctor. Put your faith in science. You'll be all right."

He pulled her down into a hug, and she sobbed like a child.

"You're gonna get through this," he murmured against her hair. "You will."

She leaned back, wiping at the snot dripping from her nose. "How do you know?"

He smiled at her, a full brilliant smile. "Because you're my daughter."

HE SAT IN darkness after the sun had set red on the horizon. The stars prickled out in sharp shards, bright overhead. He used to be able to see very well in the dark, like an owl. Now . . . things just grew fuzzy and indistinct, and he would stub his toe on the edge of the futon when he went to bed.

Gabe sat at Petra's kitchen table, staring through the window. He expected her home any time, and he knew that they had to talk. The crumpled-up wanted poster was burning a hole in his pocket. He wondered how to make her understand that he didn't want to leave her, that he wanted to find a way they could be together without her getting arrested for aiding and abetting a known felon.

Now that Sal was gone, now that Gabe's tie to the Lunaria was broken . . . he felt a curious light-headed freedom. It was possible that he could flee Temperance, for the first time in a hundred fifty years. Maybe Petra could come with him, and they could begin again on an ordinary life someplace else, someplace without magic and ravens and the threat of immortality. In the old days of the Wild West, that would have been possible. Now . . . he was unsure. Cellular signals and wires tracked people through ephemeral data and invisible networks in an ever-shrinking world. Was it still possible to disappear in this day and age?

The lights of Petra's truck came down the gravel

road, washing over the trailer windows. He watched her get out, Sig bounding in the snow. Seeing no trailer lights on, she automatically went to the back field to look for him.

He watched her, as she looked up at the sky, her hair curtaining her face. Orion glowed softly above. He remembered that was the title of her favorite poem. Orion. She wasn't a sentimental sort, but she had moments of deep feeling. There was a curious kind of romance about her, not the florid descriptions of poetry. But some of the stripped-down simplicity of prose clung to her, some grace.

She crossed back to the trailer entrance to unlock the door. Sig bounded inside, tracking snow across the linoleum, and she turned on the kitchen light switch.

She was startled to see Gabe at the kitchen table.

"How long have you been sitting here?" Petra went to hang up her coat. She glanced at Sig's dog bowl, and it was already full of kibble.

"Since sunset. It was a pretty sunset."

She slipped into the chair opposite him. "We have to talk."

"Yes."

Sig jumped up on the third chair and sat upright, as if he was also a party to the discussion.

"It seems Sig has things to say, too."

"Likely. He has an opinion about pretty much

everything." She reached over to rub Sig's ears and blurted out: "I went to the doctor yesterday. He says I have leukemia."

He blinked, tasting something like ground-up glass in the back of his throat. "What does that mean?" he asked.

"It means . . . I have to go get treatment. Probably chemotherapy. Could be some surgery, too, or something else. I won't know until I talk to the specialist. From what little I understand about it, it's gonna be an intensive process. I don't know what the odds of success are." She looked down at her hands. "So, yeah. Not awesome."

He reached across the table for her hands, scarred and beautiful, and lifted them to his lips. "I will take care of you. Whatever you need me to do."

Her eyes glistened. "You can't. You can't fix this with magic and immortality potions."

He sifted through his memory. He'd come to Temperance a century and a half ago as a Pinkerton agent, to investigate rumors of alchemy. While the town's founder, Lascaris, had figured out how to conjure gold, he'd been unsuccessful in creating immortality, beyond the botched experiment of the Hanged Men—to which Gabe had been the first unfortunate sacrifice. And that wasn't an option for Petra; that magic was all emptied out. "If there's a way, we'll find it."

"You can't go chasing after magical solutions," she said. "Someone will be looking for you, for what you . . . for what happened to Sal."

"They are. But it doesn't matter."

She pulled back, disentangling her fingers. "You have to get out of town, then. You can't let them find you and try you for Sal's death. You'll wind up on death row or life in prison."

"I know how to lay low."

She stood up, covered her mouth with a hand, and began to pace. "No. I won't be responsible for them catching you. Not because you're tied here to me, out of some foolish sense of chivalry. I can't . . . I can't deal with that now." Tears spilled out of her eyes and down her fingers.

He stood and reached for her. He placed his hands on her shoulders. "You are taking no responsibility for me. I make my own choices. Got it?"

"You can't take responsibility for me, either." She shook her head. "I can hire in-home help. Likely, I'll be barfing my guts up on a hospital floor for a solid month. I will have people around."

"No," he said. "I will go where you go for treatment. I will feed Sig and read newspapers to you in bed. We will get through this."

He could see her leaning forward and back on the heels and balls of her feet, the way she did when she was undecided.

"They won't catch me," he said. "I have a few

years on the sheriff." But a worry did work deep into his mind . . . Would they find her, and charge her as an accomplice? Harboring a fugitive was serious business.

"But . . ." She reached up to touch his face. "This is going to be terrible. For me and for you. It makes no sense for you to stay."

"I am staying with you. That's not up for debate. What is up for debate is . . . how we minimize risk."

She pressed the heel of her hand to her eye. "Well . . . I can take treatment at the university, far from here. Or even farther away, depending on how it works out. My insurance is pretty good. Maybe that would be good—getting away." She sank to the edge of the futon, her hands knotted in her lap.

He sat down beside her. "Maybe we should get married."

She blinked at him. "What?"

"If I do get caught . . . they wouldn't be able to make you testify against me. Or force me to testify against you, with respect to any aid you gave me. And I could make sure that all your treatment wishes were carried out, since your father is in no shape to do that, yet."

This had none of the staged pomp and circumstance of a modern era proposal. There was no romantic walk in the park and getting down on one knee with a sparkling ring, asking for her well-manicured hand. Not that she'd ever wanted such things. There was too much dirt beneath her fingernails to play the role of a princess in a happily-ever-after fairy tale.

"Erf." She stared out the window, at Orion sinking in the black, for what seemed a long time.

"Just think about it," he said.

"It does seem like it would alleviate a lot of our mutual problems," she admitted. "But I just never thought, well . . . I never planned on getting married."

"It changes nothing," he said. "And if you like, you can dissolve it after you are healed."

"I wouldn't, I just . . ." She gazed up at the dark sky. "If I were to get married, I want to be married for the right reasons."

"These are damn compelling reasons."

She nodded, chewing on her lip. "You know that I love you, right?"

"Yes. And I love you."

It should have been that simple, but it never was. He reached for her face, turned it to his, and kissed her. She was as warm and alive as she had been yesterday, the day before. He had to keep believing that she would live for tomorrow and the next day. His fingers traced her collarbone, over the constellation of freckles of her shoulder. He kissed her wrists and her callused palms. He felt alive. He wanted her to feel that, too.

She kissed him back, with an unexpected heat. Her palms slid up his chest and her fingers laced in the hair on the nape of his neck.

He pulled her down to the bed, wanting to savor every sigh and freckle, as Orion stood guard just outside the window, shining down from the cold, remote depths of the sky.

GABE SNORED SOFTLY into the back of her hair, while Petra stared out the window. Moonlight filtered softly down on her, and she watched all that burned-out light from dead stars glittering on the snow.

When they made love, Petra usually fell asleep right away after, tangled in his arms and legs. But this time, she'd drifted off into a muzzy half-sleep, then slipped awake. Her mind whirred around what he'd suggested. Marriage. He'd cast out the idea as if it was a simple solution to a simple problem, something as clear and utilitarian as purchasing a lock for a door.

Petra had never given much thought to the idea of marriage. Her parents' marriage certainly hadn't been wine and roses. The best parts of it had been when they both managed to leave each other alone. And that's what her father had told her: "A man wants a woman who will leave him alone." Since Petra had a deep, introverted need for solitude, she could find that a workable notion. She had little understanding of the fights they flew into. It became clear to her that her father wasn't giving her mother something she desperately needed. She needed his time, his undivided attention. She needed to be first in his life. And whether it was conscious selfishness or a side effect of how he was wired, it just didn't happen. Petra had hoped she would eventually find someone she could live her life with, but she knew it wasn't a given, and she certainly wasn't motivated enough to go hunt a man down with a harpoon and drag him back to her cave. She was fine with her own company. She had never felt incomplete without a man.

She slipped out of bed, dressed, and let herself out of the trailer. Sig plodded sleepily after her, never one to pass up the opportunity to go pee. The cold air skimmed over her face, stealing her breath. She walked around to the back of the trailer, craning her head to take in the sequins of stars above. Orion had one boot over the horizon, and the moon had moved far beyond him.

She hadn't given much thought to the qualities she wanted in a partner. She wanted someone who was loyal, capable, and who would be kind to Sig. Gabe was those things, and so much more. They'd seen amazing things together, and shared a bond that she could never replicate with another person. She was content with their relationship—and the sex was amazing. He explored her body as if she was an unknown, fascinating country, and she craved the feeling of his bare skin against hers. If he had asked her to marry her under any other circumstances, she probably would have said yes. At least, she *thought* so.

If she admitted it to herself, she was afraid to be marrying him because she needed him. She didn't want to be taken care of. And she didn't want him to marry her just for legal cover. She thought that was a lousy way to get married, each immediately becoming a burden to the other.

Sig completed a ritual of circling the trailer and peeing at all the corners. In the canine brain, she was certain this was a ritual for mighty protection from skunks and foxes. He came to join her in the field, leaning against her leg.

She looked down at him. Sig had given up much to be with her. He was a wild creature who had come to trust her enough to love her and sleep at the foot of her bed. She still didn't know entirely why. But she loved him more for it.

She looked up at Orion. She had no ideal to compare Gabe to. She loved him, without question. He was, at the present, her world. Her world would be shrinking, soon, and she wanted him in it.

After some time, she turned around to go back to the trailer, Sig on her heels. Gabe didn't awaken as she slipped back into bed, not even when she stuck her cold feet behind his knees.

She fell into a deep sleep almost immediately, the sleep of the dead . . .

. . . and was awakened by a knock sounding at the door.

Petra blinked up at the ceiling. At first, she thought she'd dreamed it. Milky grey light had filled the trailer, suspended in a buzzy warmth as she pressed her cheek against Gabe's chest. She was listening to his heart beating slowly, savoring the sense of stillness around her.

It was peaceful, this dozing with her legs tangled in his and the coyote draped at the bottom of the bed. It wasn't much, and yet it was everything. It was an illusion. She knew that, underneath her skin, abnormal cells were silently dividing deep in her marrow. Underneath Gabe's skin, he was human. But deep in his skull, he had a hundred fifty years of regret and magic churning around.

Was that what had prompted him to suggest marriage as a solution? The accumulated weight of regrets, and not wanting to cause more damage?

And how fair would such a thing be to him? She knew that he had been married before, that his wife was long dead. As things stood now, he might outlive her. And then . . .

At the sound of the second rattling knock, she reached over Gabe, fumbling underneath the futon for one of her guns. There were two Colt .44s somewhere down there, communing with the dust bunnies . . .

Gabe placed his hands on her shoulders, stilling her.

Sig had awoken and was slinking across the floor with his teeth bared. Petra reached down and snagged his collar with her other hand. Sig strained against her, but she didn't let go, didn't know what was on the other side of the door. She sure as hell wasn't expecting anyone.

"Ms. Dee?" An unfamiliar voice sounded on the other side.

She craned her head. Though the slats of the blinds, she could see movement. She glanced at the window over the futon. The blinds were mostly drawn, but she thought she could detect a shadow twitching underneath the last slat.

Shit. So much for that avenue of escape. She handed one of her guns to Gabe.

"Ms. Dee, this is Sheriff Rutherford from the county sheriff's office. We just want to talk."

A chill rattled down her spine. She glanced at Gabe. He watched the door, not moving except to hold her shoulder. His meaning was clear: *Be still.*

The knock sounded again.

Voices sounded again, circling around the trailer. She jumped when someone tried to jiggle the window over her bed. Sig turned, and she wrestled to keep him still, throwing a bare leg over him to keep him from pressing his nose to the glass.

Something scraped at the door, and then there were the sounds of boot clomps heading away. An engine started, then receded.

But she didn't relax. She didn't dare move.

It was probably a good fifteen minutes before she disentangled herself from blankets, Gabe, and the coyote. Gabe slid out and padded noiselessly to the door. He checked through the blinds and all the other windows.

"They're gone," he said.

She sank into the nest of blankets on the futon. "They know."

"They don't know anything. Not for sure. If they did, they'd have a warrant, and they'd be breaking down your door."

"Then what the hell was that?" Her brow wrinkled.

"A fishing expedition. They'll be back. Maybe not today, but soon."

Petra got dressed and peered out the window. To convince herself, she cracked open the door a sliver.

A business card fluttered down, from where it had been wedged in the door frame behind the weather stripping. It was a simple embossed card with raised lettering and a black star. It said:

SHERIFF OWEN RUTHERFORD
COUNTY SHERIFF

The phone number and address were printed in capital letters below. She nearly dropped it, as if it were hot. On the back was scrawled, with black ink: *Call me.*

"Shit," she swore.

CHAPTER 6

The Underworld in Sal's Backyard

Owen knew that he was being played.

He'd been going door to door with his deputies, looking for evidence. Fishing, but fishing sometimes yielded a trout. He'd gotten a nibble at the post office, where a postal worker said that he'd seen the man in his wanted poster in the company of the town's geologist last week. It had been a simple thing to look up Petra Dee's driver's license and find her address. There had been a couple of reports of her trespassing on Sal Rutherford's property when Sal was still alive. She clearly knew Sal's people, and maybe she knew them well enough to have intel on their current whereabouts.

He liked to knock on doors early in the morning.

Most people were usually still too fuzzy with sleep to come up with good lies. He knew she should be home; her truck was parked outside, covered with a skiff of snow. He'd thumped on the door and his deputies had circled around to the windows, but there had been no movement inside. Maybe she'd spent the night someplace else. Maybe. But it piqued Owen's curiosity, and he was determined to talk to her.

He couldn't force it. He could intimidate, though. And he'd do that, if he had to, until he got some answers.

"What do you think she knows?"

Anna sat beside him on the passenger seat of his SUV. She looked out the window, wisps of her blond hair almost translucent in the growing light. She traced a bit of frost on the glass with her finger, but it made no smear.

"I don't know," Owen admitted. "She might be involved with Sal's men, hiding them."

"She might be in danger," Anna suggested.

"Could be." Owen had seen it before, women in relationships with bad guys who controlled them. He didn't have that sense here. By all accounts, the Dee woman was not a shrinking violet. But he'd keep the door open on that idea, just in case. He hoped she didn't come up missing. That would be entirely too convenient for this Gabriel guy. It would keep her from talking.

His grip tightened on the wheel. He sure as hell didn't like where any of this was going.

His radio crackled to life:

"S-1, this is Base. What's your twenty?"

He reached for the radio. "Base, this is S-1. I'm heading back your way."

"K-9 requests your presence at the Rutherford Ranch."

Owen's eyebrows lifted. "10–4."

He'd asked one of the dog handlers to get out there and see if the dogs found anything weird at the ranch. They had one dog, Daisy, who was actually supposed to be a corpse-sniffing dog. They'd purchased her with Homeland Security grant money, but she hadn't ever found much that wasn't wrapped in bacon. Daisy was cute, though, and they'd decided not to turn her back in for a replacement. Owen had let her handler keep her, since she was useful for PR campaigns, visits to schools, and such. And she was actually pretty good at pursuit of live suspects. One took what one could get in the backcountry.

He pulled off the road by the house and was given directions by a deputy to Sal Rutherford's back forty, toward the curiously burned tree. It stood in stark, black contrast to the snowfield around it. The dog, a German shepherd, was digging in the snow, only her tail visible above a cloud of white.

Owen popped the SUV door open and jumped out. He'd given a list of sites for the K-9 to search, not expecting much. Sal's land was vast. But he'd asked the K-9 to start with the house, the barn . . . and this weird tree that he kept circling around in his mind.

"Whatcha got, Deputy Farris?"

Farris gestured to the dog. "Daisy's been digging at this spot. Won't leave it alone. Not even for bacon."

"Let me see."

Farris pulled Daisy back, and Owen stared at the ground. It looked like dead, singed grass to him, glistening under the removed layer of snow. He crouched and fingered it. He didn't see any sign of disturbed earth. But that didn't mean that there wasn't anything down there. Maybe there was some bit of trace evidence the dog was zeroing in on.

As he groped around, he felt something—a seam in the dead turf. It was straight, as if carved in the ground. And then the chill of metal—a ring.

. He pulled, attempting to free it from the frozen ground, but it wouldn't give. Grumbling at it, he braced his foot on the ground and hauled with all his might. The ground gave way, a crack popping the frozen turf up a single inch.

"Farris, get me a tire iron," Owen panted.

Farris scurried away to the back of his SUV, returning with the tire iron. Owen wedged it into the gap and stomped down hard. The turf gave way around a perfectly symmetrical hole big enough for a man to crawl through.

"What is it?" Farris murmured.

"It's a door." Owen stood over it, cold chills bristling down his spine.

"To what?"

Owen didn't answer. He'd seen some weird shit, growing up around the Rutherford Ranch. His momma had always accused him of having an active imagination, with his never-ending cast of invisible friends. Come to think of it, there had never been a time when he wasn't muttering about ghosts and odd creatures slithering about in the tall grass. That worried him now a lot more than it did back then.

He remembered when he was about eight, going to the ranch to visit Sal and his family. He'd never enjoyed playing with Sal very much, and pretty much avoided him whenever possible. Sal was the kind of kid who pulled the legs off frogs just for kicks, and would hit anyone in the junk when they weren't looking. Owen thought of him as something of a spoiled prince, given free rein over a vast kingdom.

On this particular occasion, Sal had pissed Owen off by putting a dead snake in his sneaker. Owen had beat Sal bloody, and Sal had gone running back to the house. Well, about as fast as the kid could run. Sal had been a pudgy kid. He liked to throw his weight around, but he really wasn't much more than dough. But Owen knew he was in deep trouble this time, and had taken off into the fields to get away from his cousin and whatever punishment was awaiting him.

He'd run as far as he could, into the summer grass that came up almost to his chest. He fantasized for a brief moment about what it would be like to hide in this grass, to build a fort and live among the cows and the ravens that always seemed to mass over the land in swarms, like flies.

He crouched in the grass, making a nest. No one could see him here. He could be out here forever, and no one would ever find him. This world of sunshine and grass and sky would be far preferable to dealing with Sal's petulant wrath and the anger of his aunt and uncle, who treated Sal like he was the heir to the universe, a young King Arthur wielding a Popsicle stick.

Maybe he was. Owen remembered peering through the grass walls of his hideout into the valley below, at all the vast land and green and gold. He felt a pang of jealousy, but then he saw it.

Something weird.

A man walked along a beaten-down path in the grass along a barbed-wire fence. He looked odd— like he had no arms. The sleeves of his plaid shirt hung at his sides like wet laundry, and he trudged along, looking up at the sky. Ravens swarmed overhead in a seething mass, cawing.

And then Owen saw them dive toward the man.

Owen gasped and clapped his hand over his mouth. The ravens were about to attack that poor crippled man, were going to tear him apart. He crawled forward out of his nest, terrified but compelled to watch.

The ravens slammed into the man, a dozen of them, one after the other, whacking into his body from the front and back. The man stumbled in the flurry of feathers, turning like a scarecrow in a storm as they assaulted him. But that was the funny thing—they didn't bounce off with chunks of meat in their beaks. They just . . . disappeared.

The man staggered upright, surrounded by a miasma of dust and a few feathers. With a start, Owen realized that his arms had grown back. They'd grown right down past his sleeves, with pale hands that opened and closed.

Owen squeaked.

As if he heard him, the man in the field turned toward Owen with a black and distant gaze.

Owen scuttled backward in the grass, clawing through the stems, and scrambled to his feet. Keeping his head down, he ran as fast as he could back toward the house. His aunt and uncle's punish-

ment were nothing compared to . . . to *that*. Whatever that was.

He'd come around the edge of the barn, fists
and legs pumping, and got caught in a tangle of
arms. He fought for a moment, then recognized his
mother's perfume. Dior.

"Owen, where have you been?" She knelt and
smoothed his sweaty hair back from his eyes. "I've
been looking for you."

Winded, he blurted out what he'd seen: the man
with the ravens who'd grown his arms back, right
in front of him.

His mother grasped his shoulders and forced
him to look at her. "Owen. Your imagination has
gone wild again."

"But it was real! I swear!"

"You're exhausted. It's time to go home." She
rose and took him by the hand.

Owen stomped along, frustrated. "But what
about . . ." He remembered Sal now, his bloody
nose and the shiner he'd given him. Surely some
gawdawful punishment awaited him.

"What about Sal?" He kicked a pebble along the
gravel path.

"Don't worry about Sal. Sal has enough on his
plate." His mother's gaze was distant, contemplative.

"Sal's a brat. He says that all this is his." Resentment churned in him.

"Yes," she agreed readily. "But he will have challenges that you will not have to face." She seemed so certain of that, then.

"It still sucks."

She laughed then, a small dark laugh. "You have no idea what you've been spared." She kissed the top of his head and took him home.

His parents never took him back to the ranch after that. He saw Sal and his family at holidays, and they always came to Owen's house.

Owen wondered about that for many years after. His mother had gotten into several arguments with his father, hushed whispers long after he'd gone to bed, about whether he should be allowed to go to the ranch unsupervised. His father hadn't been raised on the ranch, hadn't stood any chance of inheriting it. He was the youngest son, and had become county sheriff, like his father before him. Owen's mother seemed to think that was entirely enough adventure for the household.

"He has to be told someday," his father hissed.

"But not today," she insisted. "Not today."

And it seemed like "today" never came. Owen's father died of a stroke many years ago, and his mother had nothing to say. Not then.

Not today.

But today, there was a hole in the ground. A gaping mystery. Did it lead to a moonshiner's cellar?

Some stash of Gold Rush treasure? A Cold War era bomb shelter?

Owen stared into the darkness. He plucked the flashlight from his belt and shone it inside. He spied a mass of tree roots, gnarled and charred and twisted. He reached down and shoved at them with his flashlight. They seemed sturdy enough to contemplate climbing.

"I'm going down to take a look," he said.

"Are you sure, Sheriff?" Farris looked dubious.

"I'll squawk if I find anything. Maybe we'll hit it lucky and it'll be full of rum."

Owen stepped down into the dark, clinging to the roots, shining his flashlight before him. His light caught a spiral of tendril-like shapes, and he focused on not losing his footing. He finally could make out a dirt floor below, and jumped down to the frozen earth.

It was then that the smell hit him: the unmistakable smell of death. Winter could damp it down, slow it, but it always crept up from somewhere. Nothing ever dies pretty.

"Ugh." He pressed the sleeve of his coat over his nose and swept his light around. It stilled on a figure on the floor, about a yard away. It looked as if someone had flung the body down the hatch, and made no effort to move it. He could make out decomposing flannel, a rope around the corpse's neck, and a face blackened with rot. He knew better than to touch it, but it sure looked like it could be Sal. There was the glint of a gold ring on his right hand that Owen recognized as his grandfather's.

"Everything going okay down there?" Farris called down.

"Stand by. I'm gonna need a body bag."

He turned the light around and scanned what seemed to be a chamber carved into the earth. Dark tree roots curled around the perimeter, like Medusa's hair. The beam stilled, and Owen squinted.

"Fuck."

There were more corpses strung up in the tree roots. Bits of white tooth and bone and hair were interwoven into the twisted roots. He couldn't tell how long the bodies had been here—maybe as long as Sal, maybe more. Maybe these were the ranch hands he hadn't been able to find. And that was weird as hell—the sheriff's office hadn't received any missing persons reports on these guys. It was like they had no family or friends—and they were all down here, rotting away. Nobody had cared enough to report them gone.

Owen looked down at Sal with mixed feelings. Sal was a fucking bastard. Honestly, Owen wasn't sorry his cousin was dead. But a murder was a murder, and family was family, and he had to do something about it.

And it was looking very possible that he had a serial killer on his hands.

He shone his light up to the hatch.

"I think we're gonna need a lot more body bags."

"YOU CAN'T STAY here. They'll find you."

Petra clutched the wheel of the Bronco in her gloved hands. Gabe sat in the passenger's side, with Sig between them on the bench seat. Sig looked pleased to be out and about in the wintry bluster, bouncing around and snooting on the windshield, but Gabe sat low, the collar of his coat turned up and hat pulled down over his eyes. He'd always been very good at being invisible, but Petra wondered how much of that had been due to supernatural influences.

"Eventually, they will," he agreed. "So where are we going?"

"The safest place I can think of at the moment is the reservation. Owen hasn't got any authority there." She drummed her fingers on the wheel, impatient at getting stuck behind a slow pickup. "And I have reasonable confidence that if the reservation police pick you up, they won't beat you to death and leave you in a ditch for revenge."

"Good point," he agreed. "But have you given any further thought to my suggestion?"

Her mouth twisted. "About getting married?"

"Yes."

She chewed her lip. "It would be convenient." Her stomach flopped back and forward as she thought about the possibility.

Gabe frowned. "That is, more or less, how it was done in my day."

"Mail-order brides?" Of course. She felt her cheeks burning a bit. Gabe was not one given to grand, romantic gestures. Perhaps this was simply a business arrangement to him.

"More than one man never laid eyes on his bride until she stepped off the train," he admitted. "It wasn't very romantic."

"How did it come to be with you and your wife, then? Did she step off a train?"

His wife from long ago. Petra tried not to pry about that relationship. She felt no pangs of jealousy. There was no use having enmity for dead lovers, especially ones who had been dust for over a hundred years.

"Jelena was the daughter of one of Pinkerton's clients. We met at the theatre after exchanging letters for some months. I think it was the Invisible Prince that we saw."

"So no arranged marriage for you?"

"I wouldn't say that it wasn't arranged. Our meeting was, but affection grew from there. Jelena was under some . . . unusual circumstances. She was looking for an arrangement that would permit her to dodge some of the social requirements of the time."

"You can imagine how my imagination runs wild with that."

"Jelena's love, first and foremost, was her music. She was a pianist and a composer, a learned woman who knew her own mind. I respected that. She wanted to be able to continue her work without interference from a husband and children. I could offer that."

"Pinkerton agents didn't stay home much?"

"No. I was always on a train to somewhere, and we were content with the time that we had together."

"Did you love her?"

"I did."

"This idea of marriage you suggest—it's not what I had in mind whenever I thought of marriage."

"No?"

"No," she confessed. "You could say it wasn't ever really on my bucket list . . ." She trailed off, and it took her a few moments to come back to herself. "Anyway, I'm coming to realize that life isn't exactly what I'd planned. And it may be a helluva lot shorter than what I thought."

He reached across the seat to touch her shoulder. "No matter what happens, I'm not leaving you."

"Even if I do my best to drive you away?"

"You're stuck."

Snowplowing stopped abruptly at the edge of

the reservation land, as if the plow had simply vanished into thin air. Petra relied on the four-wheel drive and a rough estimation of where the road might lie between mailbox posts to get them to Maria's house. The wood-sided cottage was tucked into drifts of snow, the front walk and porch freshly shoveled. Maria's green Explorer was parked in the drive. Petra parked the Bronco beside it and Sig immediately slipped out, running up the steps of the cottage.

Gabe took his time, trudging after Petra. She rapped sharply on the frame of the storm door, and the front door opened behind it. A grey and white cat stretched up to peer through the glass at Sig, who slobbered at her. In disgust, she dropped down to all fours and trotted away.

A silhouette behind her laughed. "Pearl's not the welcome wagon today."

"Hi, Maria. I hope this isn't a bad time."

"Not at all. Come in."

Maria, drying her hands with a dish towel, bumped the door open with her hip. She was dressed in a long-sleeved velveteen tunic, with leggings and colorful knitted socks to the knee.

Petra took her boots off just inside the door. Maria's house was full of bright yellow paint, quilts, and the smell of bread baking.

"How have you been?" Petra asked, pulling up a chair at the kitchen table.

"Work's been busy." Maria put a pot of coffee on. "Seems like cabin fever hits everyone this time of year. Saw fifteen clients yesterday. My favorite was a family fighting over the contents of a grandfather's estate. The estate consisted of a bowling ball, a bonsai tree, and an iguana."

"An iguana?"

"Yeah. He's ten years old. His name is Seth. At least we got the custody of the iguana figured out. He now belongs to the eight-year-old granddaughter, who was really the only sane person in the room."

"No rest for the weary in social work," she said.

"Eh. You have your own stuff going on," Maria said. "I heard from Mike about that weird wolf thing you found at the park."

Gabe was on the floor, rubbing Sig's belly with one hand and Pearl's with the other. "What weird wolf thing?"

"Oh, yeah." Petra rubbed her temple. "We haven't talked about it yet. I found a wolf skin in a tree while out working yesterday—and it was weirdly staged. Stretched over an armature of sticks, like it was meant to be seen."

Gabe went still. "Where was that?"

"Near Mammoth Springs." She described the site in detail. "I used the Locus on the wolf's remains, and it registered the presence of magic of some sort."

"Horrible," Maria said.

"I've seen something like that before," Gabe said. Both Sig and Pearl lay on their backs on the floor and turned their heads toward him, annoyed that he'd stopped petting them. He climbed to his feet and pulled out a chair at the table. When he sat, his thumb traced the stubble on his chin, as if he was caught in the depths of his deep memory.

"There was a man, back in 1861. He came to be known as Skinflint Jack, the Jack of Harts."

CHAPTER 7

The Legend of Skinflint Jack

Jack Raleigh was fleeing from the law in the late 1850s. He'd been wanted for bank robbery in Boston, but had slipped through the fingers of law enforcement and traveled west. Rumor had it that he'd been robbed himself on a stagecoach and arrived in Temperance penniless and pissed about the lack of honor among thieves. But still, he found a wife and had a couple of children, and made his living as a trapper.

"Jack was a man interested in a quick buck, but the backcountry is a harsh place to try and make a living. He was a cheap man, willing to gnaw the fat off any skin he took. He'd pick up odd jobs, sometimes working as hired muscle for rich men, like Lascaris. I was working as a Pinkerton agent at the time, and I briefly considered arresting Jack and collecting the reward still on his head from Boston. But that would have blown my cover in my investigation of Lascaris.

"Jack left his wife and children to go on a trapping expedition in the winter of 1861 and returned to find them dead. He blamed the incident on wolves, and swore revenge by any means necessary. The townsfolk didn't believe him, and a warrant was issued for his arrest. The bodies were said to be found missing their bones, the skins left behind . . . and wolves do not kill like that. We all knew he would have sold them to Lascaris for a dollar and a half-blind mule.

"Jack skulked back to Lascaris, to see what might be done for his situation. Instead, Lascaris began experimenting upon the hapless fellow. No one would miss Jack Raleigh if he was gone, and no one would believe any tales he told.

"Lascaris had been experimenting with the union of opposites, which is often represented in ancient texts by the Stag and the Unicorn. He'd been gathering bits of horn from local hunters and had sent away for what were purported to be unicorn horns, at great sums. I examined them, and concluded that they were nothing more than narwhal and goat horns. But I kept silent, curious to see what he would make of them.

"Lascaris promised Jack power. He invited him

down to his lab, where Jack, being a greedy soul, realized that gold was being made. There was gold dust in the alchemist's athanor, gold nuggets in his glass beakers. He attempted to steal it when Lascaris's back was turned, but the alchemist caught him. As Lascaris told the tale, there was a great fight that ended with spilled potions, broken glass, and Skinflint Jack impaled on a set of antlers.

"Figuring that he might as well put the body to use, Lascaris used a separation process to pull Jack's body to pieces, then re-formed him. This was not a satisfactory experiment, as Lascaris had been hoping to create a unicorn by embedding a piece of horn in Jack's flesh. Lascaris was a little optimistic about his abilities, and his imagination frequently outstripped his reach.

"Unfortunately, a piece of stag antler from the altercation remained in Jack's neck, contaminating the experiment. It became the touchstone for the creature he became: the Jack of Harts. He broke free of Lascaris's basement and vanished into the night.

"The Jack of Harts remembers only gold and revenge. Since he is more spirit than flesh, he has lived a long time, haunting his old land. Once a decade or so, some huntsman or wanderer will describe seeing him, a man with antlers, wearing the skull of a stag, in the forest at night. These stories are usually chalked up to too much drink and imagination.

"The ones who have seen him from a distance are lucky. The ones who get close are not heard of again. Their bodies are left behind. If there is any gold or precious metal on them, it's stripped. There was a hunter found thirty years ago, dead, with his ring finger removed. I guessed that it might be Jack's work, for that reason.

"There's a story that went around about fifty years ago about a pond south of Fawn Creek. The myth is that if one throws a piece of gold into the pond, Jack will appear and either grant a wish or kill the querant." Gabe leaned back, seeming lost in thought. Petra wondered if he was trying to recall exactly how many years it had been.

"So . . . the Jack of Harts has been killing wolves and granting wishes like a demented tooth fairy, all this time?" Petra's brow wrinkled, digesting the tale.

"In the beginning, he was quite prolific. With the wolves, anyway. Carcasses would be found stretched over skeletons of twigs, as you describe. But there have been many years in which the park had few or no wolves, and I assumed that he slept. He seems to be awake now . . . and I wonder if that has something to do with wolves crossing into his territory. For a long time there were none there, as men hunted them nearly to extinction in this area."

"Not just *any* wolves." Maria stirred her coffee. "Mike said that this is the Nine Stars pack."

Petra planted her chin in her hand. "These wolves . . . Mike said they were shy, that the scientists had a hard time tagging them."

"More than shy. The Nine Stars pack were in the area long before Temperance was a town. Tribal legend says that they used to be men and women—a lost tribe of Navajo Skinwalkers from down south, who were just passing through. They changed into wolves to survive a harsh winter, and forgot how to change back."

"They changed into wolves?"

"There's a whole Navajo mythology about Skinwalkers. The Arapaho don't have an analogous legend. But they are supposed to be terrifying creatures—able to change into any shape they choose and steal power from their victims. Needless to say, I told Mike to stay away."

"Did he listen to you?"

"Of course not."

"They don't seem to be doing well up against the Jack of Harts," Petra said, sipping her coffee. It still disturbed her that Skinflint Jack was hunting these creatures, even if they were remnants of a terrible legend.

Maria spread her hands out on the table. "If they believe that they're wolves, maybe they can't fight back. Or maybe they're just ordinary wolves. I don't know for certain."

"Hard to know whether the Locus thinks the

wolf is magical itself . . . or whether something magical killed it, and the residue remains on it," Gabe said.

"I told my dad about the wolf," Petra said. "He suggested it might be some kind of separation operation."

Gabe seemed to mull it over. "Could be, but it's crude as hell. And if they are Skinwalkers, then Jack may have signed on for more than he bargained for."

Maria poured more cream in her coffee. "So, are you two off to chase Skinflint Jack into the wilderness?"

"Actually . . ." Petra grimaced. "It's more of an issue of being chased by the law at the moment."

"Oh, no." Maria's spoon stilled in her coffee, ringing against the porcelain rim. "What happened?"

Petra took a deep breath, her heart hammering. "I'm afraid that I have to ask you for a favor."

Maria took a sip of her coffee. "This is gonna be good."

THE STAG WAS hunting them.

Nine knew it; so did the others. The pack had fled to a valley shielded from the west wind, in an effort to protect the pups and retreat to safer ground. The pups were slowing, and many of the adults were injured. Nine limped on her front left leg, hopping through the snow. In ideal circumstances, she'd fold herself into a warm den to recover. They all would. Out here in the snowfield, however, they were too open, too easy to stalk. The afternoon was bright with sun reflecting off the snow, creating a glare with margins that danced at the edge of her vision. It played tricks on her, she knew.

Ghost had set about finding shelter, someplace to hide from the Stag. Ghost and Falling Stone had cleared the snow from the entrance at a shallow cave at the foot of the mountain. Once they'd opened the cave, it smelled like bear, and the pack recoiled. There was no way to tell how deeply a bear was hibernating, and such a thing was not worth the risk.

They continued onward down the valley. Nine glanced back, thinking she spied antlers in the trees, and whimpered an alarm. The ragtag pack picked up the pace, moving to find a more easily defensible area. There was no digging a new hiding place in this frozen soil.

They paused only to snipe at a den of voles and to find water. Most of the water in this area was frozen solid, as the creeks were shallow. The pack needed water more than it needed food or shelter or sleep; Nine felt her muscles aching and the headache of a bone-deep dehydration stealing through her. She tried to take mouthfuls of snow, but it was very little, and very cold.

At last: a possibility. A small pond appeared in a soft valley, reflecting the late afternoon sun in the sky. It was slushy, not completely frozen over yet. It must be deep, with roots far enough into the earth to be able to hold the warmth of the sun overnight. Or it might have some of the disgusting metallic tang of the brightly colored springwater, and be terrible to drink. Nine could smell nothing human about it, and none of the stink of sulfur, from this distance. Four large stones ringed the perimeter of the pond, each one as large as a wolf.

Ghost trotted down the slope to investigate, barking at the rest of the pack to stay behind in a stand of trees. Nine followed, close on his heels, eager to steal a taste before the pack nosed her out of the way. Her paws crunched in the frozen-over slush, and she peered into the water. She dipped her head to take a drink.

But it smelled wrong. All wrong. Her lips drew back immediately, and a growl shook through her chest. She peered down at her reflection in the pond. There was a curious yellow bloom below the ice that churned like smoke. She thought she saw the outline of an antler below, and she whined.

This place. It had to belong to the Stag.

Nine whimpered and backed away. Ghost followed, and they trotted back to the pack. His eyes were narrowed. She was certain he'd seen what she had seen.

Ghost shuffled forward. Nine could see that he was exhausted, but they had to get away . . . get away from *that*. They were deep in the Stag's territory and they had to escape before he returned.

A sound echoed across the snow plain. An engine, a machine belonging to humans. This could be good for the wolves, or it could be very bad.

A snow machine roared across the landscape. There was a man riding it, a gun strapped to the back. Nine's nose twitched. She wanted nothing to do with men and their guns and machines. She followed Ghost along the path they'd made in the snow to investigate the pond, slinking low to avoid the interloper. Cold snow scraped her belly, clinging to her fur in clumps.

Ghost turned around the corner of a drift. Nine ran into his backside and nearly fell down.

It was the Stag. He rose up from the snow, shedding white in a sheet from his antlers. He'd been waiting for them just under the crust of snow.

Ghost growled, backing away, his tail lashing. Nine howled for the rest of the pack, panicked.

But the rest of the pack didn't come.

Instead, the engine roared closer. Nine looked right and left, not sure which direction to turn. The man on the snow machine roared toward them in the glare of snow, skimming over the snow faster than any wolf.

"Leave them alone!"

There was the crack of a rifle, a warning shot. Nine jerked in panic. Flattening her ears, she turned tail and ran for the safety of the rest of the pack beyond the tree line, Ghost behind her. Adrenaline overcame exhaustion, and she raced as fast as she could with pain lancing through her wounded leg.

She'd made it nearly to the tree line of pine and stripped aspen when she dared look back. The man on the snow machine had dismounted, was aiming a gun at the Stag. He was shouting something she didn't understand. Another shot rang out.

Then the Stag took two steps toward him and engulfed him in darkness.

"YOU GUYS WEREN'T shitting me."

Maria stuffed her hands in her coat pockets, chortling at Gabe and Petra. The three of them stood on the steps of a courthouse four counties distant from Temperance, but still within the state of Wyoming. Petra figured it would be less likely that Gabe's wanted poster would be plastered all over the place a hundred miles away from Temperance.

"I don't think so?" Petra was still feeling oddly weird about the whole thing. She opened the glass door and shuffled down the marble-tiled hallway stained with dried slush. There was a sign perched in a window that said LICENSING, and Petra stepped uneasily up to the clerk at the long counter.

"Um, hi. Is this the place where one would get a marriage license?"

The young woman behind the counter nodded, her ponytail bobbing. "I can also set you up with a car title, hunting or fishing license."

"Just the marriage license, I think."

"Okay. Please fill out these forms, sign here and here. Your witness signs here. And I'll need drivers' licenses and birth certificates for the two of you."

Now, that part would be interesting. Petra dug her license and certificate out of her wallet, and snuck a peek at Gabe. He said that he had papers, but she was curious to see what they'd say. They clearly wouldn't be the originals—there had to be some degree of forgery involved, somewhere along the way.

But these looked really good. He had a birth certificate from Massachusetts and a well-worn Wyoming driver's license. Maybe when he'd been in good with the Rutherfords, Sal had seen to it that they all looked like legal workers.

It was then that Petra realized she didn't know Gabe's last name. Not for certain. She'd scanned his wanted poster but had no idea if any of that info was correct. She glanced surreptitiously at the license as he handed it over to the clerk.

Gabriel Manget.

She'd have to ask him later if that was really his birth name. And if he was really born in Massachusetts. Later. That was a topic for a time when she wasn't vaguely freaked about getting a marriage license with a guy whose last name she didn't know.

Gabe pulled thirty dollars from his wallet and folded the birth certificate and license back into it. Petra signed the forms with a pen chained to the desk and passed them back to Gabriel to sign.

The clerk got out her notary stamp, stamped the paperwork, and slid the license across the counter to Gabe. "You have one year to get hitched in the state of Wyoming. Your marriage must be solemnized by a registered member of the clergy, a judge, justice of the peace, or court commissioner, who will file the paperwork with us."

"That's it?"

"Yup." The clerk smiled. "Congrats, you guys."

It felt pretty surreal. They headed out of the empty hallway to the lobby and the Bronco parked at a meter out front.

"So," Maria said. "You guys got an officiant? I could ask one of the tribal elders, but I'm not sure if they can marry people who aren't of the tribe."

"I think we have that covered," Petra said, popping open the door. "I think."

If this was the right thing, then why was her heart hammering a thousand miles an hour? She climbed in and closed the door. Sig wormed out of the blanket he'd been napping in while they took care of business. He wriggled into the backseat to cuddle with Maria.

"So . . . is there something you guys aren't telling me?"

Petra swapped glances with Gabe. She hadn't told Maria exactly why he was wanted by the law. Or about her illness. She didn't want to draw any more people in to get hurt. Eventually, Petra would tell her everything. Eventually. But not today.

"Yes. A lot."

"I figured. Do I want to know?"

"Noooo. Trust me."

She cranked the ignition and put the Bronco into gear. They saw a McDonald's on the way out of town and she ordered cheeseburgers, fries, and Cokes all around. Sig dearly loved cheeseburgers, and dismantled his on the floorboards to eat the meat first, like a kid with an Oreo cookie. Maria slurped her Coke noisily in the back as they tooled down the road.

"You know," Maria said, "you guys have a whole year to pull the trigger on that thing. You both have been through a lot. Maybe a cooling off period—Oh my God." She stopped slurping on her straw and swallowed some pop down the wrong pipe, coughing so hard that Petra nearly pulled over.

"You're not pregnant, are you?" Maria croaked.

"No!" Petra and Gabe said it in unison.

"Okay, then. Far be it from me to stand in the way of true love. Or insurance benefits."

Or something like that. Petra glanced at Gabe's profile. She loved him. She really did. Not the way that she had loved anyone else. She loved him in a very strange way. It wasn't the roar of lust, though he sure damn well curled her toes in bed. This was something else. Something quieter. She trusted him entirely, in a kind of still and placid way that she couldn't see changing.

It was more than most people had. Maybe that was enough.

Hours later, when the sun had dipped below the horizon, the Bronco pulled into the parking lot of the Phoenix Village Nursing Home. Visiting hours were still on—her dad should have finished his dinner of Salisbury steak, mashed potatoes, canned peas, and yellow gravy. The stars had begun to prickle through the violet canopy of night, and everything seemed muffled, still, and perfectly quiet. White Christmas lights were wound around the trees at the entrance, shining amid icicles clinging to the gutters. She'd come to Temperance to find her missing father, and he'd wound up here, in this tucked-away place of artificial cheer. Early onset Alzheimer's, they'd said. Took some of the sting about the how and why he'd left Petra and her mother. But not all of it.

She hopped out of the Bronco and clipped a leash on Sig. He muttered his complaints, but didn't struggle too much. She was hoping she could pass him off as a dog, that he would behave that well.

Gabe came around to the driver's side of the Bronco and offered her his arm. "Ready?"

She looked up at the stars, at Orion overhead.

"Yeah. I'm ready."

They turned toward the freshly shoveled nursing home walk and went inside.

The nurse at the front desk smiled at Petra and nodded as they came in, averting her eyes to Sig. His toenails clicked on the recently waxed floor tiles, and Petra could see him turning his nose up at the lingering meat-loaf smell. Maria slipped by an arrangement of white amaryllises that someone had put in a wall niche and snagged one. She handed it to Petra.

"Humor me," she said.

Petra took it. She paused before her dad's door and knocked. "Dad?"

"Come in."

Her dad was sitting in his wheelchair by the dark window, looking a little befuddled. A splash of gravy stained his sweatshirt. A man in a black suit stood beside him. The man looked barely over twenty-one. Maybe a priest in training some-where?

"I'm Pastor Cowan," the man said, extending his hand.

"I'm Petra Dee. This is Gabriel Manget, and my friend Maria Yellowrose." She made all the intro-ductions. "Thank you for seeing us."

"You had good timing. I just finished up on last rites for Mrs. Moore in Room 242." The young man grinned. "I haven't done a wedding before."

"That's . . . um . . . great."

"But I know how to do it," he said, recovering quickly. "There are instruction sheets on where to mail the stuff and all."

"Great." Her heart was still pounding. She glanced at her father, who was in the middle of a stare-down with Gabe. Petra reminded herself that her dad had left her and her mother before she'd started dating, and that he'd never had the oppor-tunity to participate in the ridiculous paternal rite of boyfriend hazing.

"It's nice to meet you, Mr. Dee." Gabe extended his hand.

Her father took it and shook it. "Good evening. And this must be . . . Sig."

Sig was snooting all over the floor and had paused beside her father's wheelchair. He got up on his hind legs and slurped at her father's face, which sent the old man into paroxysms of giggles. So much for the paternal rite of sternness.

"You have the license?" The pastor was clearly in the mood to get going, glancing at the time on his cell phone.

"Yes." Gabe handed it over. Petra expected to be fidgety, her heart hammering. But she felt peaceful, serene. Her heart slowed, and she felt the way she did when she was taking a nap in sunshine. Warm.

"Short and sweet, you said on the phone when we talked earlier?"

"Please."

Petra held the amaryllis stem in one hand and Gabe's hand in the other. The thick stem of the flower felt like a cold piece of celery, but Gabe's hand was unexpectedly warm.

Pastor Cowan pushed his glasses up his nose. "Do you, Gabriel Manget, take this woman to be your lawfully wedded wife?"

Gabe looked at her with his bottomless amber eyes. "I do."

"Do you, Petra Barbara Dee, take this man to be your lawfully wedded husband?"

"I do."

"Do you have the rings?"

"No rings," Petra said. She hadn't gotten that far along in this adventure.

"Then, by the power invested in me by the state

of Wyoming, I pronounce you man and wife. You may kiss the bride."

She leaned forward on tiptoe to kiss him. This felt good. It felt right. He reached down to touch her face, and his was shining. He tucked the amaryllis flower behind her ear, and she grinned as he tried to negotiate the unwieldy stem into her hair. Her hand landed on his chest, and she could feel his human heart beating beneath her fingers.

A cell phone rang. Petra was dimly aware of it—the ringtone was CCR's "Fortunate Son." The pastor signed off on the marriage certificate, which was still warm from the laser printer, likely from the front desk.

"A gift for you," her father said. He took her open palm and poured something into it with his palsied hands.

"Oh, Dad," she said. "You didn't need to—"

"Hush."

She opened her hand. There were two marbles in her palm. One solid white and scuffed, the other clear with a gold cat's-eye. They rolled in her hand like a sun and moon—they must have been treasures from her father's bedside alchemy set, or something he'd found in the hall.

"Put one under your pillow tonight, and one under your husband's," he ordered, a twinkle in his eye.

Her brow wrinkled. "Okay, but what—"

"Oh, my God," Maria said from across the room.

Petra turned to see Maria blanch and sit down heavily at the end of the bed.

"What's wrong?"

Maria covered the receiver of her cell phone with her hand. "It's Mike. It's bad. I've got to get to the hospital."

CHAPTER 8

In the Dark

Keeping control of the crime scene was more difficult than Owen anticipated.

He'd radioed a half dozen of his most discreet crime scene techs and deputies to come collect Sal's body and cut the others out of the tree roots. They'd zipped Sal up in a body bag and taken a Sawzall to the roots, trying to keep the right body parts together by tagging them before putting them in bags. A generator had been hauled in by truck, and the sound drowned out much of the chatter. Orange electrical cords snaked down through the hatch to power steaming yellow lights. Photographs were taken. A fingerprint tech tried to take prints from the remaining surfaces and hands. A few squirts of Luminol suggested that the whole place had been doused in blood at some time or other. Owen watched in wonder, flickering around his men like a shadow. He'd tied a hand-kerchief smeared with Vicks over his face, but he quickly forgot the smell.

He formed many impressions in those hours—that this thing, this tree, had been here for a very long time. The bodies—not so long. Winter could slow decomposition, but these were reasonably fresh, in corpse-time. Probably not more than a few months.

And this chamber . . . he could not tell if it was man-made or natural. A tunnel split away from it, and Owen placed yellow crime-scene tape over the opening.

"We should look down there for more bodies," one of his men suggested.

"No." Owen knew that he had to get the bodies out of there, but he felt curiously protective about the rest of the site. He had the sense of standing in the center of a great hive of inexplicable things, and he didn't want to share them with anyone. Not yet.

"But there might be more evidence . . ."

"I said no."

"All right, then."

But he knew people would gossip, that word would get around the department and beyond about the weird mass murder scene. No matter how much Owen reminded his people of the confidentiality of ongoing investigations, there were no secrets that were kept long here.

When the last truck had moved away across the snow to the morgue, full of body bags, Owen remained beside the burned tree. What was this? What had it meant? What had Sal and the others died for?

He turned the heater on in his SUV and fished his cell phone out of his belt. Then he did what any wise man would do in inexplicable circumstances: He thumbed through his contact list and dialed his mother.

"Hi, Mom."

"Owen. How are you?"

"I wanted you to know before you heard it anyplace else. We found Sal."

There was a silence at the end of the line for a few moments, and then he heard his mother sigh. "Is he alive?"

His mother was not the kind of woman for whom one needed to sugar-coat things. She was steel coated in Dior, and she would lose little sleep over Sal's demise. She'd have a glass of sherry and order a flower arrangement for the funeral.

"No. We found his body at the ranch. Under a tree, of all places."

"Owen. Be careful."

He played with the heater now that it had begun

to warm up, cranking it full blast. "Do you know what's going on here? Did Dad?"

"Your father . . . when he was alive, talked in his sleep. He talked about dead men walking, about the Tree of Life. About magic."

"What did he mean?"

"He didn't like to talk about it when he was awake. And your father's story is not my story to tell. I just knew there was something . . . off about that place. And to tell the truth, I was glad that Sal inherited it, and not you. Nothing good ever comes from there. Just . . . just leave it alone, Owen. If you're smart, you'll sell it the instant it gets out of probate and wash your hands of it."

"I can't promise that, Mom."

She sighed again, and the sound rattled across the receiver. He heard the clink of porcelain teacups in the background. "Shall I go ahead and call Doug Harrington? Harrington's did a nice job with your father's funeral."

"Yeah." Owen rubbed his forehead. Harrington's was the best funeral home in town. There was really only one place to send Sal, and that was to hell in a velvet-lined coffin.

"Open casket or closed?" his mother asked. He heard her shuffling with what he assumed was a phone book and the scratch of a pencil on paper as she cradled the receiver on her shoulder.

"Closed. Definitely closed."

"Well, that'll be less expensive. Do you know when Doug and his boys can come pick up the body?"

"Not for a few days. The coroner will have to do an autopsy. But when she's done, they can get the body from there."

"Okay. When that happens, I'll run an announcement in the paper. I'll ask Doug what kind of flowers they can get . . . probably amaryllises, this time of year. And when you get a chance, get a suit of clothes from Sal's closet. Socks, shoes. The whole nine yards."

"Gotcha."

"Don't bury him with your grandfather's ring. That belongs to you." His mom was not given to sentimentality. She was all business. He only remembered seeing her cry once, when deputies had showed up on their doorstep to tell her that his father died. She had waited until they left before she broke down in tears. He admired that about her. Admired it, and feared it just a little bit, if he admitted it to himself. She was a tough lady. Had to be.

"Yeah." He stared down at his right hand, which now bore Sal's ring. He'd taken it off the corpse before they'd zipped it up, in a twinge of spite. It had been a little sticky, but he'd rubbed the residue off on his sleeve. Good as new.

He hung up when he could feel his toes again and when he heard his mother's teakettle whistling in the background.

This place. He let his eyes rove the desolation.

There was something here, he was sure of it. And he was sure he wasn't getting the whole story from his mother.

Anna sat on the passenger seat of his SUV. "Are you going back down there?"

"Yes."

"I don't like it underground." She chewed on the tie of her hood.

"You don't have to come."

He turned off the engine to the truck, locked up, and let himself back down the hatch, into the empty chamber that now smelled of fresh sawdust and chalk. He turned on his flashlight and stood before the tunnel that he'd taped off, pulled a corner of the tape down, and stepped through.

He rummaged around in his coat pocket for a piece of crime-scene chalk to mark an arrow on the tunnel wall. He had no idea where these tunnels went, but he sure as fuck didn't want to get lost in here and freeze to death.

Pulling his collar up around his ears, he began to explore. Some of the tunnel structure was round, and rough-hewn, while other sections were square with supporting beams chewed by termites and stained with wood rot. Water had sunk in here,

bits of melting ice shining overhead and treacherous slicks formed on the floor. Owen estimated
that the temperature here was warmer than above
ground, about fifty-five degrees. The ice was melting and slushy as it filtered through the ground,
and he was glad that he'd worn his waterproof
boots today. All hail the mighty Gore-Tex.

He turned left and right, marking his choices
on the walls. The tunnels seemed to slope down,
down. He figured he'd walked more than a couple
of miles. He reached for the compass application
on his cell phone to show him what direction he
was walking, but there was no signal here.

He heard something up ahead, something that
sounded like running water.

The tunnel banked sharply to the right and went
down in a series of stone steps. They were oddly
worn, as if they'd been trod on by many feet. Owen
minded his footing, shining his light ahead of him,
and the beam bounced off water.

Not just water—a river. The steps descended to
the gravel-strewn bank of a river that ran down a
passageway larger than a train tunnel. The river
was easily thirty feet wide, the current moving
lazily to his right. A thick grey mist clung to the
surface of the water, soaking deep into the damp
stone walls.

"What the hell," he muttered. He knew of no
aquifers here on the ranch. Just little above ground

streams that dried out in summer and bloated with rain in the spring.

He felt something dripping into his face, a spatter that rattled against his hat. He swept his beam up. A grey cloud was clinging up to the vast ceiling, and it was raining. Raining in an underground tunnel.

"This can't be happening," he said to himself. All he knew about meteorology he'd learned from the people in windbreakers on the Weather Channel. But he was pretty sure that this just didn't *happen*.

"Well, it is." Anna had appeared beside him, looking cold. She'd pulled the sleeves of her hoodie down to cover her fingertips and wrapped her hands around her elbows. He didn't know if ghosts even got cold, or if this was just some residual habit left over from her life. But she sure was convincing.

"I thought you were staying topside."

She shrugged. "What's this place going to do? Kill me?" She walked to the edge of the river and peered down.

Owen took this as an opportunity to gently poke at her. "Does this place bring up any memories?"

"Memories of what happened at the well?"

"Yeah."

"I told you that I can't remember who did it."

"That's not what I'm asking."

She lifted her head and rain speckled her face. "It did rain while I was down there. It felt a lot like this. Grey overhead."

"Were you alive for that?" Owen's heart pounded. The coroner had never been able to say definitively if she'd been alive or not when she'd been dropped into the well.

She closed her eyes. "I remember that I had a sunburn, and that the rain felt awfully good."

That sounded really corporeal, as if she'd been alive. Owen waited for her to go on, but she didn't. Instead, she stuck her finger out over the riverbank, into the darkness. "Do you see that?"

Owen shone his light where she pointed. Apparently, ghosts could see in the dark. His light picked out something pale and gleaming on the shore. As he stepped toward it, he saw that it was a bone—more than one.

"Shit." Owen had had enough of bodies today. A collection of bones stretched along the river silt, worn clean by water. He tugged one piece free of the mud, and lifted it to inspect it.

It was a long, light bone, attached to another, with a spine of finer bones splaying out from it. It looked like a bird wing, held together with a lacing of desiccated leathery tendons. But birds didn't grow that big. He tugged at it, and a socket popped free of the mud, sending the assembly clattering away like the sail of a kayak.

"What is that?" Anna asked.

"I don't know." He dropped it and took two more steps. There was another set of bones here—a skull. He worked it free of the mud with his boot. It looked like nothing he'd ever seen: a flat skull with a raised ridge that ran from snout to crown. It had a double row of teeth, like a shark.

"Jesus." He dropped it, plucked his hat off his head, and rubbed his suddenly sweaty forehead. "What is this place?"

Anna hovered motionless beside the river, staring at the mist. Owen was going to ask her to stand back—who the hell knew, there could be sea monsters in there—but he had to remind himself that she was dead. He stepped up beside her. "Look, I think we ought to—"

He spun his light into the mist, following her gaze. "Oh."

"That's what it looked like. From the bottom of the well," she whispered.

The mist swirled around a full-moon circle of light. Birds flew across the circle. Clouds scudded past, and the sun set. A moon rose jerkily, studded with bats, and stars spun around.

Owen's brow wrinkled. "That's what you saw?"

"Yes."

The moon and sun swung past at a dizzying pace. Owen guessed that months were passing in fast-forward before his eyes, maybe even as many as six or seven months—and then the sun eventually moved away from the mouth of the well.

"The screaming stopped after a week or two,"

she supplied, with what sounded like the intent to be soothing.

A shadow stopped over the well, leaning in.

And then a ripple formed in the surface of the water, shattering the image.

"Who was that?"

Anna looked away, shaking her head. Blond hair lashed against her cheek. "I don't remember."

"Try."

"I can't."

He reached out for her hand, but his fingers passed through her. He kept forgetting.

"How did you do that?"

"I didn't do that. It was the river."

Owen turned back to the water and squinted into it. It seemed as if something moved underneath the fog and the opaque surface. He stepped closer to the edge, peered in.

Ravens flew across a bright white sky. Ravens. It now occurred to him that there had always been hundreds of them at the ranch, but he hadn't seen a solitary one since Sal died.

The ravens swept over a field, the field at the base of the burned tree. They began pecking at Sal's prone form, pulling the flesh from his bones. Sal didn't move or flinch, not even when one of them waddled off with his finger.

What did this mean? Ravens couldn't kill Sal. Someone—or *something*—had done that.

The image misted over and vanished, replaced by ripples of water.

Owen realized with cold shock that he'd waded into the river up to his knees. Anna floated beside him, her sneakered foot barely skimming the surface of the water. His light lanced into the water, at the pebbles beneath.

And something glittered back at him.

He squinted hard and plunged his hand into the shockingly cold water, fishing around in the silt. It came back with a stone about the size of a gum ball, shining in the diffuse light.

"What is it?" Anna asked.

Owen stared at it in wonder. It was perfectly round, with a nacre sheen. "Damn. I think . . . I think this is a pearl." He jammed it into his pocket and swept his flashlight down to look for more . . .

. . . when something lunged out of the dark water at him. Something dark and massive that roared at him as it latched onto his sleeve with teeth. He stumbled backward, splashing in the water, while Anna screamed.

His flashlight dropped in the water and went out. Owen scrabbled in his gun belt for his gun and fired blindly into the darkness. The thing roared again, with an almost musical voice, and let him go with a wet smack into the gravel. He scrambled up the bank and found himself pressed to the cold stone wall, inching along it, trying to find the

mouth of the tunnel. He'd become completely dis-
oriented in the total blackness, his heart hammering in his chest. All he could perceive was the cold
and the rustle of the water, and he had no idea what
stirred within it. He heard a distant humming, like
a woman trying to remember a tune.

"Anna," he whispered. "Anna, help me."

"This way." Her voice emanated from his left,
and he followed it, stumbling, until he plunged
into a flight of steps on his hands and knees. He
climbed up them on all fours, and it felt like he was
in the smaller space of the tunnel, the river behind
him. His ragged breath echoed all around him.

"Come on," she said.

With his arms out in front of him, Owen staggered into the black. "Anna?"

"I'm here. Just keep following me."

She began to sing, a little off-key. She sang some
Katy Perry songs that Owen recognized and others
he didn't. He was just grateful to have something
to fill this interminable darkness. He wondered if
this was what sensory deprivation tanks felt like.
He could understand how this would drive a man
mad within an hour. Owen was pretty sure that he
was already entirely mad, and that it didn't matter.
He just hoped that the thing—whatever it was—
wasn't following him.

He bounced off slimy walls, slipped in a puddle
and cracked his tailbone on the floor.

By the time Anna led him back to the chamber with the tree, only a dim grey light filtered down from the hatch above. Exhausted, Owen clambered up the tree roots to the hatch. Once outside in the crisp falling darkness, he slammed the door behind him and plodded to his SUV. Trembling, he turned over the engine and cranked up the heat.

"Thank you, Anna," he said. "You saved my life."

She sat in the passenger seat beside him, staring out the window. She flushed and squirmed. "It wasn't anything. But . . . what was all that?"

Owen squinted through the frost that had accumulated on the windshield. "I have no earthly fucking idea."

PETRA RUSHED AFTER Maria into the hospital, leaving slush in her wake as she ran down the green-tiled halls. Her coat flapped open, zipper scraping the walls as she ping-ponged along behind Maria. They'd left the man in the wanted poster and the coyote behind in the truck, not wanting to court an argument with hospital security.

Maria skidded to a stop before a glass-walled room. "Oh, God. Mike." Petra could see nothing beyond her except for a sheet covering the shape of a pair of human feet.

A woman in a white coat with a stethoscope draped around her neck stopped them at the door. "Are you family?"

"No . . . I'm Maria Yellowrose. I was called. Mike must still have me as his emergency contact in his phone." She gestured at Petra. "This is Petra. She works with Mike."

"I'm Dr. Burnard. Mike was brought in about an hour ago."

"What happened?" Maria pressed her palms against the glass door.

"He was in some kind of accident or a bad fight. Blunt force trauma to the head and body, a fractured rib. He's got a bad concussion and we're watching him for swelling. It was lucky he was found when he was—he's got some bad frostbite on his extremities."

A ranger strode down the hall, his hand in his gun belt. It was the same ranger Petra recognized from the bat rescue. Sam.

"Maria?"

"Sam? How did this happen?"

Ranger Sam gave Maria a quick hug. "I'm glad you're here, and I know Mike would be, too."

"What happened to him? Was he at work?"

"Yeah. Mike had gone out on patrol, looking for wolf poachers. He was following the radio tags of one of the pack members. He radioed in that he saw some suspicious activity and gave his position a half mile north of Fawn Creek. I tried to radio him back, and he didn't answer. We combed the area to find him and finally were able to get a ping off his cell phone. He was beat up really bad. So I'm guessing there was more than one guy, and he got jumped." Sam looked away. "I should have been there."

Maria shook her head. "I told him to stop being a fucking cowboy and running around on his own." She turned to the doctor. "Can I see him?"

"Yes," the doctor said. "He's in and out of consciousness. He's pretty agitated, and we've given him a light sedative to keep him calm—just don't stress him further."

"Gotcha." Maria opened the door to Mike's room. Petra slipped in behind her, and tried to stifle a gasp.

Mike lay in a hospital bed, surrounded by tubes and wires. His swollen face was black and blue, and his head had been shaved in a spot where stitches crossed his scalp. Bandages circled his ribs, and his fingers were covered loosely with gauze. He seemed much smaller than she was used to seeing him, shriveled somehow.

"Mike?" Maria whispered, coming close to the bed. "It's Maria."

The eye that wasn't swollen shut opened, but he didn't move his head. "Hey, gorgeous," he slurred. "How ya been?"

"Better than you." She leaned against the side of his bed and touched his shoulder. "How are you?"

"Been better." His cracked lips broke into a grin.

"But I'll take all the sympathy I can get. And soup. Will you make me some soup?"

"Jesus. I was afraid you were brain-damaged."

"No such luck on the drain bamage."

Petra felt like an intruder, hovering at the foot of his bed. "Mike, you look like hell."

"I feel like it. But I guess this'll earn me some time off. Maybe I can go bowling."

"You can go bowling all you want," Petra said.

"What the hell happened?" Maria demanded. "Sam said you were in a fight, that you got jumped by poachers. What the hell were you thinking, chasing after a bunch of criminals on your own?" Anger had tightened her posture, and Petra suspected that if the poachers didn't finish him off, Maria might. There was history there. At the very least, she was going to make him suffer for a very long time.

Mike's gaze flickered to the door, at the silhouette of Ranger Sam through the door. "You wouldn't believe me if I told you."

"Try us." Maria pulled a chair up to his bedside.

Mike's good eye rolled up to the ceiling, and he was stubbornly silent for some minutes.

"Mike. You have to tell us." Petra hoped the sedative would make him chatty. She wondered if she could flag Dr. Burnard down to give him some more.

He huffed, then winced, his hand fluttering to

his chest. "I fobbed off most of the investigation of the skiers with the burning tank on Sam. So, I thought I'd check in on the Nine Stars pack."

"I told you that was a shitty idea, Mike." Maria regarded him with narrowed eyes.

"Yeah. Well. Savor this moment. You were right."

Maria huffed at him, but said nothing.

"I thought I would take a head count of the wolves, see if it squared with what our biologists said there should be. One of them has a radio tag with half-dead batteries, so I took a tracker up to the terrace area to look. I got a hit south and west of there, and I kept going. Took me about ten klicks off the trail.

"I saw two of the wolves, ones that I thought might be from the pack . . . but there was something there with them." His mouth pressed shut in a hard line, and it seemed he was debating what to say next.

"Go on," Maria prodded.

"Promise not to tell Sam?"

"We won't tell Sam."

"I dunno what it was," he confessed. "I saw antlers and a big dark fur coat . . . weird silver eyes. I fired two warning shots, but it didn't faze the guy. He rushed me, and it was like . . . like being locked in a closet. Dark. Cold. I guess he must have hit me on the head or something. I felt like I was falling, then getting the shit beat outta me." He lifted one of his hands to his shoulder, where there were bruise marks from what could have been antler points. If he hadn't been wearing a coat and a bulletproof vest, they could easily have gored him.

"And then I blacked out." His gaze flickered to the door. "Good thing Sam came looking for me or I'd be a goner. Somebody buy that man a coffee, okay?"

"You just focus on getting better." Maria leaned over and kissed the single unbruised part of his face, the right side of his jaw.

Petra slid out of the room and leaned against the wall in the hallway. Fuck. Fuck. Fuck. She rubbed her brow.

"Hey." Maria emerged from the room and touched her elbow. "You all right?"

"Yeah, I just . . ." Guilt flooded her. "If I had told Mike that the wolf carcass was magic, maybe I could have prevented this . . ."

"No." Maria fiercely gripped her shoulder. "No. You do not get to make this your fault. Neither does Sam. Mike is a cowboy and he'll go after anything in a black hat. I told him there was something hinky about those wolves, about the shapeshifting. He didn't believe me, and that was his choice."

Petra's hands balled into fists.

Mike might not have any more choices.

But she sure as hell did, and she was going to take Skinflint Jack to the grave.

CHAPTER 9

The Chemical Wedding Night

The wedding party didn't get back to the reservation until well after midnight. A front had swept in, and snow was beginning to fall. Maria offered her house up to Petra and Gabe and Sig, but Petra refused, citing a curiosity to check out the honeymoon suite at the reservation motel. The Internet touted the presence of a massive hot tub and chilled champagne, and she said she wanted to see if they lived up to the billing.

In truth, Gabe knew that Petra didn't want to expose her friend to more trouble than she already had. He understood that. Trouble was following them around, and he was feeling like an albatross. Maybe he would have felt different as a fugitive if he was still one of the Hanged Men, powerful and invulnerable. Now . . . now, he felt like a mouse scurrying from hole to hole, hiding from the cat. He couldn't even go into the hospital to support Petra and her friend. Instead, he was stuck in the parking lot in the Bronco, keeping Sig wrapped in his blanket and running the heat intermittently. He'd whiled away the time reading the maps in Petra's glove box.

She'd tucked the amaryllis blossom from their impromptu wedding behind the rearview mirror. The cold hadn't seemed to wilt it, but Gabe wondered if he should press it in one of her map books for safekeeping. Maybe when it wilted.

The motel was a newish log structure down the street from the casino. The parking lot was freshly plowed, and there was a moose head in the lobby. He could see it looming over the front desk from the parking lot as Petra went in to get the keys. They drove around the back side of the hotel, parked behind a plowed pile of snow for cover, and went up to the room.

Sig nosed through the door first. The room had carpet, and Sig flung himself on the floor, rolling around like a dog in fresh spring grass. He made an awful face of delight as the door closed behind them.

"I don't think he's ever been around carpet before," Petra said, shrugging out of her coat.

"I think he approves."

"They were out of champagne." She sighed, sitting down on the edge of the bed to remove her boots.

"No matter." Gabe fished around in the minibar for drinks in little glass bottles and passed her one.

"Shall we toast?" Petra lifted her bottle. "To matrimony?"

"To the chemical wedding of alchemy, the union of opposites, and the secret of immortal life."

"Perfect."

The wine was sweet, like syrup on a dessert. Gabe studied the bottle.

"Did you give that toast at your last wedding?"

"Hnh. No."

"What was it like?"

"I think it would be poor form to discuss such a thing on our wedding night."

Petra laughed. "Probably. Tell me about the chemical wedding of alchemy, then." She tucked her leg up underneath her, as if she was expecting him to tell her one of his stories from the dimly lit alchemical past.

"The chemical wedding is the idea in alchemy that Sol and Luna are joined and transcend physical reality. It's a critical stage in accomplishing the Great Work, a repeating cycle of dissolutions and coagulations in which purification occurs."

"Sounds . . . romantic. Sort of."

"Alchemy, as practiced, is rarely a terribly romantic art. But the chemical wedding is said to be the union of creativity and wisdom, in which the soul is released."

She swirled her drink in the bottle, her gaze distant. "It does make for a pretty toast, though."

Gabe stood and kissed the top of her head. "I'll go run you a bath."

The honeymoon suite had a hot tub larger than a cattle trough, opposite an electric glass fireplace, and it took forever to fill. Gabe fished around in the minibar for another drink and fiddled with the wall switches until he found the one that turned on the electric fireplace. It looked a little cheesy to him, but he supposed that the maid probably didn't want to spend time scrubbing wood ash out of the plush carpet.

His wedding to Jelena had been something of a production by old-fashioned standards. Her wealthy father, thrilled to finally have her married off, put on the fête of the season at his home for all the family. By modern standards, it would have been a very small and ordinary wedding, but at the time, newly tailored clothes and orange blossoms were considered extravagant finery. White wedding dresses and floor-length veils had just come into vogue for the wealthy classes, and Brussels lace was all the rage.

Jelena had been lovely, and extended her cheek for a chaste peck at the end of the ceremony. Gabe couldn't remember many of the details of the wedding itself, which was held in the morning, or the wedding breakfast afterward, but he remembered heading out to the train station three days later for an assignment from Pinkerton. Jelena had seen him to the train station, and there had been a twinge of relief in her eyes as she waved him goodbye. He didn't take it personally; he thought it likely she was relieved that the pomp and circumstance were over, and that she could get back to her day-to-day life. He felt some of the same, truth be told. He had a great deal of admiration for Jelena, and a kind of affection, to be sure. He'd always been told that love was a kind of golden mean between lust and friendship, though his relationship with Jelena had definitely been closer to friendship.

But Jelena was not Petra. Petra was fire and life and logic, and she was an ongoing puzzle to him.

By the time the tub was filled, Petra had fallen asleep on the bed. She was stretched out, facing the ceiling, snoring softly. Sig lay beside her on his back, his head in the crook of her arm.

She was lovely, especially in her unguarded sleep. It seemed to Gabe that perhaps she was a bit paler beneath her freckles than usual. Maybe he was looking for signs of illness, for some glimpse of the invisible.

She was extraordinary in every way, and it seemed monumentally unfair to him that he'd been granted a century and a half of life, when she might not wring a full lifetime out of her stint on earth. He would give anything to change that. If the Lunaria still had any power, he would have offered her up to it without hesitation, brought her to twilight immortality. He would have let the tree devour her and remake her in whatever image it chose, and he'd have loved the result without the tiniest bit of doubt or reservation. The tree, in its heyday, would have loved her just as much as he did. And Petra would have been quite formidable undead, if she'd been able to siphon off enough of the tree's magic . . . Gabe had no doubt that she would have learned to adapt more quickly than his men had.

She wouldn't want that . . . If it had been possible, he'd have dragged her to the tree, kicking and screaming, even if it meant that she would leave him forever. A world with her in it, and pissed, was far superior to one without her. Now that he was human, he found that he missed the tree in a way that he never had as a Hanged Man. But the tree was gone, and they were stuck with their own clumsy devices in the real world, with medicine and science and hope.

He knelt beside the bed and pushed the hair away from her face. She was so dear to him, and he hoped she knew that. She deserved more—a real modern wedding, a man who had a job and a home and had his shit together enough to be able to navigate the future of her illness. She deserved more than him. She deserved more life, period.

And that was one more thing that he couldn't give her.

He turned the lights down and went to hang up her coat. The marbles in her pocket clinked against her keys, and he dug them out to inspect them. Maybe these were her father's idea of luck.

He slid the white marble under her pillow and the gold one under his. He poured himself another drink and regarded Sig, whose tongue had lolled out of his mouth and stuck to the duvet. Maybe they had the right idea.

When he climbed into bed, he felt the magic hit him the instant his head hit the pillow. He had the feeling of passing through a veil, falling a fathomless distance.

Well, damn. His new father-in-law still had the alchemical juice.

He'd need to have a discussion with the old man about meddling . . . after he climbed out of the spirit world.

WHITENESS SURROUNDED HER.

Petra could feel it before she opened her eyes— that brightness pressing down on her eyelids and filling her brain with a muzzy lightness. It wasn't the cold brightness of harsh winter—this was something else, something finer.

She opened her eyes. She was lying on a skiff of snow that had coated her skirts. Skirts—she looked down and noticed that she was wearing a white velvet dress, with a white velvet cloak.

"Huh." She sat upright, blinking. When she woke up dressed in odd clothes that she never would have chosen for herself, whether it was a dress or a suit of goo, it was usually a signal that she'd dropped into the spirit world.

She pulled her cloak around her shoulders. The hem of it brushed aside to reveal Sig, who was dozing, tangled in her skirts.

"Hey, bud." She reached out to shake him awake. He blinked at her and yawned with a squeak.

She looked up. She was on a path surrounded by ice-frosted birch trees forming a cathedral of ice about her. When she held her breath, she could hear the crackle of sun in the branches. She wrinkled her brow. She didn't feel cold, and her breath didn't steam before her.

She stood and reached for one of the tree branches. It wasn't ice—it was leaded glass. She took a piece of it and turned it over in her fingers. The glass wasn't modern—this looked like hand-blown glass, with waves and ridges in it.

"Interesting."

She hadn't been in the spirit world in months. The last time she'd been here, she'd gone to the spring behind Maria's house, a pool of blue water the locals called the Eye of the World. She was miles distant from the Eye, and struggled to figure out how she'd gotten here. She'd only been able to travel to the spirit world before with the help of the Eye of the World or when she'd been in serious physical trauma . . . And it had never looked like this. Did the spirit world have seasons, too, just like the physical world?

Her brow wrinkled. The last thing she remembered in the physical world was stretching out on the motel room bed . . .

"Did I croak in my sleep?" she blurted to Sig, who was busy chewing a paw.

He huffed at her. She took that as a negative. But she had no idea what she was doing here, or what she had to do to get out.

A path of swept snow extended before her. Maybe she was meant to follow.

She balled her hands in her awkward skirts and began to hike. Fortunately, the spirit world had seen fit to give her flat-soled boots, which was something to be appreciated. The spirit world could be capricious as hell, and she was thankful not to be saddled with stupid footwear.

Her cloak scraped the snow as she advanced down the path. Sig plodded nonchalantly in her wake, pausing to sniff at the trees and water them. Petra was pretty sure she hadn't died in her sleep—was there piss in the afterlife? Could be . . .

She stopped short. The snow was seething in front of her. It seemed to drop away into a pool of dry ice, vaguely body-shaped. The snow solidified in a black stain, the shadow of a man.

Cautiously, Petra crept forward. She reached down to shake the man's shoulder. There was no response.

She turned him over, and her heart clattered behind her ribs.

It was Gabe.

She had never seen him in the spirit world. She knew that things and people took on all kinds of odd shapes and forms, but she recognized him at once. He looked similar, but he was dressed in an old-fashioned black suit. His hands and face were pale and slack in unconsciousness.

But something about his skin had changed. It was lined in a pattern, on his cheek, on the backs of his hands, on his throat. She deciphered the pattern—it was feathers. But it didn't look like a tattoo—it looked as if the feathers were pressing up from beneath his skin. She reached for a pulse and found none.

"Shitshitshit," she swore. Maybe he'd gotten stuck in some epic shit zone of an alchemical transformation. He wasn't breathing, and that couldn't be good.

She shook him again, harder this time, but he didn't awaken. She flopped him onto his back, laced her hands over his heart and thumped on him sixteen times. She tipped his chin back and forced air into his mouth. She had no idea if CPR worked in the spirit world, but she was sure going to find out.

She counted two breaths, then felt his lips move against hers. His hand reached up to tangle in her hair, and he kissed her.

She broke it off. "Gabe, what . . ."

A smile played on his lips. He looked at her, then over her shoulder. Under her hands, she could feel that he still had no pulse. The shadow of a feather moved beneath his cheek, as if pushed by an unseen breeze.

"What the hell? Were you playing opossum?" If he said yes, she was going to slug him, *so help her God*.

"No." He raised his hands in mock surrender. "I haven't been to the spirit world since I became a Hanged Man . . . it's apparently a lot tougher than your father thought to bring me back and forth."

"What do you mean?" She sat back beside him on the snow-dusted ground. "What's he got to do with this?"

Gabe grinned. "Remember the marbles he gave you?"

"The ones I was supposed to put under our pillows . . . Oh. You did?"

"Yes."

"Why did . . . Oh." It began to dawn on her. The white dress. The cathedral of glass.

"This is your father's wedding gift to us."

A lump rose in her throat. Her father had nothing to give to her. No contribution to a lavish wedding—not that she would have accepted it, anyway. But this was something he could do—open a gate to an experience that might be of their own making.

"And you are lovely in the spirit world, by the by," Gabe said, touching her hair. She realized there were flowers braided into it. Amaryllis. Sig leaned in close to her and pulled one free. She snatched it from him before he ate it, dimly recalling that amaryllis flowers were poisonous to dogs. She had no idea what effect they had on spirit-coyotes.

"And you." She turned back to Gabe and pressed her hand to his cheek. "But you're different, here." And it wasn't just his skin. His eyes were still amber, but the irises were larger, like a bird's.

He shrugged and looked down at his hands. "I suspect we're changing all the time, in the spirit world. At least I didn't appear as a turtle or a weasel. That would have been decidedly unromantic."

"Dad would have found it funny," she admitted.

Gabe climbed to his feet and offered her his elbow. "Shall we find what else your father has built for us this evening?"

"I shudder to imagine it."

They wound their way through the cathedral forest, down the snow path. It was silent here, feeling shielded and muffled by the snow. The path stopped at stone steps that led up the edge of a mountain to a terrace.

She climbed the steps, mindful not to trip on her skirts by keeping them clutched in her left hand. Sig bounded ahead of them, and she heard a happy yip in the distance.

The terrace opened up to a fantastic view of mountains at twilight. Petra had no idea where in the world this could be. If it had come from her father's mind—he'd been everywhere. She suspected these were the Dolomites, but she couldn't be certain. Her dad didn't seem to have fussed much with the architecture—the terrace grew out of the side of the mountain, and there was a lit structure glowing behind it, as organic as a cave.

The doors to the terrace were flung open to a dining room with a table set for two. Well, three . . . Sig had hopped up on a chair and planted his face in a soup tureen. Petra plucked it from the table and set it down on the stone floor. Sig was content to slurp noisily from it.

"Your father has interesting taste," Gabe said as he took her cloak. She thought she'd be cold here, but a fire blazed with warmth at the other end of the small room, tended to by no one.

She glanced down at her exposed arms. She'd

expected to see the scars there from her waking
life, but they were gone. Her skin was freckled and
milky . . . but beneath it, she could see the suggestion of her veins. Instead of blue, they were a dark
violet, like faded ink on a map. She wondered if
that was some sign of her leukemia, here, in the
spirit world. If the spirit world showed everyone
as they truly were, whether divine or decaying . . .

Gabe bent to tenderly kiss her shoulder on one
of the inky veins. "Don't think about it," he whispered.

She turned her attention to the rest of the table
and laughed out loud.

All the courses were laid out: soup, a pheasant,
fresh baked bread with apple butter, vegetables . . .
and a bowl of Froot Loops in the center, poured
into a silver bowl.

"That was my favorite, as a little girl," Petra
said as she took a seat. She pondered the food for
a moment. Persephone had gotten in a big heap of
trouble for eating a pomegranate in the spirit world
and had ended up stuck with Hades for half the
year. But this was a gift from her father. She knew,
in her heart of hearts, that he wouldn't want her
trapped in the spirit world, no matter how prettily
gilded the cage. This had to be safe.

"That looks . . . inedible." Gabe eyed the Froot
Loops with suspicion.

"Try it."

He gingerly took a spoonful. "Not bad."

"See. I knew you were the one for me."

Gabe's eyes roved over the pheasant, and she thought she saw a flicker of sentimentality on his face. "The rest of it . . . it's what might have been served in my era."

"Then we should have at it . . . though I'm certain Sig will want to try, too."

The dinner was perfect. Petra had never given thought to eating in the spirit world; she'd usually been too busy running from predators and trying not to wind up in the Underworld to appreciate its more pleasant sensory delights. Everything here was thought out down to the smallest detail— the lemon oil sheen on the table, the height of the chairs. There was even a half-open door that led to a darkened bedroom with a four-poster bed and the flicker of fire in a grate.

"Ohmygawd," she murmured around a mouthful of bird. "This is amazingly real butter."

Gabe grinned. "And an excellent brine."

They meandered through the courses. On the sideboard, a cake had been left for them— chocolate, Petra's favorite. They took their dessert to the terrace to gaze at the mountains, leaning on the stone railing. The air swept up in drafts from the valley below, chasing crumbs from her plate.

She felt alive. Which was patently ridiculous, since this wasn't a real place.

"How did he do this?" she murmured.

"Some alchemists created pocket universes by accident . . . I suspect your father is rather skilled at this. Given the tools he has at hand in our world, I suspect that he's figured out some way to stash a magical tool set in the spirit world, somewhere."

She gazed out at the snow trickling from a far-off mountain peak and licked the frosting from her fork. "Could we stay here?" she said suddenly.

"Probably not," he admitted, after seeming to think it through. "This is likely a time-limited construct. Unless it's constantly fed energy, it won't last. I can't see where your father has an ongoing energy source at the nursing home, unless he's tapping into the life force of every other resident on the floor."

"Nah. That's not his shtick."

"But we have it for tonight." Gabe set his plate down and pushed a piece of hair back behind her ear. "Let's not worry about the future."

She leaned forward and kissed him. She wanted to feel his arms around her, his curious skin against hers. Her fingers traced the outlines of feathers beneath his skin, and she sank into his hot mouth.

This little kingdom wasn't forever, but it was theirs for tonight.

EVERYTHING WAS HIS, now.

Owen stood in Sal's living room, a tumbler of

bourbon in one hand and a bottle of Ambien in the other. The lights were turned off, and he looked out through the glass at the white landscape and black sky spreading below him. He thought it odd as hell that Sal had never put up blinds or curtains in his massive house on a hill; he didn't like the idea of oppressive night converging on him or the thought that he could be spied upon. Especially since he didn't know what was in that night. Likely, something pretty awful.

"Are you going to live here, now?"

Anna swung her legs on the edge of Sal's cowhide couch. She was looking around, at the antler chandelier dripping with crystals, the travertine floors, the trophies of elk and bear and antelope mounted on the walls. Maybe she was trying to decide if it was a place she was willing to haunt.

"Maybe," he said. He didn't have any great attachment to his own house in the county seat. He'd moved there five years ago and still hadn't finished unpacking. It was a new building in a cookie-cutter gated community on the touristy side of town, which was inhabited entirely by skiers in the winter and was a ghost town in the summer, with wilting hyssop planted near the mailboxes. His mother had known the realtor, and it seemed the thing to do at the time.

"It's kind of ugly," Anna said, peering up at the stuffed head of a warthog on the wall. The warthog's lip was pulled back in a permanent grimace. Owen wondered if the taxidermist had done that specifically for Sal's benefit.

The house was pretty hideous, to Owen's taste. It wouldn't have been his first choice in places to frequent. He'd been told that other houses had stood here, over time. But Sal had the previous house nearly torn down to the foundations and built a new structure of faux-rustic timber and electric lights on top. Which was something of a shame; Owen remembered the old house, which had been quite grand in its own right, but it was quieter. A lodge that faded into the hillside, with scarred floors and a few inoperable gaslights still peppering the ceilings.

"Yeah. It *is* kind of ugly." There was a chandelier in the bathroom, for chrissakes, right above the toilet. "But it's kind of interesting, too."

"You mean the tunnels," Anna said.

"Yeah. The tunnels are interesting. Also terrifying."

"I don't like being underground," Anna declared again, shuddering.

"I know. I don't think those men we found liked it much, either."

"But you still want to go back down there."

"Yes." He wondered now—what was here, what Sal had known, and what he hadn't. He hadn't yet broken the passwords on Sal's computer, to see if his cousin had kept any records of what went on here. That would come in time.

But he was conflicted, even as he rinsed the grime and blood off his body in Sal's palatial marble shower. He wanted to get to the bottom of it. But he wanted to do it *himself*. He didn't want to share this with his deputies. He didn't know what he was dealing with, and it felt as if he was on the cusp of some great mystery, some secret that was his and his alone.

He slugged a couple of Ambien down with a chaser of bourbon and stared at the gash in his arm. It looked like he'd gone a round with a bear. And that giant pearl in his pocket that was likely worth a small fortune—those were real. Real and entirely inexplicable.

But Sal was dead. And fifteen other people, give or take a leg or two. He wouldn't know for sure until the coroner got back to him, but he was pretty sure that Sal had been killed straightforwardly, hanged. The others . . . he didn't see how it was possible to embed a man in a tree. The crime scene folks had peeled part of a kidney from a fist made of roots. They'd even found ribs wound underneath a skin of bark. It just wasn't possible. But they were dead, and he wanted to know how.

He had a pretty damn good idea who the killer

was. His deputies were looking for Gabriel, and they would find him, sooner or later. Owen just wanted an hour in a room alone with him, video camera off. Not to beat a confession out of him, or even to know why he did it. He wanted to know the *how* of it.

Owen's cell phone rang and he bent down to the lacquered coffee table to pick it up. "This is Owen."

"Sorry to bother you so late, Sheriff. But you told us to call when we got some prints back."

"Yes. Whatcha got?"

"We found some partial prints on some of the stone surfaces down there. Some really old prints. Some partial archival matches to crime scenes back from Prohibition, even. No names on those, just hits on the archive database that some data nerd is working on. Those guys are long dead."

"I wonder if this wasn't some rum runner's tunnel."

"Could be, Sheriff. Especially since we did get another hit, a print belonging to a Pinkerton agent from the 1900s."

"Wow. That *is* old."

"FBI says that the Pinkertons were experimenting with fingerprinting back then and printed some of their agents. It's more of an historical oddity than anything else."

"You got a record number on that?"

"Yeah. FBI should be faxing what they have to your location as they dig through their files. Looks like a bunch of dead leads so far, but maybe the coroner will have something interesting for us."

"Thanks."

"Good night."

Owen wandered to Sal's office. It was entirely paneled in mahogany, covered with books that Owen was certain he'd never read. Some of them weren't even real—one whole bookcase was actually just papered in textured wallpaper that looked like book spines. A fax machine was buzzing away in the corner, spewing out thermal pages.

Owen picked the pages off the floor, thumbing through the blurry photocopies of archival records. He'd always been curious about law enforcement history, and the Pinkertons were a particular source of interest to him. He paged through the blurry prints and the archivist's notes on the Pinkertons' handwritten files. If nothing else, this would be educational. When he was a schoolboy, he'd read about Pinkerton and his agents foiling an assassination plot against Abraham Lincoln, about how the agency eventually grew to an army of private police. Over time, he'd picked up a collection of badges that he kept in a frame in his office, next to his American flag decorated with gold fringe and a picture of him shaking hands with the governor at a fund-raiser. The badges gave people who visited his office something to look at while he sized them up.

He picked up a page off the floor and squinted at a photocopy of an old Pinkerton Investigative Services ID card. The agent's name was Gabriel Manget and he had worked for Pinkerton in "Special Cases." Owen sat down hard. The description was nearly identical to the sketch of Gabriel his men had been papering Temperance with: a six-foot man, 185 pounds, black hair and brown eyes. The ID card was too early for a photograph, but it was a strange coincidence. Maybe this guy was a great-great-grandfather of the Gabriel he was looking for now?

In Owen's study of the organization, "Special Officers" had often been hired on the spot to chase outlaws and break strikes—some were shadier than others. He wondered if Gabriel had been one of these men, or if he was involved in something else. The elegantly inked notes accompanying the file listed places that Agent Manget had presumably been sent to on assignment: Boston, Paris, Savannah . . . He scanned the list and his finger stopped on the last entry: Temperance. There were no notes on what he'd been doing there, no dates or indication what his mission might have been.

"Did you find anything?" Anna drifted into the

room and began running her fingers down the spines of the faux books.

"Yeah." He sat back in Sal's chair and poured himself another drink. "Things just got real interesting."

CHAPTER 10

Relics

Petra awoke, staring at a popcorn ceiling and listening to the hum of the electric fireplace. She was back at the motel, with a view of the Dumpster in the parking lot and not the Dolomites. Sig had fallen asleep curled around her head, like a fluffy hat. She took inventory and realized that she was still in her street clothes, with a blanket tucked up around her chin.

She rolled over to reach for Gabe, but he was gone.

She reached under the pillows and fished around. She came up with two marbles.

"Hell of a gift, Dad," she muttered.

She sat up, running her fingers through her hair. A pang of worry lanced through her. Where was Gabe? He'd made it back from the spirit world

okay . . . right? She climbed out of bed and walked
to the window. The Bronco was still there, covered
in a couple of inches of snow. At least that would
serve to hide the license plates from any suspicious
passersby.

Maybe Gabe had gone out for ice or something.
She clicked on the television with the remote and
surfed to the weather report. A major winter storm
was predicted for later today, but it was expected
to slide south of them. That could be good, or that
could be bad. Good, in that perhaps the cops would
be out doing other things, or hunkered down to
wait out the storm. It could be bad in that it would
make what she wanted to do more difficult.

The hotel door opened, and Gabe came in with
two cups of coffee and a paper bag. "Good morning."

"Good morning yourself."

"I brought breakfast." He handed Petra the bag,
smiling. "It's not wedding cake or Froot Loops, but
man cannot live on spirit food alone."

"Thanks." She grinned and reached into the bag
for a muffin. So it hadn't been a dream. There was
also a handful of bacon wrapped in napkins, which
immediately got Sig's attention. Gabe sat down on
the bed beside her and kissed her shoulder while
she fed Sig bacon.

"You're probably not going to like what I want to
do for a honeymoon," she said.

"Probably not," he agreed, draining his coffee. "And it'll be less glamorous than the Dolomites. But I think I know what you have in mind. You want to hunt down Skinflint Jack."

"Bingo." Petra nibbled on her chocolate muffin. "After what he did to that wolf, after what he did to Mike . . ."

"And that's why I love you," he said matter-of-factly.

She leaned forward to kiss him. "But we need a plan. We can't just go plunging into the backcountry after it."

"That would be inadvisable, under any conditions."

"Well, I've been thinking . . . we can't track the Nine Stars pack with Mike's radio tracker. I don't have access to that. But I do have the Venificus Locus."

"That's a good start. We might be able to find Skinflint Jack, but what then?"

"I was hoping that you might have some thoughts on that."

Gabe stared into space, as if sifting through memory. "I never confronted Skinflint Jack myself. But there must be some way to bind him, to keep him from causing harm."

"Would my father know?"

"Maybe. I don't know how far his alchemical adventures led him."

Petra reached for the hotel phone and punched the code for an outside line.

"Why not use your cell phone?" he asked.

"I took the battery out. I don't want Sheriff Owen to be able to track me via GPS. Just in case he's snooping around."

"Ah."

She dialed the number for the Phoenix Village Nursing Home and asked for her father's room. The receptionist patched her through, and her father picked up.

"Hello?"

"Hi, Dad. Thanks for the wedding present."

The old man chuckled. "So you followed instructions."

"Heh. Gabe did."

"Good man."

"The Froot Loops were a nice touch."

"Glad those came through. What are you kids up to today?"

"Um . . . something less alluring than the Dolomites. Are you alone?"

"I'm anticipating a sponge bath with a highly attractive aide in about an hour, but other than that, my schedule is clear."

Petra rubbed her eyes, not wanting to picture that. "I've got some questions for you. About alchemy."

She heard the sound of his wheelchair wheels

squeaking across the floor and the door closing. "Hit me."

She sketched out the parameters of the legend of Skinflint Jack to him and punched the speakerphone button so that Gabe could listen in. "Apparently, Skinflint Jack is still chasing wolves, and managed to fuck up one of my friends last night. I'd like to figure out a way to neutralize him. My husband suggests a binding." Man, that felt weird to say. *My husband . . .*

Gabe smirked and she elbowed him.

"Hmm. Well, I think he's on the right track." There was a rustling of paper. "The winter solstice is in three days. That's a good window for working magic of all kinds. Jack was last seen close to Sepulcher Mountain."

"Lascaris used to work there," Gabe offered.

"I think you might stand a good chance of disassembling him on that date, in that place, with a separation operation. You'll have to lure him or drag him there. Gabe, you're familiar with that?"

Gabe nodded. "I've never done it, but I've seen it performed a couple of times."

"Good. I can sketch it out for you, if you'd like. You'll need tools—you'll need something that belonged to Skinflint Jack in his life, and something to lure him across to death."

Petra glanced at Gabe. "I think I have an idea where I might be able to find some relics of Jack's past. Or at the very least, something to lure him with."

STAN'S DUNGEON WAS the cultural hub of Temperance, the repository for all its accumulated history. Most pawnshops were keepers of personal scraps of often-sordid history: musical instruments and guns pawned to fund drug habits, unwanted jewelry from ex-boyfriends, and military surplus sold to make the mortgage. But Stan's Dungeon was special. It was run by the county historian, and he kept particular track of every scrap of minutiae that crossed his desk. Some of that minutiae had historical significance. Stan had plenty of storage space in a paid-for building, and he didn't particularly care about stock turnover.

The bell tangled in the door handle chimed as Petra entered, wiping her feet on the threadbare doormat. She was relieved that the shop was open; Stan kept erratic hours in this erratic place.

The merchandise was constantly changing. This winter, Stan had stocked up on a metric fuck ton of military surplus: coats, gloves, boots, ammo boxes, you name it—he had it jammed into the racks on the floor and the shelves lining the walls. He must have gotten a good deal at a federal auction, somewhere. Above the shelves perched old photographs of the town's founders, a dusty kayak, and a few guitars with signatures rendered in felt-tip marker. A mechanical bull with worn paint sat in the corner. The whole place smelled of dust and a little bit of mildew.

"Good morning, Ms. Dee." Stan was behind the gun counter, chirping cheerily.

"Hey, Stan. That's new." She gestured to a Civil War era cannon in the middle of the floor. "Does it work?"

"Fired a few cantaloupes from it over the summer. That's gonna take forever and a day to move. I'm hoping a military reenactor with a trailer happens by. I'll cut him a deal."

Petra sifted through the racks. She picked out a couple pairs of gloves, socks, and warm gear for herself and Gabe. She was pretty darn sure that the sheriff was staking out her trailer, and she had no intention of returning there before going on the hunt for Skinflint Jack. If it wasn't in her truck parked in the alley, it wasn't going with them.

She gave Stan the side-eye. He wasn't a trustworthy sort, like most chatty people. She had no other options—he was the only gun dealer in town. But she had every expectation that he'd dial the sheriff to gossip about her as soon as she left, given that the sheriff was knocking about town, looking to talk to her. But she at least wanted a running start. She chucked a few boxes of ammo, a pop-up tent, a couple of sleeping bags, and a thermos on the pile.

"You going camping?" he asked.

"Storm's coming in," she said. "They say it's going south, but I want to be prepared in case the power goes out." It was a lame lie, but it was all she had.

"I get that. Last year we had a storm that closed the shop for three weeks. Took forever to dig out. Of course, that was nothing like the winter of 'eighty-six . . ."

Petra let Stan natter on while she browsed. She did some poking around the guns—she and Gabe had three pistols and a rifle between them, and she thought that would be enough. Buying another would likely trip the sheriff's wire.

She peered down into the coin case and pointed at the shiny pieces below. "Are those gold?"

"Yup. Been selling a lot of them, since the stock market sucks so bad." Stan pulled out a velvet tray and showed her some of the shiniest coins. "These are American Eagle tenth-ounce coins. Those are the newest, and the best buy for gold investment. For hard-core coin collectors, I have some older bits, some going back to Rome . . ." he reached down to finger some coins in plastic sleeves. Petra glimpsed the many-thousand-dollar price tags on those and wrinkled her nose.

"How much are the Eagles?"

"The tenth-ounce coins? Two hundred apiece."

"How many do you have?"

"Let's see . . ." He counted aloud. "Thirteen."

"Okay. I like the looks of those. Give me all of them."

"Excellent. I've got some coin cases around here . . ." He rummaged under the counter for plastic cases that snapped around the coins.

She paused before the jewelry case, full of turquoise, sterling silver, and engagement rings. It occurred to her that she and Gabe didn't have rings. *Huh.*

She wasn't given to sentimentality or symbolism, but it occurred to her that she might have to make it look like a real marriage. There were engagement rings with giant rocks and stylized bands that looked like twigs and feathers. Pretty, but . . . Petra was afraid those might remind Gabe too much of his time with the Hanged Men and the Lunaria. She poked through the case and came across a pair of plain gold bands. They were clearly old, not new, with the kind of dark patina that old gold had about it. The rings were hammered, not entirely smooth, and there was something appealing to her about their imperfection.

"Can I see those?"

"Sure thing. You planning on getting hitched or adding to your dragon's horde of gold?"

"Nah. Just looking for a fashion statement."

"Those are interesting rings. Back in the day, people would make their own rings out of coins, pounding away at them over time."

"So these were gold coins in a previous life?"

"Yup. Folks had a lot more patience then. Those were probably 1850 gold Liberty double eagle coins."

Stan opened the case and fished the rings out. She put the smaller one on her right hand, and it fit well enough. Upon inspecting it, she saw that it was engraved on the inside with a row of thirteen stars, a groove, and UNITED STATES OF AMERICA. She guessed it was left over from the rim of the coin. The date was blurry with tool marks, but it began with an 18. The man's ring had the same engraving inside, and it slid over her index finger. She had no idea what size ring Gabe wore, but she figured that it could be sized.

"How much?"

"A thousand."

"Nah. They're beat up. Eight hundred."

"Nine hundred. They're old. They have history."

"I'll take them."

Stan went poking about under the counter for a jewelry box, but Petra said she'd wear them home.

"By the way, Stan," she said, gazing at his collection of antique photos. "I heard an interesting story the other day, and wondered if you could shed some light on it."

"Oh?" The man's ears perked up at the mention of the word "story."

"That there was a guy who had it out for wolves, back in the day. Skinflint Jack, also known as the Jack of Harts."

"Ah!" Stan's eyes lit up. "You stumbled upon one of Yellowstone's strangest ghost stories." He held up a finger. "I have something to show you."

Petra leaned against the counter while he scurried off to the back to dig among the boxes. To make sure he wasn't calling the cops to tip them off, she picked up the receiver of the red emergency phone on the counter. She heard a dial tone. So far, so good. She put it back on the cradle and waited.

Stan came scurrying back with a cardboard banker's box that he plunked down on the glass counter. Inside, he fished out a dusty black flat archival box. "Skinflint Jack was a trapper whose family was killed by wolves. He went completely around the bend, and made it his mission to eradicate wolves from the area that became Yellowstone Park. He's still something of a hero among ranchers who aren't fond of wolves taking down their cattle. This is Jack."

Stan slid a tintype photograph frame across the glass to her. It showed a man covered in furs, holding up a set of stag horns. A pile of bones was behind him. Petra recognized moose antlers, bear skulls, and elk skulls. He was tall and thin, with a thousand-yard stare above his dark moustache. A fur hat covered his head, and his left hand held a rifle, the butt of it balanced against the floor.

"Wow."

"Yeah. That whole coat was beaver. And the

boots, too. Amazingly water-repellent, that stuff, when it was available." Stan rummaged around in the box. "Here's a newspaper clipping."

Petra gingerly took the framed piece of brittle paper. The headline read:

FAMILY FOUND DEAD

March 5, 1881

An unfortunate family was killed in their cabin by wolves, a mile south of Fawn Creek. Trapper Jacob Raleigh returned home after a trapping expedition to make the grisly discovery of his wife and two sons, dead. Every bit of bone had been torn from the bodies of Mrs. Catherine Raleigh and the two boys, Samuel and Ezra. Only the empty, frozen skins were left behind.

Petra's brows drew together. "That's a pretty grisly description for a newspaper."

"Different sensibilities, back then. Sensationalism ruled the papers."

"Where did this happen?"

"Skinflint Jack had a cabin in the backwoods somewhere. Nobody's been able to figure out exactly where it was, but there's been speculation that he might have occupied one of the ones near Panther Creek. Legend says he still haunts the area."

"I heard about the pond that he haunts . . . that he's in the business of granting wishes?"

"There's plenty weird enough about that pond. There was an old woman who used to go out there every winter to dump a bag of rock salt in a circle around the perimeter of the pond. I saw her do it one year and asked her about it. She said the pond was a portal to an angry spirit, that the salt weakened the spirit that lived at the bottom. Nothing grows around that pond, owing to the salt."

Petra's brow wrinkled. Maybe the salt was a key to keeping him contained. "Is that woman still around?"

"Nah. She was an old woman when I saw her. She's long dead. But she did fish something out of the pond. She sold me this."

Stan dug into the box and pulled out a rusty piece of metal with teeth.

"What's that?"

"It's a trap that belonged to Jack himself. See the engraving?"

It was a wicked looking thing, and Petra didn't want to touch it. She'd had a tetanus shot within the past few years, though, so she gently took it from Stan to examine it. Sharp teeth closed in a mouth with a rictus grin, with a trip plate, and trailing a seven-foot tail of broken chain. On one of the rusted jaws, someone had etched the initials JR with a crude heart around the letters.

"That's what they used back then. The animal would step on the plate, and then, snap! The hunter would return later to collect the prey."

The live, suffering prey. Petra tried not to grimace. There was likely old blood on this, many lifetimes of torture.

"How much is it?"

Stan blinked. "It's not for sale."

"Everything's for sale, Stan," she chided. Stan always had a price.

Stan stroked his perfectly waxed moustache. "A thousand."

"For this rusty piece of junk?"

"You asked. It has historical significance. I might write a book about it someday. Or sell it to a museum."

"This thing is rusted shut. It probably doesn't even work."

"It's not legal to use that, you know."

"I know. But how much do you *really* want for it?"

"Nine hundred, firm."

"Eight hundred."

Stan screwed up his face, cogitating on it.

"Stan, if you're gonna be closed for winter storms, this is the best deal you're gonna get for a long time."

Stan sighed. "Eight hundred. Plus nine for the jewelry. Twenty-six hundred for the coins. And two hundred for the rest. Forty-five hundred."

"Thirty-seven hundred. For cash." Stan liked cash.

Stan made a face, but his eyes lit up. "Forty-one hundred. Gold is always worth money."

"Those rings have been sitting around forever. You haven't sold 'em yet for scrap. They're not stamped, and I just have your word that they're gold."

Stan harrumphed. "Four thousand."

"Four. Deal."

Petra fished a wad of cash out of her coat pocket. She always cashed her paychecks at Bear's Gas 'n Go, paid her rent with a money order, and stuffed the rest behind a loose piece of paneling on the trailer wall. Maybe she should consider adulting up sometime and getting a checking account at a real bank, but everyone seemed to really like cash here. This had come close to cleaning her out. She should think about what she was going to do for money when she was in the hospital.

Stan bagged up her purchases, making sure to find a cardboard beer box for the trap, cushioning it with wadded newspaper, like a sacred relic. She could tell that he regretted selling it. Maybe she'd sell it back to him, if it was still possible, after this trip to the wilderness.

"Thanks, Stan." She slung the tent bag over her shoulder and balanced the other bags on top of the beer box, clumsily elbowing her way out of the door.

The hardware store was just down the street. She

walked briskly, head down, heart pounding, as she thought about the story about the old woman and the salt at the pond. Maybe there was something about the salt that Jack didn't like. And she was all about getting ahold of things that Jack didn't like.

She stuck her head in the musty hardware store. The teenage girl behind the counter never said more than five words to her. She was sitting behind the counter in a paint-spattered apron, reading a book, surrounded with glittering brass key blanks tacked up on a pegboard.

"Hi," Petra said, shifting her burdens. "Do you happen to have any rock salt?"

The young woman shook her head. "Sold out. Storm's coming."

Petra glanced outside. "Do you know anyone who has any?"

"Everyone's sold out. Try Monday."

Petra frowned. "Thanks." Monday would be way too late. She'd have to get it some other way. She rearranged her packages and stepped out to the street. True to the young woman's word, there was no residue of salt on the sidewalk. She scuttled back to Stan's and walked around the alley to the back of the store, where Gabe had kept the engine of the Bronco running.

She popped the tailgate and loaded the stuff up. Paper grocery sacks were already there, full of dog kibble, jerky, bottled water, and batteries. Sig clam-

bered over the backseat to sniff the tent, sneezing
at the dust. When she got the gear stowed, she shut
the tailgate and climbed to the passenger seat.

"It won't be long before Stan calls the sheriff."

"That's okay," Gabe said. "I got everything we
needed from Bear's Deli." He hooked a thumb at
the grocery bags in the back.

"Did Bear say anything?"

"I came in with Sig, and he gave Sig a bag of beef
jerky. Told me to avoid the camera above the gas
pumps."

She knew Bear would be cool. He'd seen Gabe
with her before, and she was confident he wasn't in
a hurry to rat them out.

"But we've got supplies, a full tank of gas, and
we're ready to go."

"Great." Petra snuggled deep into the seat. "Let's
go hunt a ghost."

"DO YOU REALLY think you should be driving?"

Owen squinted through the windshield, bringing the stainless-steel coffee cup to his lips. He had
the worst Ambien hangover known to man, and
was determined not to show it. It was, however, ap-
parent to Anna. She sat cross-legged in the passenger seat of his SUV, spinning a piece of blond hair
through her fingers as he cruised down the road.

"Eh. Probably not," he admitted, fishing around
in the console for his sunglasses to block the burn-

ing brightness of day. But he wasn't going to let his hangover stop him. He just needed a while for those double-shot espressos from Sal's fancy espresso maker to seep into his system. He'd drunk the first one in the shower, and he figured that it should start kicking in. Any time.

His cell phone sang, and he cast about in his coat pocket for the source of the sound. The SUV tires skidded in the slush, and Anna squeaked. He got the SUV back under control as he found the phone.

"What is it?" he snapped.

The voice on the other end was cheerfully chirpy. "Sheriff? This is Stan, from the pawnshop."

"Hey, Stan. What's up?" Stan was one of Owen's favorite informants. He'd blab to anyone who would slip him a twenty. Owen knew that he was the kind of guy who'd play both sides against the middle, but he'd gotten some useful leads from him.

"The geologist, Petra Dee, was in here a little while ago. Looks like she's going on a trip."

"Oh, yeah?" Owen's brows drew together.

"Yeah. She came around, picking up a whole bunch of gear."

"Like what?"

"Tent. Ammunition. Men's and women's clothes. And gold coins."

Gotcha, Owen thought. "Did she say where she's going?"

"She said she was stocking up for the storm."

"Yeah, right."

"But she asked about Skinflint Jack. Bought a trap that belonged to him, for a lot more than it was worth."

Owen rubbed his temple. "That's the wolf-killer guy from the park, right?"

"Yes. Dunno if any of this info is of any use to you, but—"

"Thanks, Stan. I'll make a direct deposit to your account." Owen hung up and squinted into the glaring morning light. So she was going on a trip to Yellowstone, and with a man. Likely this Gabriel character. She would know that Owen had no jurisdiction in the park. It was federal land, and his jurisdiction ended at the gate.

Not that it would stop him. He had a nose full of a mystery, and he wanted—no, he needed—to interrogate this guy. Gabriel was the last man standing in the middle of a helluva pile of secrets.

Owen pulled a U-turn and headed to Petra's trailer. Maybe he could still catch them before they left. He drove through the single stoplight in Temperance and turned right at the edge of town. As he rolled down the gravel road, he noted that the snow was smooth. There were no tracks here. No one had been here in at least a day.

Swearing under his breath, he stopped the SUV near the trailer and jumped out. He stalked up to the door and pounded on it. As before, no one answered. He noted that his business card was gone.

Owen was not taking no for an answer. He pulled the screen door open and examined the lock on the door. It was a simple one. He didn't bother to get his lock pick set out of the glove box. He pulled his wallet out of his back pocket, found a gift card for a restaurant he never visited. He slid the plastic behind the tongue of the lock, fished around for a moment . . .

. . . and the door opened. Owen drew his service pistol and nudged his way in.

The trailer was dark and cold. The heat was turned down to fifty degrees—enough to keep the pipes from freezing, but not suitable for human occupation. Maybe someone had turned it down for a day away from the trailer, maybe longer. He glanced around the tiny kitchen, noting there were no dishes in the sink and a half-full bag of dog food leaning beside the refrigerator. Inside the fridge were a few bottles of pop, some ketchup packets, and a gallon of milk. Looked like someone intended to return sometime.

He walked back to the sleeping area. A futon bed was unmade, rumpled blankets covered with dog hair. There was a built-in dresser opposite the futon, and Owen poked through the drawers. There were mostly women's clothes—cargo pants, tank tops, and other utilitarian gear. But the bottom drawer held men's flannel shirts and jeans. It wasn't a case of haberdashery—the jeans were a different size. A man had been living here.

His suspicions were confirmed as he poked through the bathroom. There were men's shaving implements, along with unisex shampoo and soap. There were no toothbrushes, though.

The medicine cabinet yielded no interesting medications that had potential for abuse. Just ibuprofen and aspirin.

He peered under the bed and in the cabinets on the way out. No diaries, guns, cell phones, or computers. The trailer had no more secrets to yield.

But he had enough. Enough to know that the suspect he sought was traveling with Petra Dee. They were armed, and heading into Yellowstone.

Owen locked the door on the way out. They wouldn't escape him.

CHAPTER 11

The End of the Road

As much as she loved the Bronco, there was only so far it could take them.

Petra drove first to the Tower Falls Ranger Station to get her geological gear: pickaxe, chisels, hammer, and lenses. Her tools were like a security blanket to her, and she never ventured into the backcountry without them. She left Gabe in the truck to fiddle with the maps, but Sig accompanied her to the station, trotting in like he owned the place.

Ranger Sam greeted her at the front counter. He was literally up to his elbows in paper forms. There were bat droppings on the tallest stack, which didn't seem to bother him. "Hi, Petra."

"Hey, Sam. Have you heard anything new about

Mike?" She walked to the counter, her fingers chewing the edge of it nervously.

"He's doing better," Sam said. "They're still gonna keep him for a couple days, make sure his head injury is clear and his ribs aren't going to slide around. But he's chomping at the bit to get out."

"That sounds like progress."

"Yeah. He's keen to get on the trail of that wolf-killer." Sam's mouth turned down. "There are a dozen rangers already out there, looking for that guy. But aerial searches are gonna have to wait until these winds blow through."

"Hey, I've got a couple of loose ends to tie up for USGS . . . is there a good place in the northwest area of the park to rent a snowmobile?"

"Yeah, but you'd better get down there before they close for the day." Sam pulled out a map of the park and marked it.

"Thanks." She folded the map and tucked it into her coat. "By the way . . . how's Norbert?"

Sam pointed up at the rafters. She followed his gesture and spied the tiny bat perched up on a rafter . . . with two other bats. All three had their eyes closed, huddled like a litter of kittens.

"He's brought friends?"

"Yup. Pretty darn cute."

Petra grinned. "You're gonna have to rename this place the 'Bat Cave.'"

Sam chuckled. "It'll be the Bat Cave as long as they want to stay."

"Oh, while I'm thinking about it . . ." she said, as nonchalantly as she could. "Temperance is out of rock salt. Do you guys have a bag around here I could borrow?" These were ex-Boy Scouts. They were always prepared.

"Unfortunately, we're out. We keep hearing that a truck is gonna come in Monday. We got some beet juice in the back, if you wanna give that a try?"

"Ah, nah. Thanks, anyway."

Petra gathered Sig from his water dish and picked up her gear from the conference room. She checked the break room for salt packets, came up empty, and headed back to the parking lot. Gabe had kept the heater on, and she savored the warmth of the Bronco as she pulled out of the lot.

"How's your friend?" he asked.

"Doing okay, it sounds like. I'm sure that Maria will be stuffing him full of chicken soup the instant they let him out."

Gabe showed her a map, where he'd circled a tiny, unnamed pond. "This is Jack's wishing pond."

She frowned. "That's not far from where they found Mike."

"Then we stand a good chance of catching up with him."

She told him about what she'd learned from

Stan, about the salt the unnamed old woman applied to the perimeter of the pond.

Gabe seemed to ponder it. "She may have been on to something. Salt is one of the three most essential substances in alchemy, along with mercury and sulfur. Salt represents the body, the manifestation of will in the world."

"Temperance is sold out," Petra said, chewing her lip. "But I'm betting I can find some in the backcountry." No telling if that was for certain—pure halite was only found in the southeastern part of the park, far away from where they were going. But maybe, just maybe, she could dig up a suitable substitute.

She drove deep into the park, past the east entrance, northwest, to the area Mike had last been seen. Side roads were closed with chains and sawhorse barricades; the main road was a packed-down dirty slick of snow.

"It's been a long time since I've been this way," Gabe remarked, staring out the window at the mountains and terraces.

"Dare I ask how long?"

"Maybe fifteen years?" Gabe wrinkled his forehead, as if having to count back. "When we had to return to the tree every night, it limited the extent of our excursions."

Petra squinted at the map, and she came to the snowmobile rental spot that Sam had suggested. It was just off the main road near Mammoth Springs, close enough to serve tourists. The location of the attack and Jack's pond was at least six miles west.

She and Gabe had to cough up their drivers' licenses to the young man running the snowmobile shack and sign a stack of waivers, promising to have the snowmobiles back by five P.M. They also had to watch a fifteen-minute video about snowmobile operation and safety before the keys were surrendered.

Once back out in the parking lot, Petra and Gabe loaded their gear from the Bronco evenly on the snow machines. Sig looked them up and down dubiously, not deigning to pee on either one.

"Come here," Petra said. While distracting him with a piece of beef jerky, she managed to get a harness around his chest. Once he realized what had happened, he stared at her morosely. She picked him up and sat him on the front seat of the snowmobile, clipping his harness to the frame for safety. He whined and gave her a baleful look. He'd been on a motorcycle before; she hoped he'd prove to be just as tolerant of the snow machine.

"It'll be okay, Sig. Honest." She wrapped her legs around him, put the key in the engine, and cranked it over. Sig's ears drooped, and she felt a sigh reverberating through his chest.

She glanced back at Gabe, who was astride his own machine. He gave her the thumbs-up.

Petra nodded and thumbed the accelerator, moving into the white wasteland that belonged to Skinflint Jack.

YELLOWSTONE WAS A vast place. One could easily disappear into the wilderness, never to be seen again. Dozens of men and women had disappeared here, likely rotting beneath tree roots and stream beds. Others had slipped through the forest's fingers, lured to the other side and new lives, shedding their identities behind them like snakeskin. Once the park had swallowed a person, they could very well be gone for good.

But Owen knew how to improve his odds.

It took him only two phone calls to figure out which station Petra Dee used as a base for her work as a geologist. Owen showed up at the Tower Falls Ranger Station with less of a hangover, owing to the espresso finally kicking in. His left eye was twitching and he felt like fucking Superman. The station was empty, except for a single ranger peering up into the rafters with a flashlight.

Owen flashed his badge. "I'm wondering if you'd seen Petra Dee lately. And if she was alone."

The ranger at the station regarded him with suspicion. Owen and the Feds had an uneasy working relationship. He knew they tended to view his department as a clusterfuck of parochial hicks playing rock-paper-scissors for turf. Which was pretty much true. But he also knew that the ranger couldn't outright lie to him, and he was counting on that.

"I saw her. She came in to work today, and she was alone," the ranger said.

"Do you know where she's headed?"

"Why?" The ranger leaned nonchalantly on the counter. "Anything up?"

"I just want to ask her a couple of questions about a man she's been keeping company with. The man's a subject of interest in a murder investigation."

The ranger looked at him with skepticism. "Ms. Dee is a straight shooter."

"Well, she may be under the unwilling influence of this guy. He is most definitely not a straight shooter."

The ranger frowned. Appealing to his damsel-in-distress instincts seemed to work. "She's been working around Mammoth Springs. I expect her back before dark, if you want me to have her call you when she returns."

"No need. I'll head up there myself and see if she's available to chat." Owen tipped his hat and turned to leave the ranger station.

But he felt eyes upon him. More eyes than the ranger minding the station and the ghost who sometimes turned up to bother Owen. He glanced around, then up. A half-dozen bats were perched on a roof truss, staring down at him.

"Looks like you got yourself a bat infestation up there, Ranger," Owen said.

"It's for an education project," the ranger responded, sounding nonplussed.

Owen nodded and let himself out. Not his problem.

But he still couldn't shake the sense of eyes on him, not even after he'd gotten into his car and headed down the road. Whenever Owen felt that prickle on the back of his neck, he knew someone was gunning for him. It was his spider sense. Some might call it paranoia, but it had never been wrong.

He tuned his police scanner to the channel the rangers used. He caught part of a transmission.

". . . is Tower Falls base, calling Rockhound."

There was a crackle of static, and a tinny female response: "This is Rockhound. Go ahead, Tower Falls."

"Rockhound, please be advised that a local law enforcement representative is en route to your last reported position. Please maintain your position for a courtesy safety check, over."

Static hissed and there was no response.

That fucking bastard. Owen slammed his hand on the steering wheel. That fucking park ranger managed to warn Petra that Owen was on her six, alone, without violating a single fucking rule.

And there was gonna be hell to pay for that. He would make sure of it.

CHAPTER 12

Blood Engines

The Venificus Locus ran on Gabe's blood, for the first time in a century and a half. Petra's hands were already scarred and callused from working it, and he was eager to share the burden of this tool, now that he was able.

He'd slid his knife across the edge of his hand, a featherweight cut that summoned a welt of red. He dripped it into the Locus, watching as the compass grasped the droplet and rolled it around, tasting. Maybe it was his imagination, but it seemed like perhaps it had missed him. He had long suspected that the machine had some rudimentary intelligence, that it knew the taste of one kind of blood from the next. But it used them all the same.

The droplet spiraled around the groove circumscribing its border and turned northwest.

"Let's go." Petra was impatient. Behind her goggles, her eyes kept darting back the way they'd come. Sheriff Owen was not the kind of man who gave up easily; she was right to be wary.

Gabe pocketed the Locus and opened the throttle of the snow machine. It growled to life and lurched forward, pulling him across the snow beneath the leaden sky. He glanced back, seeing Petra and Sig running behind and parallel. They were leaving tracks behind for Owen, he knew, but there was nothing to be done for it.

Miles flashed by in a spray of snow and stinging cold. The sky swept darker from the west, where the wind pushed dark clouds eastward. The wind skimmed powder up over his windscreen, stinging his exposed face.

He couldn't remember the last time he'd felt cold like this before. As a Hanged Man he'd been dimly aware of the sensation. He knew it couldn't harm him, and he simply ignored it. He'd worn a coat and gloves for a margin of extra comfort, but mostly because it was part of his cover—he was expected to. But here, exposed to the elements, he felt vulnerable. Exhilarated by the sensation of his heart pounding behind his ribs at the speed and wind, but exposed in the face of it. He remembered what it was like to be human once more, to know that one wrong turn or miscalculation could lead to a painful death. It was odd how immortality had given him a kind of arrogance, a deep certainty of his own invincibility. He was conscious of its absence now, like a protective skin ripped from him.

The sun moved behind the clouds overhead, a dull coin of white light behind them. He knew they were getting close to the pond on Petra's maps, and the Locus agreed. There was more than idle gossip and stories about the presence of magic in this place; the Locus confirmed that there was something unnatural on the horizon.

They followed the frozen Fawn Creek south and east, crossing over it easily, to where the pond lay in the embrace of the valley. It was a small pond, maybe fifty feet across. Four large stones, as tall as Gabe's hip, perched on the perimeter of the water. To his eye, they lined up with the cardinal directions.

There was something wrong about it—Gabe could see that it hadn't frozen over entirely. Such a small body of still water should have been rock-hard in October. Instead, slush swirled lazily on the surface. Below the dark, mirrored skin of it, gold algae bloomed. Tracks converged around the perimeter of the pond—snow machines, men . . . and wolf tracks.

Gabe hit the kill switch on his snowmobile and dismounted. He pulled the Locus from his pocket, and the clotted blood bubbled within.

"This is where they found Mike," Petra said, shivering. "It's amazing that they found him, out here."

It seemed that Sig sensed the magic in this place. Petra had unclipped him from his harness, and he sniffed around the tracks.

"Time to make a wish, see if Jack answers," Gabe said. He crossed to the packs, rummaged through them for the pack containing the gold. He plucked a coin from a paper bag, shinier than the sun in this snow-washed place.

"I should make it," Petra said, covering his hands with hers. A wan smile spread on her face. He knew that it made sense. With her illness, death could be close at hand for her. If anyone was going to make a wish that could turn into a fatality, it should be her.

But he wouldn't let her. He took the coin and briskly crossed to the pond. He hadn't made a wish since he was a child with a penny at a fountain. He held the coin in his fist and wished silently to himself.

Let Petra's cancer be cured. Whatever it takes.

Then he skipped the coin across the water, once, twice, before it sank into the cloud of golden algae. Air bubbles flickered up from the depths, as if his message had been received. And then there was only the silence of winter around them, punctuated by the scrape of the wind.

"What now?" she asked.

"We should wait. See if he comes back to retrieve it. Hopefully, gold will prove to be more interesting to him than wolves."

Sig whined. He clearly didn't think much of the idea. His ears were pushed forward and his eyes scanned the horizon, then fastened on the pond.

The surface of the water churned. At first Gabe thought it was the wind, swirling around loose chunks of slush. But bubbles seethed from the interior, pushing through the gold algae.

He reached for his rifle and pressed it to his shoulder. He aimed it at the water, sighting down to see a black mass rushing upward, breaking the surface in a hail of spattered slush. Crowned in antlers, the creature glittered with ice, launching itself up into the daylight like a whale breaching the surface of the ocean.

Jack.

Instinctively, Gabe blew out his breath and pulled the trigger. He fired once, twice, intending to put the creature back down in the water. His rifle jolted his shoulder with each shot, and he knew he'd hit the creature dead in its center of mass.

But the shadow leapt up onto the bank, dripping, crouching. It was the shape of a man, with antlers crowning its head. It looked upon Gabe through the skull of a stag, pale and ferocious . . . and it stood up. In one hand, it gripped the golden coin

Gabe had cast into the water. A fistful of bone-pale knives dripped from the other.

Gabe ratcheted back the slide on his rifle and fired again. The creature didn't flinch. It was as if the soaking pelts of its cloak simply sucked the bullets in.

Petra was shooting at it, too, with no better results. She was shouting at Sig to get behind her.

Gabe kept firing, backing away to the snowmobiles. He had known that Skinflint Jack was a fearsome creature, but he suspected that Jack could be hurt. He'd guessed wrong.

Jack lowered his head and made a run at Gabe. Gabe dove away, but not before the darkness of Jack's cloak slapped him in the side of the face. It was like being slapped by the abyss—cold, stunning hell. An antler caught Gabe in the shoulder and he tumbled, ass over teakettle into a snowdrift.

He rolled over in the snow, the shadow looming over him.

"Hey, you! Cthulhu wannabe! Look what I got."

Jack turned. Petra was holding two glittering gold coins in her hand. She made sure that he'd seen her. He took two steps away from Gabe, toward her . . .

. . . and she pitched the coins as far as she could, into the snowy waste. The pair of them shone like falling stars on the way down.

Jack paused, seeming torn.

But he growled and scuttled after the coins.

Gabe climbed onto his snowmobile and cranked the engine. Petra and Sig had already climbed aboard theirs and gotten the engine going. He followed Petra to a hasty retreat up the valley. Behind him, he watched the dark figure in the snowfield sifting through the snow with his hands.

That had been a disaster.

But they sure as hell had managed to get Skinflint Jack's attention, for good or ill.

"ARE YOU ALL right?"

They stopped three miles upstream. As fast and fearsome as Jack appeared to be, Gabe guessed that he couldn't move much faster than an actual stag beyond his pond. The pond might be a portal of some kind that could call Jack from wherever he roamed, but maybe Jack would be weaker away from it. At least, he hoped that much was true. He'd woefully underestimated Jack. He would not do it again.

Gabe pressed his fingers to his collar and winced. "Nothing broken."

Petra shook her head. "We go back to Plan A then . . . lure him to Sepulcher Mountain?"

"I think it's our only option. Jack can't be defeated by ordinary means. We'll have to bind him, as your father suggested."

"He can be lured by the gold. At least we know that much."

"Gold and the wolves. We'll have to get between Jack and the wolves, draw him away from them and to the mountain."

"We've got ten pieces left. Hopefully, we can tease him along with those bread crumbs."

Gabe glanced at the sky. It was close and leaden now, and he could see veils of snow dragging along the mountain slopes to their west. "I think the weather forecast was wrong. That storm that was supposed to go south is heading for us."

"Awesome." Petra scanned the landscape with her binoculars. She paused. "Take a look."

Gabe took the binoculars from her. It was irritating not to be able to send a raven out to scout, but he swallowed his displeasure. After adjusting the lenses, he could make out a dark speck on the landscape, one that looked like a man-made structure.

"Could be decent shelter. Let's check it out."

The snowmobiles were noisy, and there was no way to approach with stealth in this broad daylight. They came in fast, swooping in sheets of snow, advancing on the broken-down skeleton of a cabin, half covered in snow. It was old; Gabe could see the scrapes of hand-hewn logs on the side and fractured chinking between them.

Warily, he pulled up around the blind side of the

cabin, along a wall with no windows. He killed the engine and lifted his rifle.

After Petra shut off her engine, the silence was deafening. The sound rolled across the landscape, to the feet of distant mountains. Wind whistled around the corner of the building. In the west the horizon line had gone hazy and white. The storm was coming in; it would likely be there within the hour. Perhaps they were lucky to have found this place.

Gabe aimed his rifle around the edge of the building. He stepped around the last corner of the cabin, wading through drifts up to his knees, and spied the door.

The door was badly greyed and warped from weather, and it was ajar. A drift of snow had piled up against it, flakes spilling inside. Gabe crept beneath the shuttered window, tried to peer inside. He could see nothing but darkness within. He slipped noiselessly to the door and kicked it open with a sound like a gunshot.

Gabe ducked to the safety of the door frame and aimed his rifle inside. There was a flurry of sound and movement, and his finger flexed on the trigger. But it was a mass of pheasants, warbling as they fluttered up to the collapsed roof. A terrified rodent zinged across the floor and disappeared into the wall. Gabe scanned above the sight of his gun. Nothing else moved.

He stepped into the room, conscious of Sig slinking around his knees and Petra's shadow at his back. The cabin was a single room, as many were back in his day, the remains of a fireplace dominating one wall.

But his attention was riveted by what had been left behind here: the skins.

A wolf skin was stretched over the fireplace, hung on a complicated apparatus of sticks. Antlers and skulls lined the walls, drizzling cobwebs and stained with dust. Most of the skulls were wolves. As Petra shined her flashlight above them, he saw more wolf skins dangling from the rafters, like kites, stretched out and strung together.

Sig looked up and whined.

A gust of wind swept over the house, whistling through holes in the roof.

Gabe peered out the door at the sky. The storm was moving faster than he'd anticipated, a white wall approaching them, now about a mile away.

"Storm's coming," he said. "Let's get the gear."

Petra's brows drew together. "We're staying here?"

"We haven't got much choice. Hopefully, it'll blow over in a couple of hours and we can get back on the trail of the wolves."

"But . . . what if Skinflint Jack returns?"

"If I had to guess . . . no one's been here since the last snow."

"How fast can he move in the storm, without being summoned through the pond?"

"Not sure. If Stan is right, the pond is a portal that physically summons him from wherever he is . . . but I don't see anything like that here. I'm hoping that he'll have to travel anyplace else on foot."

Sig grumbled his skepticism.

"If he comes back . . . then we'll have to figure out a way to fight him."

TIME WAS RUNNING out. Owen could feel it.

The wind was scraping in from the west, scouring away the snowmobile tracks before him. The guy at the snowmobile rental place had said it was too late in the day to rent to him one, but Owen flashed his badge. He'd been given a snowmobile in the end, and a halfhearted warning about the weather.

Owen didn't put much stock in it. The last couple of predicted storms had turned out to be little more than squalls, and he wasn't impressed by the radar on his phone when he set out.

Now, well . . . now might be something different. The radar blazed blue precipitation. He vowed to himself to catch Petra and Gabriel—they couldn't be that far ahead—and then he'd call for an air pickup. He was determined, and he didn't give a rat's ass what it cost the bottom line of his departmental budget.

That was assuming he could find his quarry before the storm hit. He could see it gathering in the distance, a white shroud drawn over the dark grey of the sky, stretching from the earth to the low-lying clouds.

He considered turning around, but he could still make out the faint feathered tracks ahead of him. He hesitated, glancing down at his emergency pack. He didn't have much in the way of supplies or provisions, just what he'd taken from the back of his own SUV. He kept survival gear there, in case he got stranded, but only enough for a few days.

But he *had* to interrogate Gabriel. He *had* to know. Owen felt the obsession building hot behind his brow. They were going to disappear into this white wasteland, never to be found again, unless he stayed on the trail.

Snowflakes spun through the air, spitting from the grey sky. The snow thickened, the wind whipping through the spaces between the flakes, which grew hard as pellets, bouncing against the windscreen and his goggles with an audible rattle.

Ice. Fuck. He fumbled in his coat for his cell phone. Snow washed over him, in a whiteout blaze, and he couldn't see or hear anything but the sound of the engine and the slide of the blades beneath him. He struggled to maintain control over the uneven terrain, but succeeded in beaching the snow machine in a drift.

There was no point in trying to dislodge it. The storm was upon him, and he could see no more than two feet in front of his face. The world was cold, white, and blank.

He had to find shelter. He stumbled in the stinging snow, jamming his hands in his pockets. There was a stand of lodgepole pine with fallen trees to his right; he could only make them out because they interrupted the snow in tree-shaped silhouettes.

He shoved his way through a curtain of ice-covered pine branches and stumbled into that wind break, hunkering down. He could smell frozen sap as the curtain closed around him. The wind cut, and he took a deep breath.

This thicket of browning pine branches was heavy enough that only frozen ground and pine needles were below him, and nearly all the light overhead blotted out. He shivered, but it was much better here, out of the wind.

He dug in his pocket for his cell phone. Stabbing at the buttons, he was irritated to find that he had no signal. His radio crackled nothing but static. Maybe it was the storm or the distance from a base station; it was hard to tell. But he was alone out here, utterly alone.

He closed his eyes, feeling the burn of the snow against them.

"Owen," a small voice said.

He opened his eyes. Anna crouched beside him, staring up at him with concern. "Are you going to freeze to death?"

"I . . . I hope not." He already couldn't feel his toes.

"What are you going to do about it?"

He stamped his feet on the pine-needle-strewn ground. The pine needles seemed dry enough. Maybe they'd feed a fire. But he might succeed in burning up his thicket shelter entirely.

He clomped out to the snowmobile for his pack. There was a miscellaneous hodgepodge of junk in this bag, but maybe there was something he could use. He dragged it back to the shelter and began digging through it. There were two boxes of ammunition. He shook out the emergency blanket and wrapped it around his shoulders. There was a roll of toilet paper, a frozen bottle of water, a knife, a bottle of cherry vodka, and a bag of stale chocolate-covered raisins.

With numb fingers, he scraped the pine needles up into a pile, hoping they were dry enough to burn. He reached up, arranging a hole in the canopy of pine branches to drain the smoke away.

Muttering dark oaths, he flicked his lighter and brought it to the pine needles. It went out. He swore and tried again, mindful not to waste what little butane was left in it. He grumbled, arranged some toilet paper on the pine needles, and dug through his ammunition box for a bullet. With his pocket-knife, he popped the bullet open and sprinkled a bit of gunpowder on the toilet paper tinder. The next try took, and Owen got down on his hands and knees to blow on the fire. The pine would burn fast, the needles already curling. But he could feel the blessing of warmth hot on his face and fogging his goggles.

He reached up to pull some of the half-dried branches down, broke a couple over his knee to feed the fire. It was a puny fire, crackling and snapping, pushed by the drafts of wind leaking in around the pine boughs.

"So you might live?" Anna asked with all the brightness of Tinker Bell. She was sitting across from him, on the other side of the fire, her hands clasped together almost prayerfully.

"Depends. If it's a short storm and if I can get the snowmobile righted, likely." He was bullshitting her, and he knew it. There wasn't much fuel. He'd planned this poorly. He fished a cigarette out of his pocket and lit it in the fire.

She gave him a look of infinite skepticism.

Why was he lying to a ghost? Trying to spare her feelings? "Look," he said, "I might have fucked this up. Do you have somebody else to haunt, in case this goes to shit?"

She turned away, and he thought she might disappear. Odd, how she seemed to have a vested interest in whether or not he lived. Maybe she was expecting him to solve the mystery of her death, so she could find some eternal peace. Owen had always assumed that was the case. Failing that, maybe she was counting on him finding a really good exorcist somewhere, or a shaman who could perform a soul retrieval and kick her soul upstairs.

But he hadn't done any of that. Not for want of trying. If he had to admit it to himself, he really wasn't as good at his job as his father had been. If his father were still around, maybe he could have taught Owen about the things that mattered: like how to plant evidence without getting caught, how to get witnesses to keep silent on the right side of a shallow grave, and where the hell to dump the bodies of his enemies so they couldn't be found.

Owen huddled close to the fire, his arms wrapped around his knees, the cigarette drizzling ash from his mouth. His eyelids drooped. He really wasn't feeling the cold anymore, just listening to the wind howl through the stand of trees.

"Owen," Anna said. "Owen, wake up."

He lifted his head to discover that his cigarette had gone out.

"You can't sleep out here. You won't wake up."

In some respects, that might not be a bad thing. "Anna, I'm tired."

"Too bad. You need to stay awake. So tell me a story."

"Aren't you too old for that kind of thing?"

"Nobody ever did it. I think I deserve one, don't you?"

Owen sighed, sifting through his memory for a story that didn't involve sex, drugs, or rock 'n' roll. Or violence. There was always that. He reached forward to relight the cigarette.

"How about Sal?" Anna asked. "Tell me a story about Sal."

Hell. There were no good bedtime stories about Sal. "I don't think—"

"Tell me about the worst thing you did for him."

Owen made a face and took a drag on his cigarette. Anna had been tagging along behind him for years. She'd seen much, but not everything. He'd sent his men to do much of the cleanup after Sal. He didn't want to get directly involved and get his hands dirty. It was the coward's way out, he knew. It kept him in his office, with a veneer of plausible deniability. But underneath . . . underneath was ugly.

He took a deep breath. "I guess there's no point in being squeamish around the dead."

Anna made a snickering noise.

"No offense. Back when I first became sheriff, I was still figuring things out. I had maybe read too many comic books when I was a kid, and I was determined to be one of the good guys. You know, the ones with the capes who could stand in the daylight with their hands on their hips and block bullets and shit.

"About a month after I took office, Sal called me in the middle of the night. It was summer, hot and sticky as hell, and my air-conditioning was out.

"Sal told me to come to the ranch. That he had a 'problem.' I probably shoulda just rolled over and gone back to sleep, or kicked him over to Dispatch. But I was eager to prove that I was now Superman with a badge, that I could handle anything. I wanted to stand in front of Sal in uniform and have him know that I finally was in charge. That I had the power. Or something like that. Anyway, I expected that the trappings of the office would finally grant me some grudging respect from him.

"I rolled up to Sal's house about two A.M. He was sitting on his front porch, in a rocking chair, drinking a beer in the dark.

"I asked him what the hell was the matter that he had to get me out of bed.

"He was being weird. All the lights were out in the house. He said that someone had broken in, that someone was still in his house. He said that the guy was in the basement and that he was armed. I'd puffed up like a fish. Sal was asking for my help. He saw my authority, damn it! Our relationship was going to change after I swooped in and took care of this situation. And it sure did.

"I entered the house, announced that law enforcement was here. I yelled for the guy to come out with his hands up. I didn't get a response, just some banging from the basement.

"I shoulda called for backup, but I was convinced that I had control of the situation. I opened the door of the basement and saw the silhouette of a guy down there with a gun. I fired and hit him.

"Then I turned on the lights. I realized immediately that I'd been set up. There was a guy down there, all right, but he was all tied up, hanging like a puppet from one of the ceiling joists. He had a gun duct-taped to his hand. And I'd shot him dead.

"I was horrified. Just fucking horrified. Sal was laughing at the top of the stairs. Turned out, this guy had a real estate deal with Sal that went bad. Sal had asked him over for a truce over drinks, but whacked him upside the head with a golf club. I never did figure out how he got him all strung up in the basement—he had to have help." Owen lapsed into silence, staring into the blinding white before him.

"What did you do?" Anna prodded.

"I yelled at Sal. I went to call the squad, but he stopped me. Told me that no one would believe me. And he was pretty much right. If I called for help, the best case scenario was that I was gonna throw my career away. The worst would be cooling my heels in prison for thirty to life.

"So . . . I helped Sal bury the body. And I was

pretty much under his thumb from then on." Owen rubbed his nose. "I'm not proud of that. Not at all. And I wondered why in hell that man's ghost never rose up to haunt me."

He gazed at Anna through blurry eyes. He felt woozy, and he wanted to stretch out on the ground to take a nap. Just a short one. But first, he had to know: "Why did you pick me to haunt?"

Anna chewed the hem of her hoodie sleeve, and it was a long time before she answered: "I picked you because I thought you were a good man."

Owen closed his eyes.

CHAPTER 13

Beneath the Fire

I t had been decades since there had been a fire
burning here.

Petra knelt on the broken hearthstone to scrape
ice from the fireplace with her knife, trying to clear
a spot to start a fire with her steel flint. Most of the
carbon black had been worn away, and the sandstone chunks that the firebox was built of were
cracked with the incursion of ice. Abandoned bird
nests crowded the flue, and she'd pushed as much
of them away as she could with a broom handle.
Wind howled down the broken chimney and
through the chinks between the logs of the walls.
Sig sniffed at the chinking, and Petra saw that
there was animal fur in the mud, like the horsehair

that often appeared in plaster in old houses. She shuddered, thinking of the wolves.

Behind her, Gabe was destroying a table for firewood. Maybe they could get the tent set up before the fireplace. It would be survivable, not terribly comfortable, but . . .

Her knife clanged against something metal. She frowned and shone her flashlight into the box. The large piece of sandstone at the bottom had something jammed under it—it looked like a file or a tool of some kind. She worked at it, mostly out of curiosity, but the sandstone floor of the firebox shifted. A draft of cool air came up . . . up from the ground.

"Gabe." She sat back on her heels, and he came immediately to her side.

"What is it?"

She gestured at the fireplace stone with her knife. "I think there's something under there."

"Let's move the stone."

Gabe levered the broom handle under the stone and pushed. It slid up and away, and bits of grit and carbon rattled down into the darkness. Petra peered into the firebox, seeing a hole yawning into the earth. It was about two feet by three feet.

"I wonder if it's some kind of root cellar under there." She shone her light down into the darkness, seeing nothing but dirt.

"Underground is always a good spot to hide things." Gabe swung his legs down into the hole.

Petra supposed he was accustomed to mysterious underworld structures, but she still said, "Be careful."

He swung into the pitch-black and she heard his boots connect with earth. His flashlight shone around below her.

"What's down there?" she called.

"Something . . . odd," he said, sounding distracted. It would have to be something strange indeed for him to be at a loss for words. Given the macabre decor of the cabin's great room, she couldn't imagine what things Skinflint Jack would have deemed worthy of hiding.

Petra tied a nylon rope to the iron front door handle. She cast the rope down into the hole, squeezing around Sig's backside as he peered in.

"Sig. Do you want to be the guard dog or do you want to explore?"

Asking a canine to make a decision was always dangerous. Sig, at least, seemed more decisive than a domestic dog. He glanced at the hole and then at the closed door. He trotted across to the door to sit down, his ears perked up.

"Good boy." She felt much better, knowing that at least someone was on watch for threats.

She grasped the rope and tested her knots. They

would hold her weight. She pocketed her light and climbed down into the darkness.

It was a hand-hewn earthen cellar, shallow. Illuminated by her light, the floor was pounded dirt, shiny and smooth as stone. She could barely stand upright, and Gabe had to stoop. Along the walls were tool marks from the edges of shovels and timber beams jammed up at odd angles. Small bones, likely from the wolves, were set into the walls: spines undulated, ribs sinking deep into the earth. Dismembered bits of thigh bones and delicate toes were interspersed in a bizarre mosaic.

"Oh," she said. "That's what happened to the wolves' bones, I guess."

"An ossuary." Gabe seemed unrattled by his surroundings, tracing a shin bone in the wall with a finger. "I saw something like it, before I came here. It was an ossuary in the Austrian Empire. That had been built over centuries, but with human bones."

Her brow wrinkled. "This was back when you were investigating paranormal cases for the Pinkertons? I had no idea that they'd sent you to Europe."

"I went wherever a client with deep pockets would send me. That place was more elaborate than this . . . chandeliers of skulls and every inch full of bones."

"I think I might have seen some pictures on the Internet . . . it was very, uh, metal."

There were beds on the floor, two of them, covered in moth-eaten and filthy quilts. Beside them sat night tables with burned-down candles and wash basins with evaporated water, like an ordinary bedroom of the time. Except the tables were made of stacked skulls and jawbones. Peeking out beneath the blankets were legs of larger animals, perhaps cattle or moose.

Inside the beds were lumps. Petra approached cautiously, shining her light over her head.

She pulled back the corner of the disintegrating quilt on the first bed. A human figure wrapped in calico fabric lay in it like a caterpillar in a dead chrysalis, hands crossed over its chest. Skin as thin as a mica lampshade had sunken deeply over the skull, with tendrils of light brown hair clinging to flesh.

"How could a body last this long?" Gabe murmured. "Maybe tanned?"

"It's been mummified . . . this environment, closed away from air and water. It looks like most of it just . . . desiccated."

Gabe crossed over to the other bed. He drew back the blanket covering two children, lying faceup in dressing gowns. One was larger than the other, and it looked as if they'd been posed that way.

"I'm betting they didn't die here," Petra said. "They must have been brought here, after . . ." After what, she wasn't entirely certain.

Gabe had none of her squeamishness. He pulled

back the sleeves on the bodies and was inspecting them in a businesslike fashion.

"If this is Skinflint Jack's family, perhaps he put them here after they were killed by the wolves."

She was struck by the terrible effort and sentimentality of it. Maybe Jack had truly loved his family, in his fashion. She was reminded of a giant white cross that had been built on a hill near where she grew up. The story that went with it was that a man who had been terrible to his wife during his marriage had lost her to an illness. In his grief, he erected a giant stone cross in her memory that was visible from the freeway. Maybe this was like that, just . . . just more morbid.

She glanced back at Gabe, who had turned one of the children over and was inspecting the corpse with the keenness of a raven with something shiny in its talons. "What are you looking for?"

"I'm not certain," he said. "The legend of Skinflint Jack said that the wolves carried away the bones of his family and left the skins. This doesn't look like that at all."

"And that still doesn't sound like wolves. If anything, they'd take the flesh and leave the bones behind." Petra frowned. She felt squeamish in the pit of her stomach, watching Gabe manhandle these bodies. He had no fear of death, while it seemed to well up sharp and acidic in the back of her throat, like bile. She turned away, to the wall, trying to make rhyme or reason of the patterns of the bones, stuck to the wall with mud.

She paused before a section facing the foot of the beds. This spot seemed more deliberate than some of the other areas. Bones—they looked like scapulae—formed sconces in the wall, crusted with years upon years of tallow from candles. The skull of what she guessed was some kind of ungulate was set just above eye level . . . a stag, she realized. Antlers spread out from the skull, like a frieze. But the resemblance to a stag ended there. Rib bones were set around a spine in an upright posture. Arms and legs extended from the torso, the arms apart and uplifted to the sky. The legs were closed, but the tiny metatarsals didn't brush the rough floor. She scanned her light over the hands. The finger bones seemed delicate and small . . . tiny. And they were uneven sizes. The clavicles appeared diminutive, as did the overall stature of the creature. The pelvis seemed the wrong shape to belong to a wolf, and she guessed that many of the bones were human.

She chewed her lip, looking up at this . . . art? Were these truly human bones, or were they animal bones cobbled together in the shape of a man? She dredged her memory for her college anthropology classes, counting vertebrae and the number of ribs. And what did this mean? Was this a self-portrait of Skinflint Jack?

Behind her, Gabe grunted.

"You found something?" She was afraid to ask.

"It's more what I didn't find. Come see."

Steeling herself, she stepped back to the beds. Gabe had pulled off the covers and peeled the disintegrating clothes back like onion skins. The bodies were facedown. Gabe had taken off his coat, rolled up his sleeves, and was wrist-deep in a gaping tear in the woman's back.

"Gah," she said, stepping back. Her flashlight shook.

"There aren't any bones here," Gabe said. He pulled his hand back from the parchment-translucent skin and came away with a handful of sticks and dried grass. "They've been stuffed, like the wolves."

Petra focused on her shallow breathing, allowing her vision to get out of focus. Thank God it was cold in here—she was sweating beneath her coat. "I think the bones are over there." She gestured to the wall with her light.

"He had a lot of time."

"What does it mean, though?"

Gabe glanced down at the bodies. "Well, these people weren't killed by wolves. All the skin is pretty much intact—I don't see any tears or rends, like you'd expect with animals. There's just this . . ." He gestured at the zipper-like cut where the woman's shoulder blades should have been, following a tree branch that stood in place of her spine.

"Do you think that Skinflint Jack did this himself? That he killed his family?" She stood on her heels and turned around, taking in the ossuary. "He sure felt guilty about it, then."

"Looks that way. There's no trace of even muscle or fat in here . . ." He poked around in the corpse's shell.

"Oh, hell. You don't think he . . . ate them? Like the Donner party?" Bile burned the back of her throat.

"Even if he did . . . it would have been one hell of a feat to get all the bones out without breaking them." Gabe glanced back down at the body and began to fish around some more. "This bothers me."

Petra lifted an eyebrow. "Just one thing bothers you?"

"It's just impossible that . . . hmmm." He paused and shone his light into the cavity. It passed through the transparent skin and bits of straw.

She inched closer to him. "What?"

Gabe reached in, with a look of concentration on his face. He pulled out his fist, fingers closed around something. He opened his hand, and there was a mineral specimen, an opaque, shiny silver cluster.

Curiosity overcame her squeamishness. She plucked it immediately from his hand and turned it over.

"What is that?" he asked.

"It's antimony. Very, very pure antimony . . . I haven't seen anything this perfect outside of a lab. When purified, it forms a starlike structure . . ." She traced the spines with her finger.

"The Star of Antimony," Gabe murmured as she handed it to him. "In alchemy, it's known as the Grey Wolf. There's a series of illustrations of this in the old alchemical texts that show a king devoured by a wolf. When the wolf is burned, the king is resurrected from the ashes."

"Lascaris had something to do with this?"

"He must have. I know that he gathered his materials for his experiments from unusual sources." Gabe's brow was in shadow. "Perhaps Jack sold his family to him."

Petra shook her head, uncomprehending.

"We know that Jack lied about what happened." Gabe was clearly in his element here, wrist-deep in a mystery.

"I just can't . . ." The air was getting close here, stifling, as she tried to wrap her mind around this horrible act. "Let's go up."

"Are you all right?" Gabe was looking at her now, the star and his autopsy forgotten.

"I just want to get topside before I barf." She was embarrassed that he was looking at her this way, like she was more fragile than hundred-year-old corpses.

He laced his fingers together for her boot as she

grasped the rope. He lifted as she climbed. She clung to the edge of the blackened fireplace and hauled herself up on the hearth, where Sig waited to slather her with kisses.

Where underground had been black and stifling, the wind howled whitely through the seams of the windows, spitting snow through the cracked panes of glass.

She wrapped her arms around Sig's ruff, promising herself that she wasn't going to cry. She wanted nothing more than to flee this place. It felt too still, like death and suppressed rage. She had the sense of wandering into a sacred place and desecrating it. No good could come of that.

Petra climbed to her feet and peered through the warped glass. Snow rattled against it like gravel.

She sank down to the floor.

They were trapped here, in this shrine to Skinflint Jack's family.

She hoped that he wouldn't return anytime soon.

BLINDED BY THE whiteness of the storm, the wolves were lost in a colorless expanse.

Nine knew they had climbed a wind-whipped hill and descended into a new valley. The Stag had chased them there, and they'd slid downhill, the edges of the valley blotting out the grey orb of the sun before the storm swept in. The storm likely had little effect on the Stag, but it was deadly to the wolves. The nine-month-old pups were flagging, and they could no longer depend on their speed to deliver them from the Stag. They had to find shelter soon, had to, or they would die.

Dancing Shadow whined up ahead. Nine plodded forward to the sound. Snow trapped between the pads of her paws had compressed to ice, and she wanted nothing more than to stop and gnaw it free. Ghost, limping, had paused. A trickle of a creek had frozen over at the bottom of the valley, and a lump had formed over the ice crust. Bent Arrow dug at it, unearthing a beaver dam. The sticks were broken and in ill repair—Nine smelled nothing fresh here. Perhaps it was abandoned—perhaps there was still a meal drowsing in it.

The wolves broke into the lodge, shaking snow from their bodies and piling in. In spring, this would have been impossible—the dome was built over a pocket of open water and a bit of piled-up debris. But the water had frozen and was covered in brush, now, forming a solid floor all the way across. Nine wormed in behind the pups, pressing her spine against the exterior of the structure. It was cold here, but at least they were out of the wind. She kicked at the litter on the floor.

Hungry and exhausted, one of the gangly pups, Sage, collapsed beside her. Nine snuggled up against the pup. Sage felt cold, too cold. She licked her ears. Sage was the smallest of the litter, and Nine wanted to offer whatever comfort she could.

As Nine began to drowse, she was conscious of Sage breathing beside her. The pup's breath was ragged, whistling through her nose. Sometime before Nine was about to slip into sleep, she was conscious that the pup had stopped breathing. Nine nudged her, nipping the back of her neck, but Sage did not move. Sorrow flooded through Nine then, following her to her dreams.

Nine's dreams had always been vivid. In most of them, she ran across the dusk landscape in summer, darting through the grasses, staying just ahead of a storm. The storm would always overtake her, and she'd yip in delight at feeling the warm rain running through her fur, shaking it off with joy.

Sometimes, she dreamed that she walked on two legs. She didn't like those dreams. She felt slower when she ran, heavier, not as light and free. She felt fearful, crouching down in the grass, peering through the tassels for threats.

In her dream, she had lost her fur. She was freezing, curled up in the beaver lodge with the rest of her pack. The dead pup lay next to her belly, and she ran fingers through her fur. She tried to hold her, clumsy with arms and hands that didn't work like paws. Her face was wet, and she rubbed it to Sage's face.

Sage was light when she lifted her. In shock,

Nine realized that Sage was only a skin—her body was gone. Nine gasped and whined, clutching the skin to her chest. She tried to wake the others but they were buried in their own sleep, their paws twitching and upper lips moving in response to dream-threats. Something odd was happening to them, too . . . Nine could see a human hand sprouting from an ankle, a pale pink ear on a head. Fur rippled, and these mirages subsided.

Nine wrapped Sage's skin around her shoulders and lay down with the pack, shivering against the cold and the memory of what it was like to walk the land on two legs.

She was Nine.

She was a wolf.

And she would survive, somehow.

CHAPTER 14

The Crucible of Fire and Snow

I f Skinflint Jack had a physical body, there had to
be a way to hurt him.

Petra tore through the cabin, sifting through
spiderwebs and clanging through cast iron cookware. There had to be something here, something
she could use to fight him. Gabe and Sig gave her
a wide berth, perhaps suspecting that she'd finally
lost her mind. Gabe spent more than an hour in the
ossuary, muttering to himself before eventually
emerging from the hole with a sack full of things
that clinked ominously. The sack was made from
tied-together, threadbare bedclothes. She chose not
to ask what was in it, and he worked on resetting
the fireplace and starting a fire.

Eventually, she worked up the guts to ask, "What did you take from down there?"

"The skull from the self-portrait," Gabe said quietly. "And the three stars. For bait."

She muttered as she worked through a box of broken canning jars, cast them aside and flipped through a candle box full of melted wax. She had the beginning of an idea—the antimony star Gabe had uncovered. It was something precious to Jack—and perhaps something precious to him could hurt him, the way lead could not. She considered breaking off the points and using them as arrowheads, but had been unlucky so far in finding something that could be transformed into a bow. She'd found an axe, a handful of fireplace tools, and some rotted baskets. Nothing she could use to make arrows, but . . .

"Oh."

She sat back on her heels, holding a device that looked like a pair of pliers. She squinted at it, opening them to look at the cavity inside.

"Hey, Gabe. What do you think of this?"

He crossed the room. The fire had begun to warm the room and cast light, even as it was failing outside. He crouched and looked at the tool.

"That's a bullet casting mold," he said.

"That's what I was hoping. Will the caliber work with your rifle?" She peered inside. The casting hollow was round, not shaped like a modern bullet.

He frowned. "No. These were sold at the same time guns were, so that people could cast their own bullets. This looks like it was made for a Kentucky rifle, a .44."

"If it's still here, can you help me find it?"

"What are you thinking?"

"I'm thinking that if I can use one of the Stars of Antimony . . ." She pointed to the sack. ". . . to make bullets, would that hurt Jack? I mean, we can't go far in this storm anyway. And we'll need a way to defend ourselves if he comes back. Otherwise, we're sitting ducks."

Gabe seemed to think about it. "I think so. If the Jack of Harts was created in a separation process, as I suspect . . . the star is a more advanced process."

"More advanced?" she echoed.

"Jack was created in the separation phase, the phase in which unworthy material is cast aside. The true essence of a thing, usually symbolized by a black bird, splits into two white birds. Matter and spirit are divided. In Jack's case, his humanity seems to have been split out and left behind.

"Antimony represents the black earth stage of alchemy, the fermentation stage. Fermentation is the fifth stage, and is a finer, more powerful process that can destroy the results of the prior stages. If the antimony is chemically blackened, it might work. But no guarantees."

"I'll try it."

"If you found the bullet mold, the gun has to be here somewhere."

They pulled apart the remainder of the room, scattering a squirrel's stash of shriveled walnuts and a collection of tin plates. Petra might have felt guilty about ransacking the house of anyone else—like, a person who didn't have wolves strung up as ceiling decorations. She just reminded herself not to look up at the shifting shadows above, and focus on her task. She found a rotting leather pouch of round lead bullets and a powder horn that was half full of black powder that made her sneeze.

"Got it." Gabe held a rifle over his head, an old flintlock and a ramrod. He sighted down the barrel. "But there's bad news."

"Let me guess—it's rusted to bits?"

"Partially. And the stock is rotted. It's not usable in this condition."

"Shit." She sat down hard on the dirt floor. Her idea, once so sharp and shiny, was beginning to fade.

"I can probably restore it to working order, if I swap out some parts from my gun. And if I clean away the rust. There's probably enough beeswax in that candle tin to make a go of it."

"Are you sure? I don't want that blowing up in your face."

"Nor do I. But I think it can be done." He glanced down at her. "But how are you going to cast the bullets?"

"Yeah. The melting point for lead is about six hundred twenty-two degrees. Iron, like these casting tongs, is about twenty-eight hundred degrees. Antimony is . . ." She dug around in the file cabinet of her brain. When she was in a college art class, she'd become fascinated by gothic rose windows made with refracting stained glass that had included antimony. She'd been determined to figure out the recipe, but had failed. "Antimony is one thousand sixty-seven? Sixty-eight?"

"Okay. The casting will work."

"Maybe not." She stood before a fireplace. "A controlled fire in a furnace with a bellows, under even optimal conditions, with perfect pine and charcoal fuel, only gets up to about a thousand degrees. I don't think it could get hot enough in a sustained enough fashion to do this." She drummed her fingers on her lower lip.

"But." She had an idea. "A car fire can get up to one thousand seven hundred degrees, for a very short period of time."

Gabe's brow wrinkled. "You want to burn one of the snow machines?"

She brightened at the thought of setting something on fire. "Yeah. I think I do."

"Well . . . we can both ride on one. With Sig," he amended, looking down at the coyote. "We might have to sacrifice a bunch of gear and a lot of speed."

"But it could get us some magic bullets."

"It's worth it, then."

Petra dug through the iron cookware, finding a small cook pot with a lid. She scraped rust away from it and placed the Star of Antimony inside. It fit reasonably well, and there was a lip to pour from.

Handling it . . . that would be a trick. She found a pair of long-handled fireplace tongs that she thought would work to add the pot to the fire and remove it. In a laboratory, she'd have heat-resistant gloves. One slip up here and she'd be horribly burned. She practiced lifting and handling the pot with the tongs. Its wire handle would likely dissolve in the fire, and she didn't want to spill any of the antimony.

So far, so good. She gathered a frying pan and a griddle, digging away a skin of rust with the fireplace poker. She put the antimony star on the griddle, then put the bowl of the frying pan down on top of it.

"Beware of shards," she warned Gabe and Sig, and gave the star a hard whack.

It shattered into several pieces. She whacked it a few more times, imagining striking Jack in the chest. The star crunched into powder, with a few larger pieces as big as her fingers. She carefully swept them all into the small iron pot with the handful of lead bullets to stabilize the mixture.

"Do you want the other stars?" Gabe asked. He'd already disassembled the stock of the rifle on the floor with his pocketknife.

She shook her head. "I don't think I'll have time to use all the antimony here. If the hottest part of the fire burns for an hour, we'll get maybe four or five bullets out of this, before it cools too far."

She bundled up and headed for the door. Gabe lurked in her periphery with Petra's pistols. There wasn't a lot they could do if Jack returned now, but she appreciated the thought. She put her gear in a bag and shoved open the door.

The wind snatched the door and slammed it open against the side of the cabin. She struggled with it and succeeded in nearly slamming it in Gabe's face. They pushed it back in place and faced the storm.

Petra couldn't see more than two yards before her. The snow howled along the field, uninterrupted. She had to trace the side of the cabin with her fingers to keep her balance in the snow. They found one of the snowmobiles covered in snow. They dusted it off, dumped the gear, and got it started. Petra swung her leg over the machine, adjusted her goggles, and wrapped her arms around Gabe's waist.

They roared into the blinding white. She wasn't

certain how far they'd gone, and she felt a momentary flare of panic welling in her throat. What if they lost the location of the cabin? And Sig?

Gabe stopped the snowmobile and killed the engine. Petra popped the hood, while he took her bag of casting gear from the back and moved it away. She could see little through her goggles, but knew she didn't have much time until the snow made it too difficult to see anyway. Gabe aimed a flashlight on her hands, but dark had fallen, and the light was little use.

Petra eyeballed the pot she'd brought with the pieces of star still inside. She placed it carefully on the seat, near the gas tank. It didn't seem that it would tip over; that should work.

She had brought a splintered willow stick from a basket the cabin and torn off a piece of her scarf to wrap around it. She opened the gas cap and dipped the stick in, soaking it with gasoline. Squinting at the engine, she pulled the spark plugs and let them lie on the engine. Gently, she placed the stick against the spark plugs. Holding her breath, she started the engine.

On the third crank, flame flickered out over the stick. She briefly considered yanking the stick away and jamming it in the gas tank, but figured that would likely just cost her an arm. She moved away from the snowmobile to stand with Gabe.

"Nicely done," he remarked.

"Yeah, well. We'll see how well this works."

The flame licked along the housing and caught the gasoline fumes. She hoped to God that the snow machine wouldn't explode, like cars did in the movies, and spill the precious antimony. But she was lucky—the fire skimmed up along the carriage and the seat began to burn, all around the pot. They moved upwind of the plastic fumes.

It took a good twenty minutes for most of the gas to burn off while the fire blazed. Snow melted around them as it thawed, and she shivered.

"You know the way back, right?" she asked Gabe.

He held up the Locus. "It knows."

The fire burned almost forty-five minutes before it began to smolder, reaching its highest temperature. Petra arranged the iron griddle and frying pan as a work space, reached for the fireplace tongs and approached the fire gingerly. The heat was shimmering at close distances, but upwind it was sufferable. Through the black smoke, she grasped the iron crucible and pulled it away, placing the red-hot metal on the frying pan. It steamed and hissed spectacularly.

Brow knit in concentration, she removed the lid with the tongs. Liquid metal sloshed inside, and she sucked in her breath.

Gabe placed the bullet mold on the griddle. Petra took a deep breath and grasped the small pot with the tongs. She poured a bit of the liquid metal into the mold cavity, slopping only a few drops. Sweating, she put the pot back on the frying pan with the tongs and put the lid back on.

"We need to cool this gently . . . or it could shatter. Or spontaneously combust."

"That might be something useful to know if I'm to use this as a bullet."

"If it blackens, it should stabilize."

"'Should'?" he echoed.

"Really. It should."

She waited for the heat to stop shimmering, for the drops of spilled antimony to harden, before cracking the mold. A round ball of black metal popped out, bouncing against the iron griddle.

"Fuck," she swore, wincing.

"I guess it's not going to explode." Gabe fished it out with the tongs. The black bullet steamed in the frigid air. "I can work with this."

"Good," she sighed.

She got two more bullets out of the crucible before the metal began to cool. The last one cracked, and they had a total of three usable bullets. They stared at them, cooling on the griddle, as if the bullets were a fine confection of 1860s vintage.

"Good work. You might have been a gunsmith in a previous life."

She snorted, wiping sweat from her brow. "Yeah. I'd like not to do that again."

When they were cool enough to handle, Gabe pocketed the bullets. He would figure out the propellant, from the black powder horn they'd found. Gabe knew guns; she knew chemistry. It seemed an equitable division of labor.

He kicked snow over the snowmobile, ensuring that all the smoldering bits were entirely out. She didn't want to leave the antimony behind—who knew what kind of animal might find it? She carried the container under her arm, where it felt luxuriously warm as she and Gabe trudged back to the cabin. The storm had swept away all sense of direction, and she relied on the Venificus Locus in his hand more than she wanted to admit.

"Honey, I'm home," she announced when they returned to the cabin.

Sig nosed up to her, and she was relieved to see him. The fire had burned down in the fireplace grate, but not out. She went to stir it, while Gabe began to work on the antique gun.

She shed her gloves and wrapped herself in a blanket. The drowsiness of the heat licked over her, and she stretched out on the floor.

"Gabe," she said.

"Mmm?" he muttered over the sound of filing.

"Why did you become a Pinkerton agent?" It occurred to her that she'd never asked.

There was a small, almost imperceptible interruption in his filing. "I wasn't much interested in

being a lawman. It was more the chance to investigate the strange that caught my fancy. Being ac-
quainted with Allan Pinkerton allowed me to do
that."

"Why?" She knew why she'd fallen into the
weirdness of the supernatural—she'd come to
Temperance to search for her missing father. She
knew Gabe had come here to investigate Lascaris,
but she was curious to know why he'd become involved with the strange in the first place.

He took his time answering, and she thought he
might be weighing what to tell her.

"I was one of four brothers, the third oldest. As a
child, my family lived in the North End of Boston.
We would often go play in the tunnels beneath the
streets. They ran from houses to churches, con-
necting wells in basements and burial grounds.
They were used by smugglers, grave robbers, and
other unsavory types.

"As you can imagine, this was nigh-irresistible
to a group of young men determined to dare each
other into more and more audacious pranks. We
followed the tunnels to a church and stole the
Blood of Christ. We slipped into houses through
wells, teaching ourselves to swim. We prowled the
cemeteries after dark, daring each other to sleep in
freshly dug graves. We had developed, I think, a
morbid fascination with the forbidden. Our father
worked for the railroad as a doctor and was seldom

home enough to box our ears as often as they should have been. Our mother was very sickly. I suspect, looking back, that her symptoms were largely psychosomatic. Regardless, I rarely saw her out of bed."

"You sound like a proper group of hooligans."

"We were. Once, when I was twelve, our oldest brother had dared the rest of us to come look at something he'd found in the tunnels. He said he'd found liquor, which was of immediate interest. We let ourselves in through the tunnel that ran through the graveyard and followed it to where he'd seen the crate of bottles.

"There was no crate, but we found something else. A pale woman, dressed in black from neck to toe. Her eyes, too, were black, and her hands were like the claws of a bird. She slipped through the dark like an eel. When she opened her mouth, it was with a terrible shriek that sounded like glass breaking.

"We ran from her. My older brothers were much faster than I was. I struggled to keep up, but I lost track of Henry, my little brother. We were nearly to the graveyard by the time I gave a thought to him. I turned back to find him and saw the woman of the tunnels. She was standing over him, with his heart in her hands."

"Gah," Petra said, involuntarily.

"She was eating it. I knew at once that he was

dead. And I fled." Gabe was silent for some time, rubbing beeswax into metal in even strokes. "When I returned to the house, my brothers had already alerted the constable to look for him. Henry's body was never found, though his shoes were found perched on the top of a gravestone in the cemetery."

"I'm sorry," she said.

"It is my greatest regret," he said. "I didn't wait for him. I didn't save him. I let him be devoured by that . . . revenant. I had told my brothers and the constable what happened. My brothers believed me. The constable thought I was mad, thought that I had something to do with it. I spent two weeks in an asylum before my father returned to town and got me out."

Petra remained silent. *I'm sorry* seemed inadequate here. She simply listened, waiting for him to continue.

"In that time, I saw true madness. I also saw many who had witnessed terrible things and could not overcome the shock. It made me realize that the perimeters around an individual's reality are more fluid than I thought. And that there were things in the world that could not be explained."

"And you went to work for Pinkerton . . . to avenge your brother?"

"On some level, yes. So did the rest of my brothers, in their fashion. One became a priest. The other became a sheriff in Arkansas. We all chased our own demons, in our way.

"My parents did not speak of Henry ever again. I never knew if they believed me, but I know that they blamed the rest of us for what had happened. There was a palpable distance that grew. There were many meals after that eaten in silence, and all his belongings were removed from the house and burned.

"As an adult, I went back down to the tunnels, armed with holy water and silver knives. I wanted to see if that revenant was still there. There had been stories of a woman in black who appeared at the bottom of wells and wandered the church-yards, who stole stillborn infants from the ceme-tery and left empty graves behind."

"Did you find her?"

"No. I searched for her for many months, but I found no trace of her. All I found was a scrap of rotted black lace in a crypt and a huge nest of stolen rosary beads. I never solved that case."

"It wasn't your fault. You have to know that. You were a child."

"It was a long time ago," he said.

But she knew that time erased nothing.

CHAPTER 15

Waking Up

She dreamed of an ache in the marrow of her bones, so much deeper than frost.

In her dreams, Petra had dropped into Skinflint Jack's hand-dug cellar, his underground ossuary. It was cold and silent there, and her breath made ghosts in the darkness. Light emanated from the bodies on the bed, from beneath their parchment-thin skin, moving like drifting fireflies underneath the surface. The bodies sat upright, heads turned toward her with empty gazes.

Petra would have run away, but she was pinned to the wall. Bones laced over her body like shackles, splitting through the skin of the dirt to wrap around her wrists, ribs, and legs. She tried to turn her head, but it was enclosed in a helmet, the Stag's skull, and she blinked through the eye sockets of the Stag.

What had he seen? What had he done? She struggled against the weight of the bones, torn between wanting to know and wanting not to know.

Jack's wife stood, walking across the floor to Petra in a dress of black lace. Bits of her skin fluttered to the floor, disturbed by Gabe's autopsy efforts. In her hands, she held the Star of Antimony, gleaming in the shifting low light.

"What happened to you?" Petra asked, her tears blurring her gaze. The tears slid down her cheek, underneath the skull-mask.

The woman didn't answer; only gazed at Petra with those empty, vacant eye sockets.

And Petra realized that her mouth had been sewn shut.

"It's all right."

Petra awoke with a start, her fingers wound in Gabe's coat. She blinked, orienting herself to the main floor of the cabin, with a fire snapping in the grate. She was covered in rough Army-surplus blankets from their packs, with Sig draped across her legs. The fire had warmed the room to a decent temperature. Sig wasn't curled up in a tight ball. Instead, he was half stretched out with his feet tucked beneath him.

"You were dreaming," Gabe said, pushing a piece of her hair behind her ear.

She looked away. He seemed worried, and she couldn't stand that, the idea that he felt the need to guard over her sleep. But when she looked away, all she saw were the wolf skins. In the flickering firelight it seemed that they moved and danced above them, the darkness pressed close. It had to be an illusion—she knew that the pheasants they'd frightened earlier slept up there. It had to be.

She pulled her knees up to her chest and wrapped her arms around her knees. "I'm okay. Really. I was just dreaming of the basement . . ." She forced herself not to shudder.

He made a noncommittal noise and reached forward to stir the fire. She saw that the Kentucky rifle had been cleaned and reassembled, leaning against the wall like a prop from a Western film.

"You fixed it?"

"Yeah. I think so."

"What made you think I was dreaming, anyway?"

"You snore when you dream. And sometimes you talk in your sleep."

She flushed, and chided herself. Why should she be embarrassed? She'd been listening to him snore for weeks. And . . . Jeez. They were married, for God's sake.

That reminded her. She stripped off her gloves

and dug into her pocket. "Oh, hey. I almost forgot. I got us something at the pawnshop." She held her hand out with the rings. "I have no idea if these will fit, but . . . I thought . . ."

It had seemed like a good idea when she'd bought them, but she felt sort of dumb now. Sentimental.

Gabe took the rings from her, holding them up to the light. "They're beautiful." He took hers and slid it on her finger.

Clumsily, she took his and slid it on his ring finger. It fit, miraculously enough.

At her feet, Sig yawned loudly. Human rituals, unless they involved dining, held no interest for him.

"Thank you," he said.

"I thought we should look legit." She glanced back at the fire, feeling the metal warming to her hand. Aside from her father's pendant, she never wore jewelry. She expected this to feel heavy and annoying, but the edges of the ring had been polished smooth with time, like the borders of a river stone.

"We *are* legit." He said it, matter-of-factly, as if it was as evident as day or night.

"Are we?" She rested her chin on her knees, staring at the popping embers. It looked like the back of a chair was disintegrating in the fire now, or maybe those were rails from a crib. When Skinflint Jack got back, he was sure gonna be pissed about them dismantling his house and desecrating his ossuary. They had to be gone by then.

"Of course." He seemed startled. "It may have been a very long time since I've worn a ring, but I think I remember how it goes. Priest, paper . . . done."

"I mean . . . what about the future? What about if we go someplace else, and Sheriff Owen eventually gives up? What if I get through treatment okay? What then—do we stay married?"

He gave a small shrug, and she thought she felt him pull away from her a bit. "It only changes if you want it to change. Once you're well . . . you can tell me to go away. I'll abide by your wishes. And you can keep custody of Sig."

"I didn't mean that. I just meant . . . you're human now. You have a whole lifetime to lead, and I don't want you to feel shackled to me. Trapped. Or anything." She was tired and rambling, but she let herself.

He reached up to push her hair from her shoulder, a familiar gesture. "I will be happily married to you for as long as I can have you. I know not to tempt fate beyond that." His hand slipped up to her cheek and he kissed her, silencing the roil of doubts and worry thundering in her skull.

PETRA EVENTUALLY FELL back asleep, and Gabe dozed beside her. He glanced down at the ring on his left hand. It seemed to mean something different for him than it did to her. In his day, a marriage with affection was a rarity, and something to be savored. They had that, even love. He knew she found him attractive—she was the most enthusiastic lover he'd ever had. In his time, women had a tendency to lay like logs and count dust motes on the ceiling. He thought he pleased her as well—his back still bore scratches from her fingernails.

He laid down and stared at the shadows churning among the wolf-kites on the ceiling. He noticed that women in recent decades seemed to want something of romance, but he knew that Petra wasn't given to such things. On the hotel television, he'd seen a commercial of a man selling soap who was shirtless on a horse. If he'd asked her to marry him shirtless on horseback, she'd have laughed at him outright or gone running away until he'd managed to find the rest of his laundry and his dignity.

Maybe this was fear of the future that he saw in her. And he could understand that. He feared it, too. He feared the idea of her treatment, what little she'd said about it. It would involve scalpels and poisons of various kinds, finding the endurance to outlast the cancer in her marrow and wherever else it had wandered. He knew no answer to that, other than surrendering to modern technology. Alchemy was not an art that dabbled in healing. It transformed, razing from the ground up.

But all his imaginings about that were moot. There was no magical solution. Gabe knew death on an instinctive level, and he knew that it had clotted in her shadow. It would take a great deal of science to make it let go of her. He'd had little use for leeches in his former life, even his own father, but he accepted that times had changed since then. Magic was dimming out of the world—not just his world, but the world at large. He could not depend on magic to save her, not anymore. Science could produce things that even alchemy could not; perhaps it could preserve her if he gave it enough faith.

Besides, he'd made a wish. In Jack's pond. That had to count for something, didn't it? He was quite certain that Jack would want him dead now . . . and that would satisfy the bargain. As would Jack's own death.

The wind howled overhead for hours and eventually died. The windows were covered in snow, but blue light began to lighten almost imperceptibly behind the crystalline crust.

Sig sensed it. He rolled over, stretched, and yawned with a whine, arching his back and pulling back his ears. The movement woke Petra, who rubbed at her eyes with her palm.

"Did the storm stop?"

"I think so."

Her gaze grazed the macabre ceiling. "Let's get out of here."

"We could stay. Wait for Jack to return. He'll come back, eventually."

She shook her head. "No. He's hunting wolves. And Sheriff Owen is hunting us. I want to keep moving."

It took little time to gather their belongings. Petra tied up their bedrolls and blankets, while Sig inspected her pockets for the presence of beef jerky. Gabe set about sweeping snow into the firebox to kill the embers. He took the time to carefully load the Kentucky rifle with powder, one of Petra's bullets, a cloth circle he'd cut from a scrap of fabric, and the ramrod. He loaded some powder in the pan and covered it with a sock to avoid accidental ignition. It had been a long time since he'd used a weapon like this—he estimated that it would take him a good three minutes to reload. Best to be ready.

Gabe took one last glance around the place. There wasn't anything else here that they could pragmatically use—just bits of iron and rotting wood and the materials they'd used to cast bullets. He hid those, not wanting to tip off Jack in case he returned.

But there were the things they might need, things to trap Skinflint Jack. He reached for the bag he'd left by the fireplace, the things he'd hauled up from the ossuary. The sack clinked as he knotted it shut.

Petra tugged the door open, and a drift of snow flooded in, up to their knees. She made a face.

"You reconsidering moving on?" he asked, slinging the pack over his shoulder.

"No. Not at all." She slogged into the snow, Sig padding behind her.

Gabe was about to tug the door shut against the snow drift, but decided against it.

If Jack came back before they caught up with him, he wanted to leave a challenge for him. He wanted Jack to know they had been there. That they were hunting him. That they knew what he was.

Dawn had not yet burned through the cloud cover. The world was perfectly silent, wrapped in snow that gleamed violet under the sky's shadow. They dug the remaining snowmobile out and dusted snow from the engine exhaust. Gabe estimated that nearly two feet of snow had fallen, on top of the snow that had already been there. The fresh snow was dense and wet, pierced by only a few rabbit and fox tracks in the broad expanse.

Gabe swished some blood into the Venificus Locus as the engine warmed. The blood drop circled agitatedly in the groove circumscribing the rim. It clearly was focused on Skinflint Jack's house . . . hopefully, as they gained distance from it, it would be able to home in on Jack himself, or the wolves he was hunting.

Petra climbed up behind him on the snowmobile, and Sig clambered up between his knees like the figurehead on a ship. He noticed that Petra had wrapped Sig's ears with a scarf tied around his neck, and he smiled. With a quick wrench on the throttle, Gabe plunged into the frigid predawn.

He mulled strategy in his head. Jack had been human once; he had a human intelligence, motivated by emotion. It would be critical to get ahead of him, somehow, to lay a trail that might lead him to Sepulcher Mountain, for the ritual that Petra's father had suggested. He hadn't admitted it to Petra, but he wasn't certain how this was going to come together. In his time as a Pinkerton agent, he'd researched the dark arts and rubbed elbows with necromancers and summoners. But he'd typically been an observer, not a practitioner.

If all else failed . . . He glanced back at the gun lashed to the snowmobile packs. If all else failed, perhaps they could destroy the Jack of Harts with brute force. Or, at least, maybe they could hobble him long enough to get the wolves out of his way.

THE WORLD HAD gone white, a screaming white that burned through Owen's eyelids and seared into his brain with blistering fingers.

"Owen."

A voice cut through the white noise, a hiss over the static that suffused every cell of his body.

"Owen. Owen, wake up."

He cracked his eyes open, and the light became more blinding. He thought he'd given himself a bad case of snow blindness, but he fixed on Anna's face, peering at him.

"Owen. Get up. Get up, or you're going to die."

He looked past her, at the fire. It had blackened the side of the pine tree, red embers glowing. He coughed and rubbed his face with numb fingers. His gloves came away with black soot. Smoke had blackened his clothing and his exposed skin.

"Get up, Owen."

He struggled to get his legs under him. They felt swollen. Not particularly cold, just unwieldy. It took him three tries to crouch, then grasp the overhead pine branches. Snow had formed a crust over it, an igloo of ice where the fire had melted and it froze again. Above the fire, water dripped from a hole the hot smoke had burned into it.

He pulled the branches apart, snow sliding down over the remnants of the fire. He dug with his hands, panic rising in his throat. He was buried. Buried alive, in ice and sticks and pine sap.

"Lemme out," he panted, his hands slamming into the frozen sheets. They'd melded with the branches, forming an unbreakable wall.

"Lemme out." He kicked at the walls, doubling up his fists.

"Lemme out!"

The snow was heavy. He made a dent, and thick

chunks of it slid down from above. He could feel himself hyperventilating. How much oxygen was in here, anyway, that hadn't been eaten up by the fire?

"Lemme out!" he howled, then whimpered.

Anna was standing at the far side of the shelter, cowering from his rage. He didn't care. He was going to fucking die in here with a ghost, and wind up haunting this godforsaken hillside with her. He'd have forever to apologize.

If she was even real in the first place. Maybe he imagined her. He discarded that thought immediately. Anna was real. He was real, too. The weird shit underneath Sal's ranch was real. He had to find the answer to it. He would not die like this. Would not.

He took off his belt and began to hack at the ice with the buckle. Slivers of ice spewed back at him, cutting his face. He shouted as he swung, the belt biting into his prison in a wrathful rhythm.

"Let.

"Me.

"Out."

This fucking storm. It shouldn't have been here. It had come to test him, to try to stop him. Damn it. He wouldn't let it. He was going to uncover all the Rutherford Ranch's secrets. He would not be defeated. Not by something as stupid as fucking snow.

His belt buckle chipped away at air, and a thin trickle of grey light slid in. Owen jammed his fist into it, feeling the ice chew into the knuckles of his glove. He began to strike it with both fists, howling and screaming. His screams echoed tightly in this space, sounding like Friday night at the jail under a full moon.

The ice cracked. He jammed his bloody fingers into the fissure and ripped it open, spattering the pristine white with red. He made a void of about the size of a bowling ball, got his arm and shoulder through, as the structure creaked and groaned. His shoulder split in a blinding pain as he forced it, like breaking down a door.

Finally, he stumbled out, into a drift of snow up to his knees, howling. He collapsed to the snow, gasping and bleeding.

"Goddamn it. Goddamn it," he kept saying, over and over again, stupidly, riding the bright edge of that anger.

Dawn had begun to lighten the horizon. Anna floated above the snow, her arms wrapped around her elbows. She made no tracks, her toes not brushing the cold surface.

"You're crazy," she said, and she looked afraid.

He began to laugh. A ghost—a ghost was calling him fucking crazy.

He'd show her.

He climbed to his feet, staggered to the snowmobile, a lump with handlebars clearing the topmost drift. Summoning that white rage, he scooped the snow away from the machine, his breath burning in the back of his throat. He could feel his heart hammering against his ribs, hard enough that he thought his chest might explode of a heart attack.

But he slammed his battered hands into the snow, over and over, until he cleared a ski. In pure wrath, he slammed his shoulder against the jammed rear track. The snowmobile shook, the track shivering loose from the ground.

The machine came free, sliding from the snow and causing him to stumble. Snarling, he grasped at the handlebars, determined not to let it defy him. He swung his leg over the seat and cranked the engine to life, turning back to Anna. A feeling of invincibility surged through him, pounding through his lungs and his skull.

"Are you coming?" he snarled.

She looked down at the ground with an expression of unfathomable sadness. She faded away, like dry ice in a stiff wind.

"Go back to hell, then. I'll do this alone."

Leaving the cracked-open shell of his shelter behind him, he struck off into the frozen wasteland, into the burning white unknown.

CHAPTER 16

The Pack

The Locus looked behind them, like Lot's wife, for miles.

Gabe had begun to despair that it would ever turn away from Skinflint Jack's cabin. There had been incredible magical gravity there, and the Locus was behaving like a compass held too close to a magnet. Perhaps their disruption of the cabin, the opening of the ossuary, had let the power leak out over the land. He scraped frozen blood from the Locus and added fresh from a slice at the edge of his hand every mile. If he was honest with himself, he was unaccustomed to seeing his blood this way. As a Hanged Man, it looked red in ordinary sunlight, but glowed in shadow. Now, it was simply red. He was rewarded for his efforts as a droplet finally, reluctantly, turned away from the cabin to the north.

Sun burned through the tatters of the clouds, lighting the desolate land before them. The plain at the foot of the mountains had begun to break up in pockets of pine forest and rills of uneven ground as they descended into a shallow valley. They were forced to travel more slowly, winding through trees and sliding over frozen creek beds, avoiding clumps of underbrush hidden by a skin of snow that could hang up the snowmobile. The snowmobile was already slow and heavy with three passengers and all the gear they could cram onto it.

"We should stop here," he suggested, at a spot where frozen creek met forest. This place was shielded from the wind, and perhaps they could take a few minutes to consult a map and eat something.

Sig dismounted immediately and began nosing in the packs. Petra dumped some dog kibble out in a dish for Sig, while the coyote made a face. Gabe slipped him some beef jerky when Petra turned away to unfold a map.

"The creek is here," she said, tracing a spidery vein with a gloved hand.

He saw that she'd marked the location of the cabin and traced out their route with times. He didn't blame her for not fully trusting that the Locus might suddenly fall silent and leave them stranded.

"And the mountain my dad mentioned is here."

She circled a triangle with her pencil. She looked north and squinted. "It's still too far away to see with the haze, but maybe . . ." She dug into her pack for some binoculars. "There it is."

She passed them to Gabe. "Doesn't look like anything much is going on there," he said. Through the binoculars, he spied an eagle's shadow on the snow of the sloped peak and the shapes of elk. But nothing out of the ordinary.

"I'll take that as a good thing, though—"

She was interrupted by Sig's growling. The coyote had strayed away from the snowmobiles, pressing his nose to the ground. His hackles had risen and his ears were perked forward.

"Sig, what is it?" Petra approached and knelt beside him. Her right hand reached for her sidearm.

Gabe plucked the rifle from the rack on the snowmobile and scanned the forest's edge with the sight. Slowly, he approached Sig and Petra.

"Wolf tracks," he muttered. He brushed the toe of his boot in the snow before Sig, who slithered in front of him and peed on the tracks.

"How recent?"

"Pretty fresh. Since the snow settled, and before the wind's had a chance to soften them."

Something moved in Gabe's peripheral vision, and he immediately drew his rifle to his shoulder.

A grey shape was moving between the trees,

light as smoke. It was a wolf. She was thin, her golden eyes bright in her rough coat.

Gabe froze. A wolf would not attack a human, especially not one by itself. This one looked stringy and hungry, though, and she had zeroed in on what she wanted.

She ducked behind the snowmobile, slinking low, her tail brushing the snow.

Sig continued to growl, so loud he practically vibrated. Petra had wound her fingers in his collar, but he strained forward as the wolf sidled up to the dog dish and devoured his dog food in three quick gulps. She didn't lift her eyes from Sig and the humans as she licked the dish.

Petra was down on her hands and knees, talking to the wolf. "We know that something terrible is after you. We want to help."

The wolf backed away, nosing through one of the packs. She grasped a plastic bag full of jerky and turned to flee.

Sig wriggled free of Petra's grip and gave chase.

"Sig!" she shouted, and took off after him, plunging into the woods.

Gabe had no choice. Rifle in hand, drawing his sidearm from his belt, he followed.

NINE RACED INTO the pine trees with her prize, kicking up snow as she ran. Her jaws salivated around the treat, distracting her as she zinged right and left through the forest.

The coyote was behind her. She had no desire to confront the coyote or the people. In another time and place she might consider the coyote prey, but . . . there was something odd about him. He reeked of the humans, but also of something else that she couldn't readily identify with her heart thumping and feet skimming over the landscape.

She just wanted to escape, to catch up to the pack with the badly needed food. It wasn't much, but it would stop the loud belly growling among the pups. She would be a hero, she knew. This would elevate her status, and she thrilled to imagine it.

She plunged through the woods, keening around the plastic in her mouth. She could see the wolves just ahead on a ridge. They turned at her sounds of distress and began to race down the slope to meet her. Her heart soared to see them, knowing they had not left her behind.

The coyote howled behind her.

Ghost cocked his head quizzically. Nine was allowing herself to be chased by . . . prey? A flicker of a smile crossed his mouth, and his tongue lolled.

She turned, skidding in the snow, with the wolves above her and the coyote running flat-out behind her. The sack of jerky swung in her mouth, and she regarded the smaller canine with narrowed eyes. The tables had turned. She had a wall of wolves at her back. Even if they found her ridiculous, they would stand behind her.

At first she thought the coyote was angry because she'd stolen his food. He looked well-fed enough. But there was something about him . . . something shimmery and otherworldly.

The coyote had slowed to a stop, lifting his head, scenting the air and huffing.

She cocked her head. The wolves surged down behind her in a ranging line of breathless fur, but the little coyote held his ground.

Nine dropped the sack and stepped toward him. She lowered her head and body, instinctively falling into a nonthreatening posture as she crept to him.

The coyote stood still, waiting for her to come, still and alert, ears up and tail swishing in the snow. He was unafraid.

Nine's tail was low around her ankles, ears flattened, as she extended her nose toward him. The coyote's nose made contact with hers . . .

. . . and she realized, with a jolt, who he was. Some bit of atavistic memory rattled loose in her feral brain, a memory from a time when she walked on two legs.

He was Coyote. Maybe not a fully embodied Coyote, the entire god on earth poured into a fur suit. But this creature was certainly a piece of him, roaming the backcountry for his own divine amusement. He was beyond magic, beyond the pack and the humans he led.

She remembered the tales of him from the people on two legs—how Coyote was responsible for the moon and stars in the sky, and how an offended Coyote could cause great devastation.

Nine threw back her head and howled.

PETRA HEARD THE howling ahead of her.

First it was one solitary howl, then it was many. A whole pack of wolves, howling victoriously in the daylight.

"Sig!" she screamed, running harder into the woods. Her breath burned her throat, and she was clumsy in her thick boots. He'd gone chasing after that wolf, angry about his food, and he must have run into the pack.

Please let him be okay. Petra wasn't given to prayer, but she hoped something, somewhere, would hear her, would keep him safe.

She ran into a clearing, fumbling for her gun to fire a warning shot to scare them, swearing . . .

. . . and stopped short, stunned.

The ground was a writhing mass of yipping, grumbling wolves. They tumbled over each other, tails flickering, bellies wriggling. She realized, in shock, that they were playing.

And in the center of them was Sig, rolling around on his back, displaying his golden belly. The bag of jerky beside him had been disemboweled and licked clean.

"Sig?" she whispered.

He heard her, rolling up, covered in snow. One ear turned back, and it seemed he was laughing, his tongue lolling from his mouth. He came to her, forced his head under her hand.

"Are you okay, buddy?"

His tail thumped on the snow. She ran her hands through his fur. No blood, no wincing. He seemed to be all right.

She looked over his ears at the wolves, still romping in the powder. The skinny grey wolf she'd seen before watched Petra with solemn eyes.

Petra reached into her pocket for a piece of jerky. She peeled it from its plastic backing, broke off a chunk, and threw it to the wolf. It landed about a foot away from her.

The wolf snatched up the piece from the snow.

Petra broke off another piece. By now, the other wolves were paying attention. They were all different sizes and colors—black, white, grey, and mottled. One of them had a radio collar on. Petra tossed another piece into the pack. She counted twelve wolves in all. The piece she offered was snatched away by the radio-collared wolf.

She felt a thrill of fear and fascination as the wolves closed in. Sig seemed unconcerned, leaning against her thigh as she knelt. She tossed chunks of jerky to the group. They growled and nipped at each other over the treats. Soon her pockets were empty.

She showed her empty hands to them. "No more."

The grey one sat down on her haunches. The others began to sniff the snow and lick the powder.

"You've made friends."

She realized that Gabe was behind her. He must have been watching, all this time. His pistol was in his hands and he looked as puzzled as she was. The wolves didn't seem bothered by his presence; they continued to look for tidbits in the snow.

Petra swallowed. "Look, I know that you guys are magic." She felt a little stupid, but she hadn't given any thought to how she was going to communicate to the wolves when they caught up with them.

The grey wolf watched her, seeming to listen.

"And I know that something awful is after you. We want to help."

The largest wolf, a white one, seemed to observe her as well. She had no idea if they could understand her. It was highly unlikely that even if they held any piece of human Skinwalker consciousness, they would understand English. But she tried, anyway, hoping some of her intent would shine through.

"We want to try to protect you. And capture Skinflint Jack—to get rid of him for good."

The white wolf looked deeply at her, so much so that she squirmed. It seemed he could see through her, past her to places she couldn't understand.

After a while, her ankles began to ache. She slowly stood up, trying not to make any sudden movements. The wolves didn't react, just watched.

"What now?" she asked Gabe.

He shrugged. "I know ravens. I don't know wolves."

Sig huffed. He stood up, stretched, and walked past them, back the way they'd come. He didn't look back.

After some hesitation, the white wolf followed him. Petra guessed that he was the alpha. And then the others followed.

Feeling as if something had transpired in the great canine pile-on that she didn't understand, she grasped Gabe's sleeve and followed the entourage.

Some understanding had been reached, beyond human ken. Maybe it was something among dogs. She wasn't sure. But the wolves followed Sig back to the snowmobile. Petra found Sig's bag of dog food and spread kibble all over the ground in a broad line. The wolves descended upon it like birds on birdseed. Sig, the smallest of the group, took his place at the end of the line. The other wolves didn't push him out.

"Do you think the snowmobile will freak them?" she asked.

"I think that everything should be freaking them out . . . but it's not."

Petra pushed it a few yards away from the wolves and started it up. She winced at the noise, and the wolves started. She put it in gear, idled about twenty feet away, let Gabe climb on, and whistled for Sig.

Sig broke away from the consumed dog food line and trotted after her. He glanced over his shoulder.

The grey wolf followed him. Then the white wolf, then the rest.

Panic and optimism mixed in her. She was at the lead of a Pied Piper line of wolves. Holy shit.

She grinned and set her sights for Sepulcher Mountain.

The going was slow. She kept the pace comfortable for Sig. Still, he and the wolves were easily distracted. A group of them split off after a hare, and she was forced to stop while they plunged after it and tore it apart. But they returned, fur on their tongues. Later in the afternoon they took a try at a herd of elk, but came up empty. They were luckier with some pronghorn crossing a field. They took down a small one and devoured it on the spot.

Petra didn't want to watch. She waited with Gabe about a quarter mile away. But she made herself observe through her binoculars, fascinated that they seemed to make room for the tiny Sig.

"I'm surprised they didn't eat him," Gabe said,

matter-of-factly. "Wolves are natural predators for coyotes."

"They seem to like him." Still, it made her uneasy. Her fingers kept twitching to her pistols at the sign of any aggression. She felt like the owner of a Chihuahua at a dog park full of Dobermans.

"Maybe it's because of what Maria said they were. The remains of Skinwalkers. They have more intelligence than ordinary wolves, and they might see him as under your protection."

"Maybe." But she still didn't trust, completely.

That evening, the wolves went AWOL. As the terrain grew rougher, Petra had to be careful not to hit rocks or buried bits of rubble. Steam emanated from the north, and the wolves peeled off toward it.

"Where are they going?" Gabe shouted.

"I think . . ." She scanned the horizon with her binoculars in the swiftly falling light. " . . . I think . . . they're going for a swim."

The ground had split open to reveal a geothermal feature, a hot spring about the size of a decent-sized swimming pool. Cyanobacteria colored it pale orange, the color of a citrine, steaming in the evening. Heedless of the science, the wolves plunged in, shattering the shimmering surface.

They were likely desperate for warmth, but Petra knew it could be a trap. The warmth in the water often attracted buffalo and other creatures in harsh winters, but the fumes could kill them, over a long period of time. She bit back her desire to call for Sig, who was dogpaddling in the steaming water.

It looked like pure joy below her, the wolves nipping and swimming like dogs. A simple, magical thing that made her heart swell and her face split into a smile.

She stopped the snowmobile at the edge of the pool, where the snow had melted on the stone. Her gaze tracked down to the water, and she yelped in glee.

"What is it?" Gabe wanted to know.

She got off the snowmobile and skidded down to peer at a yellowed crusty material on the rocks. "I think we have ourselves some mineral salts." She stripped off her glove, stuck her finger to the warm material and licked her finger.

"Well?" he asked, looking over her shoulder.

"Tastes like salt. With a bunch of other stuff in there, like sulfur." She made a face and grabbed a handful of snow to wash it down. "We should check to see if there's actually much NaCl in there."

"How do we do that?"

She scrambled back up to the snowmobile for her geology tools and hauled her pack down to the crystalline residue. With her chisel, she scraped away a good chunk of it. Under her hand lens, it looked like it might contain what they needed— some pieces that looked like they were cubic. To make sure, she struck an emergency flare. It wasn't as hot as a Bunsen burner, but maybe it would give her the data she needed.

Carefully, she placed the flare on a rock and dropped a piece of the salt on the red flame. To her delight, it flared orange with a streak of purple before it faded out.

"We have halite," she crowed.

"How do you know?"

"NaCl burns orange. There's a bit of potassium in there, which is what the violet is. As long as Jack isn't a mineral purist, I think we're good."

She began chiseling off chunks of the glittering salt. Gabe used the back of her hammer to scrape off more, and they heaped it in handfuls into her bag. When it was full, it weighed nearly twenty pounds.

"Think that's enough?" she turned back to ask Gabe.

"Yeah. I think it is." Gabe grinned, took off his hat and set it on the handlebars. He shrugged out of his coat and left it on the seat.

"Where are you going?" she called.

He kicked off his boots. "Seizing the moment." He smiled at her, seeming very human, and she dissolved in this moment of warmth.

She peeled off her clothes and followed, leaving the guns at the water's edge, within reach. The air was breathtakingly cold, but the water felt above a hundred degrees, luxuriously warm. She splashed it on her face, and it reminded her of swimming in the ocean. It tasted a bit of sulfur. She deliberately tried not to think of whatever bacterial critters were roaming in it. She figured that she had much bigger things to worry about, and she'd worry about things she couldn't see later.

A wolf paddled lazily by—the alpha. He swam as easily as an otter, his great paws churning ahead of his tail. Petra had somehow expected them to be cumbersome in the water, but they were so easy with it, as if it was their second element. She tried to imagine them in a river in summer, doing exactly as they were doing now—yipping, snorting, splashing, and sliding in the water.

Gabe floated out to the center of the pool. She hadn't seen him this relaxed in a long time. Taking a deep breath, she dove under. She couldn't see anything and relied on the muffled sounds above to guide her. She came up beneath him, toppling him over in the water. He turned over like a capsized boat, sputtering and flailing.

The wolves eventually had enough fun, and pulled themselves out of the water onto the rocks, licking at their paws. Petra and Gabe and Sig followed. She dried off with her extra set of clothes and dressed, wringing her hair out on the warm stones. It was drying stiff, in waves.

In this moment, she felt . . . alive. She grinned at

Gabe. He sat across from her, inspecting his rifle. He smiled back at her.

"Don't move." A voice came from above.

Petra spun, looking up the ridge. A man-shaped creature stood at the top, glowering down at them. She sucked in her breath and reached for her pistols under her coat.

She thought at first that it was Skinflint Jack. This could surely be him—a blackened figure stumbling toward them, caked with blood, holding out a gun in a quavering grip. But glancing at the compass within Gabe's reach, she saw that the Locus hadn't alerted them. And there were no antlers. What kind of monster was this?

The wolves crouched down, their paws flexing on the stone, growling, ruffs rising.

"Who's asking?" Gabe asked. He was sitting opposite her, obscured from the newcomer's view by Petra's body. His fingers tightened on the pistol on his knee.

The blackened figure stepped down the slope.

"Owen Rutherford. You're under arrest."

CHAPTER 17

The Gunslinger and the Stag

Owen advanced down the slope to the steaming pool. His gun shook in his numb grip, but he was determined to catch this man who could unlock all of Sal's mysteries.

"You're under arrest for the murder of Sal Rutherford."

Gabriel just looked at him. The light turned just so, and Owen could see under his hat.

He recognized Gabriel, and not just from the sketch his men had been sticking to every telephone pole, bulletin board, and shop door in town. He knew this from deeper memory, from the way back machine of his brain. It took him a moment to realize that this was the man he'd seen, armless, in the cornfield, as a child. He was certain of it.

Heart pounding, he reached to his belt for handcuffs. But eagerness made him clumsy and he stumbled. That was his undoing.

Gabriel drew a pistol in one smooth motion. What Owen thought were dogs lunged forward in the snow, at him in a grey blur. Realizing they were wolves, he fired, over and over.

"No!" The woman threw herself between him and one of the canines. She fell in the snow a split second before Owen did. White teeth tore into his coat and his gun arm, and he struggled to cover his face.

Something was standing on his chest. Gabriel. He aimed the gun at Owen's face. The wolves didn't let go, their teeth tearing into his sleeves and pants. He could feel the warm trickle of blood pooling in his boot.

"Tell me why I shouldn't feed you to the wolves."

This had gone all wrong. Owen struggled, his mind flailing. He blurted the first thing that came to mind: "Because I've seen what's under that tree."

Gabriel watched him with cold amber eyes for what seemed like an eternity. Then he picked up Owen's gun. He rolled Owen over and cuffed him with his own handcuffs. The wolves crowded around him, snarling.

Gabriel looked over his shoulder for the woman. Owen assumed she was Petra Dee. "You all right?"

"Yeah." The woman was sitting upright, her arm

around a coyote. It was like fucking Omaha's Wild Kingdom here. "Sig's okay. Bastard got my hood." Her fingers worked through a hole in her fur hood as she scanned the rocks. "And the wolves . . . I don't see blood."

"Lucky," Gabriel said, turning his attention back to Owen. He rifled through Owen's pockets and took his radio, knife, cell phone, ammunition, and a can of bear spray. "You were lucky. If you were a better shot, I'd have to kill you outright."

Petra Dee came close enough to squint at him. "What the hell are we going to do with him?"

"Depends on him."

Owen stared at Gabriel and used his best *I'm in command here* voice: "What you're gonna do is let me go."

"Not an option."

"I'll send help."

"We don't need your help."

"Actually, you do." Owen gestured back over his shoulder with his chin. "I pretty well destroyed your snowmobile."

"Shit." Gabriel stood and kicked him, right in the gut. Owen doubled over and a wolf stared at him. The wolf had terrible breath. Like dead rabbit and beef jerky.

Petra scrambled up the hill to look at the machine and returned, shaking her head. "He's ripped out every wire he could find. That would be fixable."

"Okay."

"The part that's not fixable is the broken spark plug and the shit he poured into the oil reservoir." She crossed her arms and stared down at Owen. "Let me guess—was it cough syrup?"

Owen cackled at his own creativity. "It was cherry vodka."

"You're sloppy. You spilled it, and there's a nice red puddle under the machine." She turned her attention to Gabriel. "He got here by snowmobile. We take his and continue, siphon the gas from our machine. He won't die here . . . it's warm enough to survive until someone finds him. Well, maybe if we leave him some water and food. And we cuff him to the dead snowmobile. But that leaves shelter . . ." Her brow knit. She was soft.

"It makes more sense to just kill him."

Owen shook his head. "The park rangers know I'm looking for you. If I turn up dead, you'll be in a whole lot more trouble than you are now." He was making threats, but he wasn't sure they were buying his argument. But the first rule in hostage negotiation—even if you are the hostage—was never to show weakness.

Gabriel snorted. "That's assuming you turn up at all. Yellowstone is a big place. I bet I can find a place to put you that no one would ever think to look."

Petra rolled her eyes. "As amusing as I find this

macho posturing to be, do you think we can figure out what to do with him and get on with things?"

Gabriel squatted before Owen. "I want to know what he knows."

Owen glared at him. "The feeling is mutual."

"I didn't kill Sal."

"You're the last man standing. We hauled more than a dozen bodies out from under that burnt oak on the ranch. Did you kill those guys?"

"No."

"Well, what did?"

Gabriel looked away. Petra put a hand on his shoulder. "There's no reason to talk to this guy. Let's get going. When we're done, we can call someone to pick him up. We'll figure it out."

Gabriel stood up, and one of the wolves reluctantly stopped chewing on Owen's boot. It was as if Owen simply ceased to exist, as if he was no longer part of their calculus. They gathered their belongings in their packs.

"You have to tell them." Anna sat on the rock beside Owen. "You have to tell them what you saw. You'll never catch up to them again."

"I will," he said.

"No," she countered. "You won't."

"I saw the tunnels beneath the tree," Owen blurted. Desperation leaked into his voice. "I saw stuff I couldn't explain."

Gabriel paused, his back turned.

Owen continued, plunging in: "I went down a tunnel. I found an underground river. It showed me things."

Gabriel turned partially. "What things?"

"There were bones all around. Bones of weird creatures, animals I'd never seen before. And when I looked in the water, I saw a crime scene. A crime I couldn't solve, with a little girl who haunts me. And then a creature with teeth came up and tried to get me, but I ran and—"

Petra had turned to Gabriel. "What the fuck is he talking about?"

"The Mermaid," he murmured. "He met the Mermaid."

Owen sat up and scooted forward on his butt. "You know! You know there's something down there, something that can see the past, something that's guarding pearls the size of bottle caps . . ."

Gabriel glanced at him. "You'll stay away from her, if you know what's good for you. She's tricky. You were lucky to survive her. Forget about that. Sell that land and go about your life." Gabriel sounded like his mother.

"I need to know," Owen said. "I'll inherit the place. I need to know what it all is. If you tell me . . . I'll let you go free."

"You seem to think that this is some sort of negotiation."

"Everything is a negotiation." Owen leaned forward. "I found something from the past. An old Pinkerton ID. With your name and prints."

Gabriel turned away, rubbing his forehead.

"Is that you, somehow?" he demanded. "I've seen ghosts and a mermaid . . . it ain't that far to believe in things that live a long time."

"Owen. You need to forget this," Gabriel said.

Owen laid his last card on the table. "I can make the investigation go away. Entirely."

Gabriel cocked his head. "Why would you do that? Sal was your cousin. Blood is thicker, after all."

"I need to know. I know this thing is huge. And it could be mine."

"That seems . . . about as honest as any other Rutherford."

Petra grabbed his sleeve. "Gabe. You can't."

"Will you continue the deal your predecessor had? Will you keep silent about what you learn?"

"I give you my word."

Gabriel squatted before him. "How do I know that you'll keep it, and not put a gun to my head the instant I cut you loose?"

"Because I'm a Rutherford."

Petra snorted.

"We aren't going back to civilization any time soon," Gabriel said. "Maybe it would be best for me to cut you loose, and you and I settle this, later. We'll sit down over a beer and spin some yarns. But later."

"No. I'm not letting you out of my sight. Not until I have all my answers."

Gabriel glanced at Petra. "He's stubborn. Like you."

Petra was having none of it. She crossed her arms over her chest. "You do what you've gotta do. But I want no part of your deal."

"Understood," Owen said. "What he and I strike is between us. It has nothing to do with you."

"She's no longer a person of interest?"

"I'll leave her alone. Drop the investigation. All I want is the answers I'm looking for."

Gabriel paused. "All right."

He rolled Owen over and uncuffed him. He stuck out his hand.

Owen grasped it with his own frozen, sooty hand. "Deal."

"WHY THE HELL did you do that?" Petra hissed at Gabe, gripping his sleeve. The wolves seemed content to babysit Owen. Three of them sat around him in a circle, staring at him intently, as if he still might become dinner. They wouldn't even let him reach into a pocket for cigarettes without growling and snapping. She'd dragged Gabe back, out of earshot, toward the snowmobiles.

"It's our only chance," he said. "This is the way it always is when power changes hands from one

Rutherford to another. There is bargaining. Grief. Acceptance."

"Do I not get any input in this?" She was starting to feel pretty darn peripheral to decisions that were going to impact the remainder of her existence, however long it was. "I mean, if nothing else, we *are* married."

"That man is not going to let us go. That, or we kill him. It's your choice." He said it without a trace of resentment. He was turning this man's life over to her.

She quailed, rubbing her forehead. "Damn it, Gabe. I don't want to be responsible for—"

"Choose."

He waited then, a silence that stretched out over the night that had fallen. Tatters of clouds had been pushed away in the wind, revealing a sinuous snake of stars overhead. Petra stared up. If Owen was aiming a gun at Gabriel, she'd have no hesitation in killing him. None. But now, unarmed, he was just as much a threat. He was just unarmed. What was her problem? Why couldn't she just say they should bury him in a ditch, where no one could find him?

Because she wasn't built that way. She knew it, and she couldn't help it. Gabe could do it; she knew he could. He'd done terrible things without batting an eyelash.

But she couldn't allow that to change her.

"Okay," she said. "We do this your way. For now. But if he steps out of line once, just once . . ." Her hand rested on her gun belt. ". . . I reserve the right to drop him over a cliff and make it look like one hell of an accident."

"Understood." A smile twitched across his lips.

"What's so funny?"

"Our first fight as a married couple." He kissed the corner of her mouth, leaving her fuming while he approached Owen. She sighed and joined them.

"So," Owen said. "What are you guys doing out here anyway?" The wolves had finally let him light a cigarette and he was trying to look relaxed. But Petra could see that his hands shook, his fingers black with what looked like soot. Was he in withdrawal? Injured? She wasn't sure she wanted to know.

"Someone is out here killing wolves, nearly killed a park ranger friend of ours. We aim to stop him." She lifted her chin.

"Why not let the rangers handle it? The thin green line is all over poachers. And if they hurt one of their own, they'll never stop until the culprit is behind bars." Owen shrugged.

"This is no ordinary poacher. We think it's the ghost of Skinflint Jack." Gabe laid it out without preamble or apology, like throwing poker chips down on a table.

"Oh." Owen blinked, and took a drag on his cigarette. "Far be it from me to pick and choose what ghosts around here are for real. Still, it sounds like some kind of mission."

"You believe in ghosts?" Petra asked, surprised at his nonchalance.

"I've got my own. Little girl from an unsolved case. Anna." Owen hooked a thumb over his shoulder. "She's sitting right over there."

Petra saw nothing. "Do you talk to her?"

"Yeah. She talks to me. She led me out of that maze in the field underneath the tree."

Oh, God. He was a nutter butter. Not that she had any room to judge, but looking at this man, jonesing hard for a cigarette and blackened and bloody . . . yeah. She could believe it. She just couldn't decide if that would make him more or less dangerous.

"So you went under the tree." Gabe's face was unreadable.

"Yeah. Found a shit ton of bodies. And Sal. Sal didn't die like the others. Sal was hanged."

"The men hanged him from the tree," Gabe said. "After he burned it."

Owen's eyes narrowed. "Why did he burn it?"

"He wanted to kill us for not following orders. All of us. The tree is—was—the Lunaria. The Alchemical Tree of Life. It kept us alive. Sal wanted to destroy it."

"Who killed the men?"

"In a manner of speaking, Sal did. He choked off the source of their life. Once he burned the tree, they knew they were finished. They went to ground and didn't rise again."

"So this is . . . a multiple retaliatory homicide?" Owen's filthy brow wrinkled, and it seemed as if he struggled to understand.

"In a manner of speaking."

"How come you survived?"

Gabe flinched. Owen had hit a nerve, all that bright and shiny survivor's guilt. "I was the oldest, the first man hanged from that tree a century and a half ago. Whatever trickle of magic was left kept me alive. That's the only thing that I can reckon."

Owen's eyes were large and dilated as a raccoon's as he absorbed all this dark information. "What is that river . . . underground? And that thing you called the Mermaid?"

Gabe shrugged. "The tunnels are funny. They lead you in strange ways, to strange places, usually where you need to go. The fact that they led you anywhere suggests to me that the land is at least open to accepting you as a master."

"There was a monster . . ."

"A leftover alchemical experiment. She was meant to be an oracle and, well . . . the process disintegrated. Lascaris sent her to the river."

"Lascaris? The town founder?"

"Yes. This goes deeper than you can imagine. But. We should get moving."

"Where are we going?" Owen leaned forward to wash his face in the water. Petra wrinkled her nose. He smelled like pine pitch and fire, like he'd been locked in a burning barn.

"Sepulcher Mountain. To capture Skinflint Jack."

Owen looked back at them. "I'm in. But you have to tell me everything."

"Later. As promised."

Owen had done a nice job of fucking up their machine. But there were still usable parts. She siphoned as much gas as she could off into empty water bottles. She pulled the headlight reflector, bulb, and battery out. Wrapping the connections with duct tape, she could make a pretty decent lantern that would run forever on that big a battery. With a screwdriver, she ripped the hood off the defunct machine, flipped it over, and set about stringing it up with rope to make a sled to haul their supplies. As she worked, the air was cold in her wet hair, and her teeth chattered.

Sig came to lay down in the snow beside her, looking up at her with a soft expression.

"Strange alliances, huh, Sig?" She jammed her finger on a sharp edge of metal and swore. "I feel like everybody knows what's going on but me."

Sig solemnly stood to lick her face.

"I trust you. And if you trust the wolves, I trust them, too."

Sig sat back, his gold ear flipping backward. In the chill, the interior was pale pink. Petra reached out and turned it back over. She didn't want him to get frostbite.

"That guy . . . I do not trust that guy."

Sig whined. She took that as agreement.

"We should watch him. You, me, and everyone with four feet." She shook her head. She suspected Gabe was too easily trusting of anyone with the last name Rutherford, since that was all he'd known, that intergenerational line of ass-hats. But this dude was crazy. And crazy did not make good deals.

"Off the record, if the wolves decide they're hungry enough to snack on him, I won't try very hard to stop them."

One of the wolves sidled up to watch her work. The grey one. She sat in the snow about two yards distant, watching.

"Hello," Petra said. She didn't make direct eye contact, not wanting to be perceived as a threat.

The wolf didn't run away. She thumped her fluffy tail in the snow and whimpered.

"We'll get moving soon, sweetie," Petra said. It was hard not to treat the wolf as an animal, when she suspected there was a centuries-old sentient creature in there, wearing a fluffy suit. "The plan is to lure Jack to Sepulcher Mountain in a day. If we can nail him there during the solstice, he'll be kicked out to the spirit world. And you guys can go on your merry way."

But the wolf continued to stare at her, as if there was a weighty question Petra wasn't answering. And she had no idea what it was.

NINE LIKED THE woman Coyote had brought with him. She seemed gentle, and she kept fishing pieces of dry food from her pockets to feed the pack. The woman clearly loved Coyote—Nine had seen how she had thrown herself over Coyote to protect him from the Burnt Man's gun. She was a good servant for Coyote; Nine could see that he had chosen well.

Nine didn't have a strong feeling, one way or the other, about the woman's mate. He seemed much older than he looked. He had the bearing of a chief, of some kind of deposed king. He smelled like a raven, which made no sense whatsoever to her, unless he was some kind of Skinwalker. He didn't do anything threatening, but Nine didn't like his proximity to the man who smelled like burning.

They finally got their little caravan together. Coyote's serving woman rode the Burnt Man's snowmobile with the jerry-rigged sled holding their supplies behind it. The two men walked on foot with the wolves and with Coyote. The Burnt Man walked ahead of Raven King, and the Raven

King kept a gun on him at all times. Still, Nine remained ready to take him out at the knee if he made a threatening move.

She could feel magic in the air, the magic of time and stars. The solstice was coming. She'd felt the nights dragging longer and longer, felt the sun's track growing shorter and shorter during the day, sweeping lower on the horizon. In some distant memory, she recalled that her people had celebrated this time of year, calling the sun back from his self-imposed exile in darkness. She didn't remember many of the details, other than the dancing. She had enjoyed the dancing by the fire, feeling the exhilaration of crisp, cold air. She was part of nature, a small fragment working through the wheel of the year in ancient cycles.

She had not felt that way for a very long time. She felt . . . somehow apart from this. When she encountered wolves from other packs, she was conscious that they were different. They were true descendants of Wolf. She knew, deep down, that she and the others only wore the cloak of Wolf. Many of them had likely forgotten, had become Wolf in spirit as well as body over the generations, like the pups. But Nine wasn't certain. She could still remember fragments of her old life, though she didn't know if it was truly her own life, or if it was some part of a collective memory diluted by generations of wild wolf blood.

She had felt magic like this, in the distant past, when her father was still alive. Her father had been a Magic Man, fearsome and funny. She forgot his name; it had been so long ago. But she remembered that she had loved him dearly as a little girl, the way he could talk to turtles and wasps. He could become any creature he liked, as long as he had its skin to wear. Once, she'd seen him become a dragonfly when he put a pair of iridescent wings on his eyebrows, just to amuse her. He walked the Witchery Way, but she never thought of him as evil. He just *was*.

He had given her a gift, once. It was a small bag of corpse dust, ground bones and bits of obsidian and crushed sage. She was fascinated by it, opening the bag and peering inside to watch the light glint on the obsidian fragments. She knew there was power in it; she just didn't know how much. She wore it in a bag strung around her neck, close to her heart.

She understood the power of it one day when one of her sisters snatched the bag from her neck, accusing her of being her father's favorite. Nine, in her childish venom, had wished her dead at the top of her lungs.

And her sister dropped dead, a victim of the Harming. She fell over in her tracks, spilling the Harming, which scattered away to the ground, where it should have gone in the first place.

Nine was devastated. She would not eat or tell anyone what happened. But her father knew. He sat her on his knee and told her that she was a very precocious girl, but that she should perhaps be a bit older to use such tools. There was an odd tone of pride in his voice that she couldn't understand.

If she just had a bit of that corpse dust now, just a pinch of the Harming . . .

She shook her head. There was no point in such thinking. There was no point in thinking at all. They were moving toward the mountain, and that knowledge swelled in her heart as correct. If they defeated the Stag, all this could be their new territory. It could mean the future of the pack. They could hunt this land and all within it. It could be theirs.

The sky cleared out overhead and the stars bristled through. The road of stars overhead mirrored the unseen road before them. As above, so below. The mountain reached from one plane to another, from earth to heaven. Even from this distance, Nine could tell that it hummed with power. She felt that hum in her throat, wanting to vibrate out as a howl. She kept silent, not wanting to give their position away to the Stag.

But the Stag found them anyway.

They'd made camp in the foothills at the base of the mountain. The Coyote's Seneschal—the woman—had started a fire in a hollowed-out tree stump, splashed with a bit of gasoline and a spark from the machine battery. The wind screamed across the valley, and they did their best to use that machine as a windbreak. The wolves huddled together in a pile. Coyote was welcomed into the pile, as was his servant and her mate, the Raven King. The Raven King did not stay long, preferring to keep watch.

The Burnt Man was not welcome in this den. Ghost snarled at him as he tried to approach. Instead, he huddled close to the fire in blankets, talking to himself. He was clearly quite mad. Nine had hoped that Coyote's Seneschal and the Raven King would give up on him and let the pack eat him. Nine was certain the rest of the pack was thinking about it. One was either in or out in wolf culture. Us or them. Even at Nine's status, at the bottom of the hierarchy, she was in. The humans didn't even want this man in their own hierarchy, but they feared him. He reminded her of a male wolf that had tried to tag along with the pack several years ago. He tried to join, but Ghost ran him off. Fortunately, that hadn't resulted in bloodshed. But this, she sensed, would be different.

Nine curled tightly against the Coyote Seneschal's leg, beneath a blanket. Coyote was already there, but he shared. She'd nearly drifted off to sleep, in a haze of warmth in the arms of her new protectors, when the Raven King whispered, "Something's coming."

He had kept watch, pacing above them on a snow-covered hillock. He held a gun, scanning the dark horizon.

The woman climbed out of the tangle of grey and black limbs. "What is it?"

"I think it's our target."

Then the wind shifted. Nine could smell him. The Stag. She scrambled upright, whimpering. The others churned awake, stirring tails and ears and the edges of blankets. The Seneschal grabbed her guns, and the Burnt Man clawed to his feet.

"What is it?" he demanded. "What's coming?"

"Shut up, Owen," the Seneschal said.

A shadow crossed the ice field, blacker than the sky surrounding it, stark against the snow. It came at terrible speed, fast and silent as an owl, moving downwind.

"Skinflint Jack. Jack of Harts." The Raven King shouted across the expanse, his rifle lifted to his shoulder. "Stop where you are."

The shadow hesitated for a moment, perhaps startled at being named. Nine knew that names had power; in a distant memory, she recalled a great shaman being turned to dust at the mention of his true secret name. But the Stag was not summoned to dust; he swept toward them, cloak flaring behind. A whine escaped Nine's bared teeth.

The Raven King fired. Nine flinched at the muzzle flash and the report's echo across the field.

The bullet struck the Stag's antlers, shattering the right stem with a loud crack. He turned his head and howled at them, an unearthly howl like the roar of wind through a crevasse in January.

And he advanced, as unstoppable as that wind.

"Damn it," the Raven King swore. He reached for the powder horn at his side.

"That hurt him, at least," the Seneschal said.

The wolves were on their feet, surrounding the Raven King on the hillock, keening. The Seneschal had lifted her guns, eyes wide with fear. Even Coyote, tangled in the Seneschal's legs, laid his ears back. The Burnt Man stood behind them, frozen in terror.

Ghost bayed, a short, sharp bark of retreat. The wolves turned then, moving toward a frozen river that meandered to the north. Nine followed them, but paused to look back to make sure the humans and Coyote were coming. Ghost nipped her in the flank. His responsibility was the pack, not the humans.

"Follow them," the Raven King shouted to the Seneschal. "Across the river."

"Not without you."

"I'm right behind you."

They began to retreat, to move downhill, behind the wolves, toward the river.

But the Burnt Man remained rooted in place.

"Owen, come on."

He turned slowly, to follow the others. But not fast enough to catch up with them. The Stag swept up like the west wind and engulfed him.

OWEN SAW THE darkness coming, and was transfixed.

He had never seen anything like it, this shadow that skimmed over the snow, wearing the skull and antlers of a stag. It was a man, but it wasn't. Instinctively, he knew it was some elemental force of nature, some bit of wind and darkness granted form.

"Owen. You have to run." Anna tugged at his sleeve.

He couldn't speak. He couldn't run. He was fascinated by this tatter of black flag and fur, moving toward him. It seemed that the temperature dropped several degrees, and he could feel the frost on his face crackling as it came.

"Run!" Anna shrieked at him.

He had no desire to run, no wish to fight. It swept into him, over him, a wall of darkness that muffled Anna's shrieks and the howls of wolves.

All he heard was the drone of the wind. It hissed in his ears and through his body, like steam. And he was falling. With the sensation of falling from an impossibly tall height, his stomach pitched into his throat and he screamed.

Annihilation surrounded him like a thick cloak.

This was deeper than any drunk, blackout haze he'd craved when he wanted to shut out the world. He was dead. He knew it. He felt the darkness hollowing him out, like an awl. He could feel his cells disassociating, the cold oblivion sinking through him. His breath clotted and his neurons stopped firing.

He landed against the ground with a white crack, and that was the last thing he remembered.

CHAPTER 18

That Old Black Magic I Forgot
Once Upon a Time

Nine struggled to keep up with the pack as they crossed the river. It wasn't much of a river, less than twelve feet wide, but the surface was slippery under the skin of snow. She turned back to see the Stag dropping the Burnt Man to the ground like an empty shell and gliding to the bank of the river. From this distance, Nine couldn't tell if he was alive or not.

"What's the plan?" the Seneschal yelled. She'd picked up Coyote and was sliding across the ice with him under her arm.

"Reloading," the Raven King muttered, fishing bits of metal and cloth from his pocket. The powder horn was balanced in the crook of his arm.

The Stag put a cloven hoof on the ice, with a sound like thunder.

A cracking sounded from deep underneath the surface of the ice. The Seneschal put the coyote down and gave him a shove. "This is hot spring water. It's not completely frozen."

The Raven King backed away as the Stag stomped out onto the ice. His cloven hooves made deep indentations that quickly filled with water. He had to be heavier than even the humans.

Ghost had lagged behind with the Raven King. He barked and snarled at the Stag, trying to distract the monster from a pup who was dancing on crackling ice. The pup howled and yipped for its mother like a newborn. The ice split beneath it and its back half fell into the water.

Nine turned back, plunged into the water after the pup. She grabbed his ruff in her jaws. With all her strength, she backed up and drew the pup's paws onto the firmer ice. The pup scrambled, slipping. Nine put her head under his rump and shoved as hard as she could, sending him scooting across the ice toward the rest of the pack . . .

. . . but the ice broke beneath her. It splintered up against her belly like a blow, and she fell, fell into cold darkness.

"No!"

Shock enveloped Nine. Her only thought was for the pack, the need to save the pup. The pup was so much more valuable than she was; he had to survive. He couldn't die, like Sage had. She wouldn't let him.

But she knew, on a deep level, that this was the end for her. She had lagged behind for too far and too long. She was too thin and too weak to keep up, and the water would claim her. She felt her body slipping away like a milkweed pod, and she was suspended for a moment in that limbo of cold water. She knew instinctively that she was between worlds, suspended between life and death. She had no more energy to fight, and she surrendered to the water. She was without bones and form, and thought herself more ghost than corporeal, in that moment. Something slipped from her, and it felt like a skin, sloughing away.

Something grasped the back of her neck with a clumsy grip and pulled. Her head broke the surface of the water, and she gasped. It was the Seneschal. She'd wrapped her elbow around Nine's neck, was clumsily flopping on the ice as she tried to draw Nine up over the shifting lip of ice. She jammed her boot into a jagged crack in the ice and got enough leverage to haul Nine over into her lap, legs flailing.

Nine lay against the ice, gasping. She had no strength.

The Seneschal stared at her. "Oh, shit."

Nine whined. She made to get up, but her feet slid beneath her. And then she realized that her feet were no longer feet. They were hands, like the Seneschal's.

The Seneschal grabbed her hands and pulled. She pulled until they reached the opposite bank, and Coyote and the wolves grasped the Seneschal's pant leg and coat in their jaws. Nine rolled into the snow beside the pup she'd rescued, feeling cold noses pressing against her gooseflesh.

Through slitted eyes, Nine looked back at the river.

Ghost and the Raven King were battling the Stag. The Raven King was swinging his gun at the Stag like a club. The Seneschal clawed herself upright and shot the ice at the foot of the Stag, fracturing the fragile surface. The Stag plunged into the river, antlers churning. The man and Ghost tried to flee to the bank. Beneath the ice, Nine could see a dark shadow swirling and the pale silhouette of an antler as it tracked them. She howled an alarm.

The Stag burst forth in a hail of ice, up from the depths. The wolves yipped and cowered around her. Nine lowered her head, shivering, baring her teeth.

"Hey!" the Raven King said, pulling something from his pocket. It was metallic and shiny, in the shape of a star. Nine had never seen anything like it. It shone as bright as the moon.

The Stag paused, one cloven hoof on an ice floe, tipping its antlered head. Its expression was inscrutable. It could be confusion. It could be wrath.

"You know this. The Star of Antimony." The Raven King turned it in his fingers so it captured the light in its metallic facets.

The Stag made a piteous noise and reached for it. It must be a great treasure for him.

The Raven King tossed it in the river.

The Stag howled and plunged in after it. His shadow slid under the ice, churning downstream like a salmon in pursuit of a mate.

The Raven King turned back. "That might keep him busy, but . . ." He made eye contact with Nine.

"Where did she come from?"

The Seneschal was wrapping her coat around Nine. "One of the wolves fell in and . . . she came back up." Her voice sounded helpless.

The Raven King crouched before her. "Can you stand?"

Nine nodded. She thought so.

"Good. We have to move. Now."

"What about Owen?" the Seneschal asked, looking across the river.

The Raven King pressed the heel of his hand to his head. "Goddamn it." He stood to go back for the Burnt Man. Coyote grasped his pant leg in his teeth, snarling.

"He might already be dead," Petra said.

"No. Look."

The Burnt Man stood at the far bank. His expression was blank and dazed.

"Owen! Get over here. This train's leaving town *now*."

The Burnt Man stared down at the ice. He went upstream several yards and minced his way across. When he reached the bank, the Seneschal grabbed his collar. "C'mon, man . . ."

But she stopped speaking to him. His eyes were blank, the pupils dilated completely black. She let go of him and backed away.

Nine wrapped her arms around herself and cried into the collar of her borrowed coat. She felt both naked and hobbled, unable to smell or hear or use her senses.

Something terrible had been lost, and she was just beginning to understand.

"WHAT HAPPENED TO you?"

Petra paused in buttoning her extra shirt up to the woman's neck. The woman she'd fished out of the water when the wolf went in seemed to be in shock. She appeared to be in her mid-twenties, with bronze skin and incongruently silvery hair sweeping past her shoulders. Her dark eyes passed vacantly over Petra. She'd said nothing since they fled from the river, speechlessly watching the sun rise and the wolves mill about her.

Petra had put her on the back of the snowmobile. Gabe had run upriver to retrieve it from the campsite, though it had gotten water in the engine from the crossing. She'd flinched against the sound of the machine, but had held on tightly until they'd made it to a safe distance, her fingers digging into Petra's ribs. The engine had begun to miss, and Petra wasn't sure that she trusted it much further.

Petra dug her hip-waders out of her pack and knelt to put them over the woman's feet. She offered no resistance; she was like dressing a rag doll. "These are the only other boots I have, but maybe they'll work . . ."

"I can't remember the last time I wore clothes."

Petra looked up, startled. The other woman's voice was thin, low, like rain trickling on tin.

"What's your name?"

The wolf-woman's brow wrinkled. "Nine."

"Nine," she echoed.

"The ninth wolf." Nine's gaze drifted over to the pack, huddled in a knot yards away. They took turns keening over the wet pup and grooming it.

"I'm Petra. That's Gabe, and that's . . . Owen." Petra glanced over at the two men. Owen was sitting on the ground with his head in his hands, talking to himself. Gabe dug through the packs on the snowmobile, giving Owen some serious side-eye. Petra stifled a shudder and turned her attention back to Nine.

"What happened at the river?"

"I don't know." Nine looked down at her hands.

"Can you . . . change from wolf to person?"

"Not for a long time. I forgot . . . I forgot how to do it. And then it just happened." Fear lit in her eyes as she gazed at the wolves. "I'm afraid . . . I don't know how to change back."

Petra put her hand on her shoulder. "You're gonna be okay. We'll figure something out."

Petra wasn't sure how, but she had to.

She left the young woman with Sig, who nestled between her feet and trudged across to the snow-mobile to speak with Gabe.

"She's talking," Petra told him. "And she knows English, which is amazing."

"Yeah, well. Owen's talking, too." He inclined his head. "To his ghost, I'm assuming."

Petra listened as she popped the hood to the snowmobile.

". . . Blackness. It was all blackness. I can't . . ." Owen rubbed his face. "The nothingness. It was all around me, inside me. Is that what it's like, being dead? It can't be. I mean . . . you're here, right? This can't be all there is."

Petra peered at the engine, fingering the frayed timing belt and looking at the water sloshing about in the housing. It didn't look good. But she was de-termined to run it as far as she could before it died.

"Owen's ghost . . ." she murmured to Gabe. "Are there such things? Human ghosts?" She wasn't sure what was real anymore and what wasn't, but she was pretty certain her grip on reality was stronger than Owen's.

"There are," Gabe confirmed. "But he doesn't have one."

"How do you know?"

He pulled the Locus out of his pocket and stripped off his glove. He plucked at a scab on his palm and dripped blood into the device. The blood boiled in it, splitting off into tiny droplets, crowding to the left, where the wolves and Nine sat.

"Ghosts are their own kind of magic. It's a weak magic, most of the time, but a magic, nonetheless. But the Locus doesn't register anything around him."

The truth of it crawled up her spine. Given all the strange things she'd seen, the existence of a ghost seemed like a minor element. If there were alchemists and mermaids and undead ranch hands, surely ghosts were par for the course in Temperance. She didn't question the assumption, and that rankled her. It was as if she was losing her grip on reality. But not as badly as Owen.

"Owen is insane." Completely and utterly batshit.

"Sure looks that way."

OWEN HAD TASTED hell, and it tasted like a bottomless void.

He sat in the snow, rocking back and forth. He had always felt darkness, evil as a force outside of him. It was external. Something to be fought against. But now, he felt it *inside* his body. The antlered beast had passed through him, like a wind through a curtain, and part of that numb darkness remained behind.

"How do I get rid of it?" he demanded of Anna.

"I don't know," she said.

"How can you not know?"

"I've never seen anything that dark before. Not even at the bottom of the well."

He groaned. He feared it, like he'd feared nothing else. Owen had never been particularly afraid of death before. He just assumed that it was One of Those Things that happened, but he'd been pretty firm in his belief in an afterlife of some sort. He'd heard a lot of talk about heaven and hell in church as a child. As sheriff, he wanted to believe there was something more terrible waiting for wrongdoers than simply blanking out of existence, because that was too fucking easy and so monumentally unfair that it offended his sensibilities. Meeting Anna had confirmed it—there was something else out there. Life after death.

But this creature—as it swept through him, he'd felt a nothingness that was unlike anything he'd ever imagined. It was cold and endless, and evil unlike anything he'd ever known. It had shocked him, like no crime scene ever had.

If he had been a better man, Owen suspected that the evil would have found nothing to cling to. But the darkness had snagged on the rough edges of his character, tearing away pieces that curled and festered under his skin.

This evil—it was a part of him now. He was certain of it.

SHE WAS NO longer a part of them. Not like she remembered.

Nine followed in the pack's footsteps as they climbed through the foothills of Sepulcher Mountain in the bitterly cold afternoon sunshine. That part was the same as it always had been, being the last. They wove around her knees and surged past her, but they did not chirp and yip at her, as they always did among themselves. It was as if a veil had been drawn between them. She poked at the barrier, letting her fingers brush ears and ruffs, but they shied away. They knew her, but they did not. She assumed that she smelled different, and it wasn't just Petra's coat.

She paused in her ascent and closed her eyes, willing her limbs to shorten and fur to cover her naked-feeling human flesh that wanted to freeze at the barest touch of wind. But it didn't happen, no matter how hard she clenched her fists and willed it to.

She wondered if, tonight, she would dream she was a wolf.

The Raven King—Gabriel, she reminded herself— seemed to know where they were going. He carried a golden compass that smelled of magic. It smelled of metallic, man-made magic, not the wild, natural scent of the pack. She gave it a wide berth. It felt familiar to her, a memory that tickled at the edge of her consciousness.

She avoided it and the machine that Petra drove. It had developed a sound that Nine could best describe as a mechanical hiccup. Over the roughening terrain, the gear on the sled she'd made of the parts of the old machine bounced and banged.

Finally, a deafening crack sounded from the engine and it fell quiet. Nine rubbed her ears at the sudden silence, and all heads turned to it. The Seneschal swore colorfully and popped the hood. Black smoke leaked from the engine.

"It's dead," she announced, waving at the smoke with a glove. "I think the drive shaft's busted."

"We don't have much farther to go," Gabe said, pointing. "This is the mountain."

The mountain took up half the twilight sky, like a sleeping giant. It had its own special gravity, Nine had to admit. It was as if it had black roots deep in the earth and reached up to the sky with slumbering white fingers. She threw back her head to take it in.

"Why does the mountain matter?" Owen asked. This was the longest sentence Nine had heard him utter since his encounter with the Stag.

"My father is an alchemist," Petra said. "He thinks that this is a place where we can bind Skinflint Jack."

"It's magic," Nine blurted. "Can't you feel it?"

Gabe nodded. "It was named by an Army man in 1871 because it looked like a crypt. But he got the notion from Lascaris more than twenty years before. This was one of the places that Lascaris buried his faulty experiments."

"Who is Lascaris?" Nine asked.

"An older alchemist," Petra said. "We think he gave Skinflint Jack his power. He roamed around here a century and a half ago, looking for the secret to eternal life." She knelt to clean snow from Coyote's paws.

Nine closed her eyes, feeling the chill of the mountain's shadow on her naked eyelids. "I remember. A man long ago. He was sitting in a field, surrounded by the antlers of deer on the ground, pieces of what must have been a glorious hunt. He smelled like that—" She pointed to the golden compass.

"We watched him," she continued. "At first, we were curious to see if there was any meat left for us. But it was just him, in that circle of bone. And then . . . the ground shifted. It split open, and white deer grew beneath those antlers, clawing out of the ground. I remember their dark eyes and my mouth watering at the sight of them. Such beautiful flesh.

"But something went wrong. The deer tried to come up from the ground, but they couldn't. They sank, struggling, back beneath the dirt, leaving only the antlers behind." Nine shrugged. "It didn't smell right. We left."

Gabe nodded. "That sounds like him. The fleeing hart symbolizes fleeting evanescence, the union of the spirit and the body in the chemical wedding. The deer is the soul. The alchemist tries to capture it and fix it into physical form . . . which is what I suspect he did with Skinflint Jack, after a fashion."

"Are we climbing that?" Owen was looking up at the mountain. Nine watched him with narrowed eyes. Maybe it was a good thing he was coming back to himself. Maybe not.

"Yeah." Petra scanned it with her binoculars. "We're looking for a point at which the sun will rise and illuminate Jack in the solstice. The exact time of the solstice is in a few hours."

"There." Nine pointed to a crag at the edge of the peak that stood upright. Her gut pulled her toward it. She'd never seen this one before, but it reminded her of dozens of other earth-clocks her people had set up over time, before they'd become wolves.

"The Sepulcher itself," Gabe said. "Looks as good a place as any to set up. Let's divide the gear and get moving."

Nine looked behind them, at the darkening snow. The Coyote came to her and leaned on her leg. She reached down to touch his brow.

The Stag was out there, somewhere. She could feel it. He was coming, and he would not grant any of them an easy death.

CHAPTER 19

On the Witchery Way to Sepulcher Mountain

It would not have been an easy climb up Sepulcher Mountain, even in the best of weather.

They were forced to leave much of their gear behind with the machine, but Petra was determined to haul all she could. She'd filled her pack with as many supplies as she could carry, and brought a pickaxe to use as climbing leverage.

Approaching from the south, the trail ascended in a series of switchbacks. But ice had worked itself around snow and rock, making footing treacherous. She slid more times than anyone saw. Petra urged Gabe to watch Owen closely. Owen seemed to be charging on ahead with a restless energy. She didn't like it, and the wolves didn't like it, either.

They surged around him in a circle, some growling deep in their throats. She had seen his soot-blackened feet and fingers. Perhaps he was beyond feeling pain beneath his injuries. But madness was excellent fuel.

Petra walked at the back, keeping pace with short-legged Sig and Nine. Nine was determined, and had good stamina, but the young woman seemed not to remember how to walk well. Petra stayed at her elbow, with Sig bringing up the rear.

"Your father was a Magic Man?" she asked Petra.

"Yes. He was lost to me for a long time. I just found him a few months ago."

"My father was one, too. A shaman."

"I assumed that all of you were . . . shamans?" Petra felt an instinctive empathy for Nine, but she tempered it. She knew nothing of Nine or her magic.

"No." Nine laughed. "Only my father. He was very, very old. And had many, many children. He was quite wise—it was said he could speak any language of any tribe by listening through an elk's horn. He had a cloak made of feathers and could turn into an owl. He could wear the skin of a bear and become a bear. Once, for fun, he wore a crown of turkey feathers and became a turkey."

"It sounds like he had a sense of humor."

"At some times. But not at others. He was exiled from his tribe for killing one of his wives who was with another man's child. He ground her bones up into the Harming . . . it's a powerful magic, a corpse poison. The chief cast him out.

"Some of his wives and children left with him. He was a skilled follower of the Witchery Way. Winter had fallen upon us, and he taught us how to wear the skins of wolves, to survive. He told us that someday we would find our land to the north, if we kept following the stars." She shook her head, as if chasing memories from it. "I was small. I don't remember all of it. Just that wolf fur was warmer than human skin."

Petra glanced at the wolf pack ahead of them. "Is he still with you?" she asked quietly. She had a hard time trusting sorcerers she wasn't related to.

"No. He died many, many years ago. A man shot him. He changed back then. I remember seeing him lying on the ground, an old man bleeding red on the snow. The hunter, he panicked. I think he dragged him away to bury him without telling anyone."

"I'm sorry." Petra realized she seemed to be saying that a lot lately. She'd arrived at the conclusion that, no matter how charmed she thought the lives of witches and wizards were from her childhood stories . . . everyone had problems. Dead, undead, human, wolf . . . didn't matter. Everyone was fucked in their own special way.

"He taught us many things," Nine went on. "How to hunt. How to find shelter. How to listen to the voices of men. Good things. And also many terrible things. How to kill, up close and from a far distance with the Harming. But he didn't teach us how to change back," she added, blinking back tears. They spilled from the corner of one eye, and she rubbed them away with the palm of her hand.

Petra wrapped her arm around the other woman. She wanted to tell her that it would be okay. But she wasn't certain if it would be. It sure wasn't looking good. They had limited supplies, little time, and it was getting colder the higher they climbed.

One thing that they needed little of was light. The snow was bright, and the moon had risen, full and bright as a lantern overhead. The moon's gleam shimmered off the blanket of snow in a soft aura. Petra hadn't bothered using her flashlight since it rose. Sepulcher Mountain would have felt surreal on an ordinary summer night, but in winter, it stood completely apart from the surrounding land in an otherworldly glow.

They approached the summit as the moon crept high in the sky. Up close, she could make out a magnificent hoodoo at the peak. She'd seen hoodoos before—spindles of sedimentary rock that had been worn away in unusual spires. This one was massive, like a hand pointing upward, with fingers pressed together.

"This is the spot?" Owen panted, bracing his hands on his knees.

"I'd say so."

Nine had gone to the hoodoo and pressed her hands to the stone. "It's beautiful," she murmured, and it seemed she was listening to something deep in the rock. The wolves milled around her, pacing, seeming alert and full of energy.

"Let's get the trap set up." Gabe was already digging in the packs, and came up with the trap Petra had found at the pawnshop. He chucked it on the ground next to the hoodoo, where it landed with a clang and a rattle.

The wolves snarled and backed away. Nine turned toward Gabe with her hands outstretched behind her, to protect the pack. "What are you doing with that?" she demanded.

"It belonged to Skinflint Jack when he was alive," Petra rushed to explain.

"It might be able to hold his current form," Gabe said. He moved the trap a couple of yards away, with the chain snaking around it. He returned to rummaging through the packs. The wolves circled it, growling.

"It's okay," Petra said, trying to sound soothing to Nine. "Really."

Nine's face was an impassive mask. "It reeks of old blood."

Gabe had crossed to the hoodoo and was writing symbols on the dark stone with a stick of chalk. Petra recognized some of them as alchemical sym-

bols for air, earth, fire, water, mercury, and the sun.
But the others were foreign to her.

Petra opened her pack, glittering with damp
and dirty salt packed around her tools. She
planted a stick at the center of the trap and tied
a rope around the stick. Measuring off nine feet,
she figured that would be big enough to hold Jack.
She walked in a circle around the trap, sprinkling
salt as she went. The salt came out in chunks, but
crumbled easily within a fist. It began to melt the
snow with an audible crackling, leaving behind
lacy patterns that collapsed as the salt sought bare
ground. She hoped to hell that the old woman who
salted the pond was right, that if Jack touched the
salt, he wouldn't be able to get out. Or, at least, that
he'd be weakened.

She nosed around outside the circle and found
four fist-sized rocks, speckled granite. She figured
she should make this as much like the pond as she
could. Glancing at the compass on her watch, she
placed one at each of the cardinal directions: north,
south, east, and west. They seemed pathetically
small compared to the big chunks of granite at the
pond. But something in her gut told her the rocks
were significant, somehow.

Gabe was deep in concentration over his
sketched-out marks. "Owen can make himself
useful and build a fire. The light will show Jack
where we are."

"Okay. What next?"

"We set the trap. With bait."

The wolves quailed, crowding around the far side of the hoodoo, away from the circle.

Gabe pulled a deer skull from the sack. Petra recognized it as the skull that had been installed in the wall of Jack's basement. Bits of mud and mortar were still crusted in the jaw and eye socket, as if it had been torn from the mud of a wasp's nest. One of the antlers was broken off entirely.

Gabe opened the trap and set it, the rusty metal groaning. The end of the connected chain coiled around it, like a sinister tail. He placed the skull at the center of the trap, along with the remainder of the gold coins.

"All that's left is to summon Jack," he said. "And the easiest way to do that is to piss him off."

Gabe tossed the last Star of Antimony down on the rocky ground with an almost careless gesture. He stomped down on it with the heel of his boot. The fragile mineral cracked.

Somewhere in the far off distance below, something screamed, the bellow of a stag.

And the wolves answered. They howled back, all of them, even Nine, their voices rising in the darkness. It was a challenge, a mocking of that ethereal string to Jack's heart that Gabe had just shattered.

Jack had been summoned. He was coming.

THE NIGHT WAS curiously still. At this height, Gabe would have expected the wind to tear through his coat and hat and obliterate their unshielded fire. But the cold simply radiated up from the earth, from the mountain, as a relentless weight in the air.

Magic was afoot.

He watched from the south, from the direction they'd come. The bright moon illuminated everything below: the halo around it in the cloudless sky, the wreck of the snowmobile at the foot of the mountain, the stillness of the snowfield beyond. He could see the far horizon into Montana. Time stood still here, and the earth knew it. The only sound was the snap and crackle of the fire, the crunchy pacing of the wolves behind him, and the ticking of blood in the compass.

Blood churned in the compass, too quickly to freeze, like a second hand around a watch. Tiny drops swished as the wolves milled behind him. A heavy glob lay in the bottom of the rim, all around, like the stain of a coffee cup on a wood table. Gabe figured that was the mountain itself. Lascaris had liked to embroider his stories, and once told him that he'd put the hoodoo here as a grave marker for a creature he'd summoned and had to put down. That was par for the course for Lascaris's experiments, but Gabe was never able to pry more out of him about this place. He only knew that the mountain had a reputation as a place horses would avoid, if given any choice. That was good enough corroboration for Gabe.

He swept the binoculars across the ground below. This high, it reminded him of when he was a raven, when he could fly. He was struck by a pang of longing for the feel of air beneath his light body, the freedom of it.

Something moved below, and Gabe stilled. A black figure flitted across the snowfield, inexorably toward the mountain. It paused at the snowmobile at the bottom, then looked up. One antler caught the glimmering moonlight.

"He's here," Gabe said quietly, and heard the hiss of indrawn breaths behind him.

The shadow began to ascend. It didn't follow the trail that Gabe and his party had laboriously climbed. Skinflint Jack scaled straight up, flowing over obstacles in his path like water. The skull turned up, gazing at Gabe from dark eye sockets and the glint of silver eyes. Gabe could feel the hatred smoldering there. He had desecrated Jack's home and the remains of his family. Jack would do anything to kill him. Gabe hoped that his rage would render him blind and sloppy; that was their only chance.

Gabe retreated with the rest, holding his loaded rifle. The wolves had their backs to the hoodoo, huddled around Nine's legs. Owen remained at a distance from the pack, muttering to himself. Gabe hadn't seen fit to give him a gun. Petra remained before them with Sig, at the edge of the circle, guns drawn, and Gabe went to stand beside her. His heart pounded in his chest.

Gravel rattled below them, from the ledge. A clawed hand reached over the precipice, and Skinflint Jack hauled himself up. The wolves growled behind him, a chorus of vibration.

Jack pulled himself up to his full height, bellowing. His head inclined toward the circle, and he hissed. Knives made of bone glinted in his hand.

He knew.

He was smarter than Gabe had given him credit for. Or maybe Jack sensed the magic gathered here. But the darkness in his eyes fixed on the shattered remains of the Star of Antimony within the circle, and he couldn't help himself. He'd spent too much time in the body of a beast. He lunged over the salt line at the perimeter of the circle and plucked the gold from the trap, quick as a raven plucking a shiny gum wrapper from the street. He landed on one knee and coiled up to leap over the salt line, to escape the trap with the bait.

Gabe aimed and fired. Jack bellowed, and Gabe knew he'd hit him. Jack crumpled. Gabe dropped the gun and plunged forward, his shoulder striking Jack, attempting to keep him within the circle. Wolves snarled around Jack, harrying him, ripping at the hem of his ephemeral cloak. The skull at the center of the trap fractured, crunching into the snow.

Darkness fell over Gabe's vision like a curtain. Sound disappeared. Cold and all sensation vanished. He could see, now, how Owen had found this terrifying. But Gabe had spent more than a century underground. Darkness was nothing to him.

He hit the ground, hard, away from Jack. Jack reeled back, snarling, clutching his shoulder. His cloak swept the salt at the edge. Jack fell into the open jaws of the trap and bellowed, thrashing as the rusty teeth pierced the darkness of his body. Gabe crawled to the edge of the circle, beyond the edge of its containment, and climbed to his feet.

He turned around to look at Jack.

Hatred smoldered in Jack's glittering eye sockets. The trap had caught him around the knees, but he reached for the chain. He swung the chain over his head, cast it out . . .

. . . and it struck Gabe in the throat in a bright slash of pain. He stumbled and fell backward, tumbling off the mountain in a skiff of white snow and darkness. Panic sang through him as he flailed.

He heard Petra screaming behind him.

For this moment, he flew. He soared in the cold darkness, and he smiled to feel the rush of it in his face, the freedom of it . . .

Until he hit a ledge and darkness slammed over him.

"G<small>ABE</small>!"

She saw him stumble back, lose his footing. She reached for him as he tumbled back into space, a dark shape against the white snow below.

Her heart shattered when he fell, when he plummeted away from her and soared into the white. He struck an outcropping below with a sickeningly soft crunch.

"Gabe!"

He didn't move. Oh, my God, he wasn't moving. Jack had killed him.

She wheeled around to Jack. "You fucking bastard." Gabe's gun was useless to her now—Gabe had gone over with the powder horn. But she didn't care. She scooped up a fistful of broken antimony in the snow. One jagged piece was the size of a penknife blade. Small, but sharp. Rage soaked her skin, and she advanced on him.

The Stag glowered at her from the circle, head lowered, puffing like a bull ready to gore her.

"Asshole. Over here." It was Owen, behind him. He'd picked up the chain connected to the trap. There was a good seven feet of it, long enough to make a weapon. He lashed it around Jack's head, where it got hung up in his antlers. Jack snarled and pawed in the trap, and Owen approached with the remainder of the chain. Petra guessed that he meant to try to strangle him with it.

She lunged forward, the antimony knife in her hand. The blade plunged into the creature's shoulder and he howled. She pressed her knee into his side. Jack's head twisted around, and he tried to bite her throat. His stinking breath steamed over her face, and a tooth scraped her chin.

In a flash, she realized that it was her pendant he was after. The one her father had given her: the green lion devouring the sun. Gold.

"No. No, you can't." The fragile piece of antimony fractured in her grip. The creature twisted around and kicked her. Petra went skidding, landing with her spine cracking against the hoodoo. She struggled to turn over and draw breath, tears leaking from her eyes.

Owen was wrestling with the weakening monster. He'd gotten the chain around its throat, and the Stag thrashed and kicked, trying to free himself of the trap. Owen's blackened knuckles oozed red on the chain.

A gold ring gleamed on Owen's right hand, snagging the Stag's attention. Fast as a striking snake, Jack ripped into Owen's hand, biting it off as if it was a piece of jerky. Owen screamed and fell back beyond the circle, dripping red.

Nine slipped into the circle then, on all fours.

Her hand snatched up the broken jaw of the skull and scraped up the fractured bits of bone that had become dust in the trap. She swept them into her hand, advanced on Jack, and blew the bone dust into his face.

"Be dust," she commanded in an ancient and hollow voice.

Jack howled, clawing at his eyes.

Nine lunged out of the circle, landing beside Petra, who struggled to her feet, fingers scrabbling in the snow for any remaining pieces of antimony. With savagery, she thought she'd dig Jack's eyes out with the slivers, if she had to.

A hand landed on her shoulder. "Wait." It was Nine. She wrapped her arms around Petra, restraining her with a surprising strength.

Petra struggled, tears blinding her.

"Look."

Something was happening to Skinflint Jack. He thrashed in the trap, but he seemed to be melting. Black drained out of him into the ground, leaving behind the bleached whiteness of bone. Petra realized this was a twisted realization of the alchemist's White Stag. Hooves lashed into the sky, antlers twisted, and Jack's body sank below the permeable ground, as if sucked in by quicksand. Only the fractured bits of the skull remained, tangled in the trap.

Silence settled over the mountain once again, punctuated by the whimper of a wolf and Owen's sobbing.

Petra sucked in her breath. "Is it done?"

"He's gone." Nine said it with certainty, twisting to look at the hoodoo. "He's in the mountain now."

The sun peeked up over the horizon, and the light changed subtly, from violet to pink.

Petra broke free to look over the edge for Gabe. Owen was standing there, stupidly staring down, and cradling his bloody hand in the crook of his elbow. His eyes were glazed, and it sure looked as if he'd pitch over at any moment.

She grabbed his shoulder and shook him. "Help me get him," she ordered savagely.

Owen nodded. She shoved a rope into his good hand and Nine's, tied some knots into it. She looped it around the base of the hoodoo, mindful not to disturb the marks on the face or the circle, swearing the whole time.

Gabe had to be okay. He had to be. She would not let him be otherwise.

She made a quick rappel down this steep side of the mountain. She hadn't bothered with constructing any kind of a safety harness. It didn't matter. If Gabe was dead, none of this mattered.

She bounced down nearly a hundred feet to the ledge, where Gabe lay motionless. Scrub skeletons of sage clung to the crevasses splitting the rock.

She startled something in the gloom—a white-feathered eagle took wing from the scrub, sailing into the valley like a kite.

Crouching over him, she gently touched his face. "Gabe."

He didn't move. She stripped off her glove and checked for a pulse. There was one there, and she rejoiced. She pulled back an eyelid and winced. One was normal, if dilated, but the other eye was so black she couldn't see the iris, rimmed in red. She knew he had to have a serious head or spine injury. Moving him could kill him. But leaving him here would be worse.

She looped the rope under his arms, trying to be gentle. He wasn't conscious to protest, floppy and rubbery. She tightened the rope under his arms until her stomach turned. She didn't want to exacerbate the damage to any broken ribs, but if he slid out of the crude rigging, he would be dead beyond any retrieval.

"Pull!" she yelled up to Nine and Owen.

They pulled, hand over hand, the limp body rising up the mountain face as Petra watched. She winced each time Gabe's body bounced against a rock or the wall. He spun like a doll, but she couldn't look away.

Finally, they succeeded in hauling him up over the rim. He vanished from her sight as Nine and Owen reeled him in. The rope came down again, and they hauled Petra back up. The slippery nylon rope cut into her hands in deep slashes.

She scrambled over the lip and crawled to Gabe. Sig sat beside him, washing his face. Behind him, the wolves whined.

"He's in a bad way," Owen said.

"We've got to get him help. Get him off this mountain to civilization." Petra turned on her heel. "The nearest road is five miles as the crow flies, that way."

"Let's get him down," Nine agreed.

"What about . . . this?" Owen gestured to the ritual remnants on the peak. Petra squinted at it. The sun had crept higher, over the hoodoo. The sun seemed to pause perfectly there, balanced.

"I don't know anything about magic, but I think this is finished." To make sure, she dug the compass out of Gabe's pocket. She scraped some blood from her scratched hands into it. The blood boiled inside, tiny droplets clustering where the wolves stood. The deep groove was saturated with the mountain's magic.

She extended it toward the circle, taking a deep breath and stepping inside. She would not forgive herself if she unwittingly left some kind of magical trap behind for a tourist to stumble into.

Nothing happened. The compass continued beating its bloody pulse, not altering in the slightest as she approached the skull.

She pocketed the compass and lifted the skull. The antlers were broken off, and it looked like little more than a decorative piece of southwestern kitsch now. The Star of Antimony was shattered beneath it, splintered on the ground. The trap was closed and folded in on itself, harmless, as she'd suspected. The gold was gone. Maybe that was the price of doing business.

"Let's go," she said. She stepped away from the scarred circle in the snow, where all that terrible magic had spilled and faded.

Climbing down the mountain was slow going. Petra bound up Owen's hand as best she could— he'd lost the ring and pinky fingers of his right hand. He'd live. She dug a tarp out of the packs, and they used it as a kind of stretcher for Gabe. Petra carried the head and Nine the feet. Owen supported the middle, while Sig and the wolves rushed ahead. It took hours to take the trail down the mountain in the growing morning light.

When they got to the bottom, they moved Gabe's body to the sled she'd made from the hood of the old snow machine. It was too short, and she added the hood of the second beneath his body, held together at the hinges with bits of rope. She'd pitched all the gear on the ground. None of the rest of this mattered.

"See if you can get a signal." She tossed her cell phone to Owen. She'd pulled the battery before they'd begun their journey to keep Owen from tracking them, and there was still some juice left in it, thankfully. She didn't care if the cops descended on them and hauled them away to jail, as long as somebody with some medical know-how got there for Gabe.

"No good," Owen said, shaking his head.

"Do you think there's anybody out looking for you?" she demanded as she tied off her knots.

"Probably not," Owen admitted. "Being sheriff has the privilege of being able to disappear at will."

Petra unwound a long length of rope and tied one end around her waist. "Come here. We're gonna drag this sled to civilization."

But the wolves had another idea. After a consultation with Nine, they nosed Petra aside. Each wolf picked up a length of rope. Sig got in front and picked up a piece.

All eyes turned toward Petra, expectantly.

"Uh. Thataway. Mush!" She pointed to the east.

Wolf legs churned in the powder, and the sled began to move. It moved slowly at first, in a walking pace, and then Petra had to run to keep up.

Her breath burned in her throat as they ran. Petra chucked her heavy pack and did her best to keep up. Owen lagged behind. Nine was nearly as fast as the wolves. But Sig set the pace, moving quickly, but not so fast as to lose the humans.

They'd been moving for nearly an hour when Owen announced: "I got a signal."

The procession stopped and waited for him to catch up. Petra sat down on the snow, panting, next to Gabe. He was still breathing, unevenly. She didn't feel the cold anymore, and had the urge to strip off her coat.

"The rangers are coming," he said. "They said to hold position at these coordinates."

"How long?" Petra demanded.

"They've got the helo. It'll be fifteen, twenty minutes. They're already looking for you."

Petra knelt beside Gabe. She had no idea if he could hear her or not. "Hang on. Help's coming."

She only hoped it wouldn't be too late.

"THE MEN WILL be here soon."

Nine knelt in the snow among the wolves. They'd dropped the rope and come to stare at her with curiosity. With wariness. Did they not know that she was still one of them?

She reached her hand out, willing it to change. The Stag was gone. It was time to go home, to the new range, with the pack. She concentrated until tears leaked from her eyes, but she couldn't make the change come.

Ghost stared at her with sympathy and more than a bit of pity.

What to do now? She began to pull her gloves up, to prepare to follow the wolves. She couldn't bring herself to transform now, but maybe it would happen in a few hours, a day or two. And all would be right again.

Ghost continued to stare. He stepped up to her, whined, and licked her face.

Her lip quivered. She knew that she couldn't keep up with them, with her family.

"Don't leave me," she said. "Please don't leave me."

She reached out, her fingers brushing his ruff, but he shied away. Could they smell the corpse-dust on her, the spell of Harming that she'd cast on the mountain? It had been a reflexive impulse, as instinctive as spitting.

Didn't they remember? Had they forgotten what it was like to walk on two legs and cast magic in fire and dust? Would they shun her and leave her to . . . To what? Nine had not been alone in over a century.

A black speck approached in the sky, with a humming noise. That noise grew to a tremendous, mechanical roar as the machine swept down to the snowfield. The blades on the top stirred up snow in veils.

The pack turned to run. They ran, north and west, to the mountain and the new territory.

Nine ran after them, away from the terrible noise. She ran as hard and as fast as she could, fists pumping and breath steaming, her too-long hair obscuring her vision.

But the wolves were too fast. One paused to look back at her. The pup she'd saved.

Men tackled her and took her down to the snow.

She watched, crying, as the wolves retreated into the wilderness. In that moment, she knew what had happened. The pack had rejected humanity, had rejected magic. They simply wanted to live as they were, one with the world, unencumbered by that poison. She remembered it, and would be forgotten.

She was alone.

CHAPTER 20

The Dream of Wings

You gonna tell me what happened?"

Petra sat in the hospital hallway, her head on her knees. Her bandaged hands dangled in space. She felt oddly weightless, suspended in this strange interstitial place where things always fell apart.

Mike Hollander sat down beside her, offered her a cup of coffee. She took it gratefully, drank it greedily.

"Starting at the beginning? Well, I got married."

"So I hear. Congrats. I owe you a waffle iron or something."

"Heh. I wonder if Bear's Gas 'n Go has a registry."

"Good thing that your husband's insurance has

kicked in. Dunno much about your judgment in anything else, but your timing is impeccable."

"Thanks for coming to get us," she said.

"Anytime. You keep my job interesting." He took a swig of his coffee. His face was still beat to hell, and she could see bandages beyond the collar of his shirt. She was pretty sure he wasn't supposed to be back at work with a busted rib, but chiding him about being Superman had never gained her any traction. "So. The sheriff says you don't have to talk to me. That that whole thing was part of a local investigation."

"Oh, really?" Nice of him to get them off the hook. Petra's mouth turned.

"Well. He said that after he'd been tranquilized. Scuttlebutt has it that it took three times the normal amount of Haldol to put that guy into la-la land." Mike poked at his coffee with a stirrer. "You guys went up there after Skinflint Jack, didn't you?"

She was tired of lying. "Yeah. Yeah, we did."

She expected a barrage of arguments about how monumentally stupid that was, but instead he said, quietly: "Did you get him?"

"Yeah. We got him." She glanced sidelong at Mike.

Mike's jaw hardened and he stared into the distance beyond the hallway. "Good."

Her brow wrinkled in surprise, and she was

about to ask him more when a nurse walked down the hallway.

"Ms. Dee?"

"Yes." Petra stood, feeling every bone in her body ache. "How is he?"

The nurse reached out to touch her sleeve, her brown eyes liquid in sympathy. "Does Mr. Manget have any family that can make decisions for him? Or a living will?"

Petra sucked in her breath. "That would be me. I'm his wife."

"Come with me, please."

The nurse led Petra down a green-tiled hallway, to the ICU. Gabe was in a room beside the nurse's station. He lay in a bed with wires and tubes coming out of his arms, mouth, and nose. Petra stepped to his side and took his hand. It was cold and bruised purple.

"I'm Dr. Burnard . . . hello, Ms. Dee."

"Hello, again." Petra looked over the bed at the doctor. "How is he?"

"Not good, I'm afraid." Her fingernails drummed against her clipboard. "He's suffered a collapsed lung, a broken leg and a broken wrist, a fractured pelvis, and a broken vertebrae."

"That sounds . . . manageable?" Painful as fuck, but manageable.

"The primary issue is the head injury. There's a

whole lot of swelling and bleeding, and we need to take the pressure off."

"Why isn't he in surgery?"

"He will be, within hours. The surgeon is hung up on bad roads near Billings." Dr. Burnard took a deep breath. "Forgive me, but I have to ask. It doesn't look good. If we lose brain activity, what would you like for us to do?"

Petra looked down at Gabe, broken and utterly mortal. She was a rational woman. As a rational woman, she had to accept the evidence of science. If Gabe's brain activity disappeared . . . he just wasn't in there. Not anymore.

But. *But.* Her heart clenched. She wasn't ready to let go of him. And damn it, part of the reason they got married was so that he could make these kinds of decisions for her. She hadn't expected the tables to be turned. She'd expected to be lying to cops and judges, not uttering an irrevocable truth to a doctor. She pressed her hand over her mouth.

"Can I have a few minutes with him alone to think about it?"

"Yes. Absolutely. I'll wait for you at the nurse's station."

"Thank you."

The doctor moved from the room, and Petra closed the curtain. She touched Gabe's face and kissed his hand. She laid her head on his shoulder and listened to the mechanical sounds of the machines moving air and fluid through him.

"You are not allowed to die," she told him. "You're just . . . not. I won't let you."

Deep in his chest, she thought she heard something move. Something that sounded like wings fluttering.

She lifted her head to look at him. "Yes. You have to fight this," she whispered at him furiously. "You may believe that you're entirely ordinary now, but . . . you're wrong. There's got to still be something left in you that can fight. And you have to."

Her tears tapped down on the blanket, but he didn't respond.

Eventually, there was a knock at the door and Dr. Burnard came in.

"Ms. Dee?"

Petra looked up at her. "I want you to keep him alive. No matter what," she said fiercely.

And she meant it. Her definitions of life and unlife had unraveled in the time she'd spent in Temperance. Sometimes she barely knew what was real or not, under the broad sweep of this western sky. The world was a helluva lot bigger than she ever knew. She'd seen only a small fraction of it, and she'd had to develop a modicum of openness to the idea of the inexplicable.

She asked to stay with Gabe until the surgeon arrived. She was his wife; they couldn't refuse. She set up a chair beside him, dimmed the lights, and pulled the curtains around them to shield them from the views of passersby. When it felt like a warm cocoon, Petra dug into her pocket for her father's wedding gift: the marbles.

She had no idea if there was any juice left in them, if they just represented one round-trip ticket to the spirit world. But it was worth a try. She slipped the yellow cat's-eye marble beneath his pillow and put the other behind her head in the chair. She wrapped her coat around her and closed her eyes. The numbing exhaustion she'd felt crept through her, deepened her breathing.

She hoped that she could fall asleep without the irritating lullaby of his snoring, just this once.

GABRIEL DREAMED OF wings.

At first he dreamed that he was flying. He was soaring above Sepulcher Mountain, feeling the cold sun on his wings and the wind as it slipped up through the hoodoos. He felt untouchable, this high.

Funny. He'd never been able to fly this high, before. He glanced around, expecting to see other ravens.

But there were none. It was just him, soaring. He felt stronger, more powerful, as he skimmed above the clouds. He was beyond the reach of pain, of the earth and all the tangled things that had conspired to keep him there. He drifted along the tatters of a cumulus cloud, feeling the moisture soak through the ribs of his feathers.

His feathers . . . they were white.

As he flew toward the sun, he wished that he could show Petra.

She would find this glorious, all this light and all this sky.

Maybe someday soon.

He closed his eyes and felt the sunshine warm on his back. He felt free. He'd shed the dust of centuries to make this alchemical transformation. He could not have done it without Petra. He wished he could tell her, somehow. Give her a sign.

He glanced down at the valley through which he flew. It looked familiar. Snowcapped mountains lifted in a wall in the sunshine. And there was a terrace carved in that wall, where a woman in white waited with a coyote.

He tucked his wings and dove down, banking hard and lighting on the stone railing of the balcony.

Petra was there, and his heart soared to see her. She wasn't wearing a white wedding dress, as before. She was wearing a white sweater and pants. She squinted at him.

"Gabe?"

He ruffled his feathers and stuck his chest out a bit. "Like the new suit?"

"It's beautiful." She reached out to touch him, to stroke the downy feathers of his neck. He leaned into her hand and squinted past her to the dining room. It was empty, with no furniture or fire in the grate. If she'd used the marbles to get them here, it was likely that magic was disintegrating.

"Why are you a bird now?"

"I think I changed. An alchemical transformation, if you like." He shook out his wings and tucked them in. "It seems getting thrown off a mountain by Skinflint Jack kick-started my spiritual progress." He peered down at Sig, who made a grab for one of his tail feathers. "I see you brought Man's Best Friend along for the ride."

"I think he just goes where I go." An expression of deep worry was in her eyes and mouth as she reached down to pet Sig.

"Things not going so well back at the ranch?"

"No. They're not." She sat down beside him on the balcony, her hands on her lap. "Your earthly body is pretty well fucked up. They're going to do brain surgery on you in a couple hours. Whenever they can get the surgeon out here to start."

"That doesn't sound good." He paced beside her for a few moments and then stopped. "What would you like to do?"

"There's a choice?"

"There's always a choice in things."

"I told them to keep you alive. No matter what."

She looked at him levelly. "And I didn't stop to con-sider if that was what you wanted. Not for one cold minute."

He laughed so hard his tail feathers shook.

"What's so funny?"

He tipped his head. "That's why I love you. You do what you want."

"But what do you want? It seems like you've got one foot halfway through the door to the spirit world." Her lip quivered and her eyes shone. "I mean, you're a bird. Have you moved on, and are you going to find the other Hanged Men, the ravens?"

He reached forward to shush her with his wing. "This isn't about the Hanged Men. This is about you and me."

She took a deep breath. "What do you want to do?"

"Well, it's pretty much a joint decision. I can go back there, try to ride out the surgery, and hope that I'm able use a spoon at the end of it. That's the first road."

"Okay. But I believe that somewhere the idea of marriage—there's something about me wiping soup from your chin in poor health."

"That's kind of you. The other road is that I decide that my transformation is complete. That I go explore the spirit world. I seemed not to wind up in hell, which is a surprise." He looked down at his taloned feet, which were notably not burning.

"And I let you go," she said quietly.

"You don't have to," he said, just as quietly. "You could come with me."

Her brow wrinkled. "How does that work?"

"You. Me. The coyote. We decide to move on together. All three of us take a jump off that balcony . . . change into eagles, and hit the skies."

She drummed her fingers against her lower lip. "I don't know." She looked over the balcony. "Falling off mountains is what got us into trouble in the first place."

She seemed steeped in thought, looking over the edge. "And I'm scared."

"Of this world?"

"No. Of facing cancer in our world. Of losing you."

He brushed a feather across her brow. "You will never lose me. Not if it's within my power."

She smiled, a sad, wan smile.

She climbed up the balcony and stood on the wide railing, holding onto a pillar. She looked down, then back at Sig and then at him.

She inched closer to the edge and took a deep breath.

And then she vanished. She didn't jump over the ledge; she simply faded, like ink dissipating in water.

Gabe looked down. The coyote had disappeared, too.

He sighed and gazed at the horizon.

"Mrs. Manget?"

Petra stirred, sucked in her breath. Bright over-head lights had been turned on, buzzing with fluo-rescence through her sleep-haze.

"The surgeon is here now."

She moved, and the marble behind her collar fell to the floor. She reached down to grab it and had to dodge many pairs of feet as nurses and aides un-hooked wires from Gabe to prepare him for travel to the operating room. The marble rolled to a floor drain and plinked away into darkness. Petra stood up and gazed at Gabe's battered face, knowing how serene he'd been in the otherworld.

She wanted to say to him, *Wait. Don't come back.*

But they whisked him away, leaving her in a bright empty room with disconnected machines. She rubbed her face and stared down at her shoes.

There were no more choices she could make. Gabe would have to decide for himself.

She plodded down the hallway, past the ICU, and gazed at the vending machines. She made a couple of phone calls. One, to the insurance com-pany. And second, to Maria, to check on Sig. Mike had taken Sig to stay with her, and she was cer-tain he was happily asleep on her couch. She knew that she needed to call her father. She procrasti-nated with a couple of candy bars and watching television before dialing the number to the nurs-ing home. She was told that he was out at physical therapy, and she left a message. She didn't want to tell him what happened. Not now. She didn't trust herself not to dissolve into tears. She was holding herself together with what felt like chewing gum and duct tape, and she didn't want to lose her grip.

Maria came to see her, and she disintegrated. Her friend held her while she blubbered and spewed incoherent snot-strings on her shoulder. Petra had never been a good crier—when she did, it was messy. She finally scrubbed her face with a handful of tissues and took a deep breath.

"I'm okay. Really."

"No, you're not. But that's okay."

Once Petra had gotten herself together, they headed up to the patient care floors. She had no idea where Owen was being kept; she sure didn't want to see him, even if he was zoned out on Haldol. But there was one person she did want to see. She paused before Room 211. The door was ajar, and she stuck her head in.

"Hi."

Petra let herself into Nine's room. The young woman was sitting on a bed in a hospital gown, with her arms around her knees.

"How is Gabe?" she asked.

Petra shook her head. "I—I don't know. They're working on him." She felt drained of tears, hollow. She sat down on the bed beside Nine. "How are you?"

Nine stared down at her toes. She wiggled them. "Confused."

"The doctors say that you're well."

She gave a short bark of bitter laughter. "Well. They said I have worms. I have pills for that now."

"They worked for Sig," Petra said. "Look, I know you've got to be afraid. I want you to know that we're not going to abandon you."

She looked up and met Petra's eyes, but didn't say anything.

"There's someone I want for you to meet." She glanced at the door. "This is Maria Yellowrose."

Maria came in, smiling reassuringly. "Hi. I'm a friend of Petra's. And Gabe's."

"And Sig's?"

"And also Sig. He likes my cooking." Maria grinned. "The hospital will be releasing you, and I wanted to see if you might want to come home with me."

Nine looked at her, then back at Petra.

"Maria is the most wonderful person I know," Petra said. "I trust her with my life. And more than that, I trust her with Sig. He's currently taking a nap with Maria's cat."

Nine looked down at her toes. "I appreciate it. Really, I do. But this is all very . . . confusing."

"I can't say that I understand everything about your situation. Or anything, really," Maria admitted. "But I understand the need to have a safe place to gather one's thoughts. I can offer that."

It was a long time before Nine spoke again. "Thank you."

But there was a distant look in her eyes. And Petra had no idea how long she would stay.

Not that there were any guarantees about how long anyone would stay.

Maria had brought Petra a change of clothes, and Petra stubbornly remained at the hospital. She watched television in the floor lobby, paced, and slept in a chair. She received word from Mike that Owen had been taken to another facility. Mike had used air quotes when he said the word "facility." Perhaps Owen'd had enough of unreality, had lost his grip and was refocusing on what was real. In any event, deputies had not come to take her away to jail. So he was honoring his bargain, if only to keep what remained of his own sanity.

She stared down at the golden ring on her finger. She knew that the other ring was sitting in a plastic bag stapled to the foot of Gabe's bed, with the rest of his personal effects. She spun the ring around in her fingers, a loop without beginning and end. Gabe would have something deeply philosophical to say about the nature of the ring's symbolism and the chemical wedding, no doubt. And she looked forward to hearing that.

When he woke up. Not if. When.

After many hours, a man in blue scrubs with a surgeon's mask draped over his neck came to the waiting area.

"Mrs. Manget?"

She didn't correct him. "Yes?"

"Your husband pulled through surgery quite well. We were able to drain the blood that was causing pressure on the brain, and the clot that's sitting on his temple is breaking up."

She pressed her hand over her mouth. "Thank you."

The surgeon held up his hand. "He's not out of the woods yet. That clot was pressing pretty hard on the optic nerve of his left eye. We won't know if it's affected his vision until he wakes up and the swelling goes down."

"Can I see him?"

"Sure. He's back in his room now."

The surgeon led Petra back to the ICU. He left her to go find some paperwork, and she slipped to Gabe's bedside.

He looked like hell. His head had been shaved and the bruises stood out in sharp relief over his skull. She saw no trace of stitches on his temple, just a bandage, and wondered if they had been able to drain off the fluid with a syringe. She gingerly pressed the back of her hand to his cheek.

"Hello, love."

He didn't speak. But she knew, deep down, that he was in there. She glanced at the bandages covering his chest and the plastic tubing coming out of his nose and mouth, when something flickered at the edge of her vision.

The bruise on his chest. It had taken on an odd pattern. She tipped her head to look at it more closely. Something moved beneath his skin. It seemed to seethe softly, with the outline of a feather.

She leaned forward and kissed him on the cheek. Her heart soared.

CHAPTER 21

Snow Madness

Snow madness.

That's what they said, anyway, murmured behind hands and closed doors.

Owen was certain there was something more official-sounding on his chart. "Transient dissociative state." "PTSD." "Trauma-induced psychosis." Likely something like that.

But it was extremely unhelpful that they put him in a white room to recover. It was so white that he could see white behind his eyelids. He was stuck facing a white popcorn ceiling that looked an awful lot like snow, especially when he focused on one spot and let his vision get sparkly around the edges. Maybe nobody quite thought this through, from a treatment standpoint.

It wasn't like Owen was in much of a position to argue, anyway. They'd parked him in a restraint chair that was identical to the ones in his jail, where they were known as "Hannibal Lector chairs." It was an orange plastic chair covered in seat-belt straps, but the gimmick was that the seat and back were tipped back at an angle. It was nearly impossible to climb out of the chair, and an orderly or deputy could hold a person in it with one hand.

Aside from being immobilized in the chair, he was getting a whole lot of meds. Some of them, he guessed, were painkillers. He'd lost two fingers on his right hand. The hospital hadn't been able to do much about that. The fingers were long gone. They just sewed the skin over, like sealing an envelope, with black stitches. He could see it if he lifted his hand up at the wrist and craned his neck down. He had frostbite. His ears burned, which could have been a good sign. His feet were covered in thick socks. He hadn't seen those yet. But if they looked anything like his fingertips, they were likely mottled and blistered. He was lucky he hadn't lost more digits.

There were other meds, too, that they gave him. Someone came by with a paper cup twice a day with pills and checked his mouth to make sure he'd swallowed them. The pills made him fuzzy-headed. But he noticed that Anna didn't come around at all after he started taking them. She'd been very indistinct the first day, and then faded away, like an image on a shaken Etch-A-Sketch.

He suspected that he was on video camera. He didn't call out after her. He didn't take any more swings at the staff. A psychiatrist came by once a day to peer in on him and scribble notes. The shrink asked very easy questions, the same ones every day after they moved him around, dressed him, fed him, and cleaned him up:

"What's your name?"

"What year is it?"

"Are you and I alone in this room?"

"Do you remember anything about what happened to you?"

He answered the first two truthfully, and told them what they wanted to hear for the third. They were alone. No voices. No one was out to get him. He remembered little of what happened in the backcountry, just following up on a current investigation. He just remembered that it was cold and he'd gotten into it with a bear. He liked the story about the bear. People could perceive crazy as weakness. But if he survived a fight with a bear, well, hell. That was building a legend of crazy.

Owen knew how this worked. Eventually they'd have to let him up. They'd give him a bed, let him walk around. If he behaved himself, he'd be out soon with a referral to a shrink and a bottle full of pills.

After a while his mother came to see him. She walked stiffly through the metal door. Her platinum hair was an impeccable helmet, and she wore heels that clicked on the tile. Her long leather coat looked like it had just gotten back from the dry cleaners, and he smelled a puff of Dior when she got close.

Owen was sitting on the floor, his back to the wall, when she arrived. Someone had given him a pad of paper and a fat crayon to draw with. He knew that was a test, to see if he'd scribble pictures of angry monsters. He drew benign pictures of deer on a mountain, grazing, beneath a smiling sun. All the deer had antlers.

"Mother."

"Owen." She bent down to squint at him. She took his chin in her hand and turned his head right and left, assessing God-knew-what in his eyes. She didn't sit on the floor or let any bit of her clothing touch the inside of the cell. Finally, she released him and straightened, apparently satisfied. "Are you ready to go home?"

"Yes."

"Good. Get yourself together. You have work to do."

She checked him out. They gave him back his clothes in a paper bag, just like how the jail stored inmates' clothes. Unlike jail, he got three bottles of pills and a list of instructions. He shoved them into his coat pocket and followed his mother to her spotlessly black BMW SUV. He never knew how she managed that, with winter slush. Dirt never stuck to it.

Once ensconced in the silence of the car and settled in the heated leather seats, Owen spoke. "Thanks for picking me up."

"Of course." She punched the engine and pulled out onto the highway. The radio was on, a low volume, playing something atmospheric and soothing. Space music.

"You don't have to do that on my account." He nodded at the radio. "I'm not crazy."

She turned it off. "Whatever happened on the mountain . . ."

"Let's not talk about it, okay?" He looked out the window, at the miles flashing by. He changed the subject. "Did you have Sal's funeral?"

"Not yet. It's Thursday. I thought it was important for you to be there. It is, in some respects, the end of an era in Temperance. It would be good for you to be seen there, in control."

Owen smirked. "In control?"

"Of the Rutherford estate." She sighed, and he could tell she wasn't happy about it.

He had to agree. They discussed the arrangements she'd made with the funeral parlor. "We'll do a processional through town to the graveyard. You'll be in the lead, in a marked car. The ground's too frozen to put him in; they'll just keep him in the vault until we get a good thaw."

"All right." He glanced down at his hand.

"Do you want gloves?"

"No. I don't think so."

"Good thought. It would make more of an impression on folks. Also . . ." She stared straight ahead, at the road unfurling before them. "The other bodies your deputies found. Do you have any idea what you want to do with them?"

"Hm." He hadn't given any thought to that. "I suppose . . . we could just rebury them at the ranch, if no one comes forward to claim them. No pomp and circumstance. That would make the most sense."

"I agree. The sooner we're done with this unpleasant business, the better."

He expected her to bring him to his house at the county seat. Instead, she dropped him off at Sal's house. It took him three tries to work the key on the door. Missing a good chunk of his right hand was going to really screw with his life. He had no idea how he could shoot with it. He guessed he'd have to train himself to use his left hand.

His mother had been here. He could tell. Paperwork about disability payments from work was stacked neatly on the coffee table, with fluorescent plastic tabs where he needed to sign and stamped envelopes ready to go. There were clean towels in

the bathroom and a freshly stocked refrigerator
with vegetables and fruit. And she'd even stripped
the bed and had it redressed in new, crisp-white
linens that smelled exactly like summer sunshine.
There were candles placed throughout the house,
and a half-burned bundle of sage. She'd been here,
doing odd things. He saw that over the window-
sills and on top of the door lintels, lines of salt were
drawn. The whole space smelled like rosemary.
Curtains had been hung, now drawn back to let
the light in. And a small mirror had been placed at
every window facing the back field.

He was touched, even if she'd gone overboard on
the Feng Shui. His mother rarely interfered with his
life. She must have been really worried . . . worried
enough to do his laundry for him. He showered,
mindful to keep his right hand out of the stinging
water. His frostbitten hands and feet looked better
than he expected—a rosy shade of lavender. He
clumsily dressed in fresh clothes, grumbling at his
socks and his belt.

He wanted nothing more than to take a handful of painkillers, fall into that luxurious bed, and
sleep for a week. But there was something he had
to do first.

He put on his coat and boots. He couldn't fit his
swollen right hand in his gloves, so he made do
with the oversized pink rubber dish gloves from
under the kitchen sink that Sal's maid must have

used. They were lined with flannel, and he figured they'd keep the worst of the muck out of his
fresh stitches. He found his flashlight, grabbed
some extra batteries, and headed for the garage.
He chucked a ladder into the back of Sal's pickup.
He found a box of signal flares, a bag of salt, and a
crowbar, and threw those in the back.

He drove the truck down to the tree, leaving
thick tracks in the snow. Afternoon sun had begun
to beat down, and old tracks in the area from the
crime scene investigation had frozen to ice. He
stopped just before where he knew the door in the
ground was.

God damn it. This place had a hold on him. His
throat burned with thirst to know what this place
was about. He needed to know.

He clumsily hauled the bag of salt out of the
truck and sprinkled salt on the turf. The salt crackled through the snow and ice, and he was able to
lift the door in the ground easily with the crowbar. His hand ached as he lowered the ladder into
the darkness, working it until he was certain he'd
placed it on a solid footing. He dropped the box
of signal flares down, and the cardboard box ex-
ploded, flares scattering in every direction.

With his flashlight tucked into his pocket, he
climbed down. The going was slow; he couldn't
feel his feet in some places, and he didn't want to
fall. There would be some irony if he fell from the

ladder and froze to death in the exact same spot Sal's body had found. But he made his way to the floor of the chamber, and shone his light around.

It was exactly as he'd left it: the dark branches and the smell of fresh sawdust, from where the bodies had been cut. There was no smell of death lingering here. With his flashlight to guide him, he picked up the flares and stuffed them in his pockets, up his sleeves, in the neck of his shirt and the tops of his boots. He would not be left without light again.

His flashlight easily picked out the chalk marks he'd left on the walls in his last venture down here. He wound his way back to the underground river, lighting and dropping sizzling flares as he went. To what Gabriel had called the Mermaid's domain.

The river stretched out before him, black and whispering, churning around the skeletons of old bones. Cool rain wrapped over his face in a veil. His flashlight beam swept over the water, bouncing up off the opaque surface and glancing off the stone walls.

"I have something that belongs to you," he said into the dark water.

He reached into his pocket and pulled out the giant milky pearl with his clumsy rubber glove. He cast it into the water, where it landed with a soft *plink*.

Mist swirled above the surface. Owen instinctively took a step back and reached for his gun. But his aching hand only snagged air. They hadn't given him his gun back.

The mist closed and cleared around an image: a birdcage. It seemed to be a large cage, as big as a washing machine. Behind the bars paced a white bird—an eagle, he realized.

He didn't know what it meant, but he felt that it was something profound.

"Thank you," he whispered, feeling as if he'd been forgiven.

And he retreated.

His knew not to push his luck. The mysteries of this place would reveal themselves to him. He just had to be patient.

"Good job, Owen," a voice reassured him, whispering in his ear.

Anna's voice.

"You're back," he said, unsurprised. He was a bit disappointed, if he was honest with himself. Part of him wanted to believe that he was just batshit, that the meds would erase all the magic and ghosts and otherworldly presences on the ranch. Maybe he could sell the land and go back to his desk and run a fiefdom like a proper sheriff.

But he couldn't unsee what he'd seen. Through the fuzz in the back of his brain, he remembered these things. And he wanted more. He wanted to know the full depth and breadth of this world that had been revealed to him.

"I never left." She sounded accusing. "You just stopped listening."

"I'm sorry," he said.

She huffed. "You made up with the Mermaid."

"I hope so?"

"You know what you need to do, now."

His brow wrinkled. "I'm not sure what she . . ."

Anna leaned close to his ear and whispered.

And he understood now, what the Mermaid asked of him. He would deliver.

"I WANT TO show you something."

Nine sat on a bed in a warm bedroom, wrapped in quilts. She had explored it relentlessly, pawing through the glass bottles under the bed, the collection of feathers stuck in the frame of the mirror, the polished river rocks and bits of obsidian lined up on the windowsill. Pages of old books had been framed and placed on the walls. They were torn from a catalog of birds, Maria had said. They were meticulously inked and painted, and seemed almost real. Nine recognized herons and sparrows and blackbirds, perched in blooming branches.

She had spent hours in front of the mirror, peering at her reflection. She couldn't remember much of what she had looked like as a child—she'd only seen glimpses of her reflection in water. The body she wore now was shorter than Maria, muscular, with copper skin and curiously grey hair. Her eyes were dark and reminded her of her mother's, and her long-fingered hands reminded her of her father. Since she'd come indoors, her coarse hair had smoothed and the angles of her face seemed to soften more every day.

There was a dresser and a closet full of clothes here. Nine had found an old pair of jeans with wide legs that fit her and a poncho with fringe that was irresistible to play with. Maria had seen her wearing them and choked up. Nine was afraid she'd done something wrong, but Maria had given her a hug and told her that she just hadn't seen those clothes worn in a very long time.

But this place was warm. There was food. Very exotic things, which she had never tasted before: things called chocolate and pasta and rice. Nine had a special affection for the chocolate that Maria kept in a jar in the kitchen. She dipped in to steal a piece whenever she slipped through the kitchen. If Maria minded, she never said.

At night, Nine dreamed of running with the rest of the wolves. She'd awake in a warm bed with a pillow wet with tears.

And she had a roommate. The cat.

Pearl sat at the foot of the bed, watching Nine. She didn't blink, just stared. Nine had woken in the middle of the night to find the cat sitting on the bed, staring at her, eyes shining. Cats, she knew, could always see magic. She wondered how much this cat saw.

Wrapped in quilts, Nine extended a hand to the small grey and white cat. The cat sniffed at her hand but made no further moves.

That was good enough for now, Nine decided. She had, after all, invaded this cat's territory. Nine was used to being the omega. She could play omega to this cat.

Maria had come to the doorway of the bedroom, watching Nine and the cat. "There's something I'd like to show you."

She was wearing a coat and boots. Nine put on a pair of Maria's boots and one of her coats and followed her out of the house to a windswept field behind the house. They followed a well-worn path in the beaten-down snow.

"Where are we going?" Nine asked.

"It's called the Eye of the World."

In the center of the field lay a pool, shiny as an obsidian mirror. It was surrounded by a large ring of stones. Nine placed her hand on one of the stones. This place radiated magic, calm and tranquil.

"It's beautiful."

"There's supposed to be a door into the spirit world from here," Maria said, the winter wind pulling her hair free of its braids. "I've never seen it, but I believe it's there."

Nine walked to the edge of the pool and peered in. Clouds and sky, still and perfect, were reflected on the surface. And where her face should have been, Nine saw the outline of a wolf, with pointed ears and a grey ruff.

She reached out, skimming her hand over the cold water, and smiled.

A COLD WINTER night seemed like the right time to go to church.

To the Compostela, that was.

The stars were bright overhead; Orion could even be seen dancing through the streetlight outside the bar. All the parking spots on the street were full; Gabe and Petra had to walk a half block to the door.

It was the first time they'd been out since Gabe had been sprung from the hospital. Petra was glad to have him home; the small futon felt too big without him, even with Sig sprawling on the covers.

He was home, but not unchanged. She knew that he'd lost much of the sight in one eye, and he moved much more slowly, with a cane. Some of his hair had begun to grow back, but he still groused about the winter drafts, his hat pushed low over his brow. But she saw improvement each day in how far he walked through the fields, and heard his lungs breathe steadier each night. When he walked in the field behind the trailer, she noticed that he no longer bothered to try to court the ravens with cat food and shiny things.

They shouldered through the bar, finding a booth hewn of church pews to sit at near the back. The place was full of candlelight and the ring of glassware. After they were seated, their drinks arrived, unbidden, and Petra perused the menu.

She lifted her glass. "To getting better." Her treatment started next week. She was nervous, but guardedly optimistic.

"To getting better." Gabe clinked her glass with his own. "And to falling off mountains and successful chemo."

She took a drink of the sweet, cidery ale and smiled. "This will likely be my last one of these for a while." She dreaded it and at the same time wanted to get it over with. She'd put it off for as long as she could, using the excuse that she had to tie up loose ends at work, until Gabe had insisted that she begin. "Rocks can wait," he said then.

"Then you should enjoy that drink," he said now.

Petra glanced surreptitiously around. There were no more flyers posted with Gabe's likeness on them, and no uniformed deputies had appeared on her doorstep. She'd seen a picture on the front page of the paper about Sal Rutherford's funeral. Owen had been standing front and center, in uniform, looking much more stoic than he had on the mountainside. If the man was up to public appearances, presumably he was back to his regular duties.

"Looks like y'all have seen better days."

It was the bartender. He'd drifted by their table, nonchalantly scribbling on an order pad.

Gabe tipped his hat. "There have been better days. Anything new here?"

The bartender shrugged. "Big gossip has been about Sal Rutherford's funeral."

"Did you go?"

"I hung around the fringes. Lots of pretty talk about an ugly guy." He shrugged.

"Well. Sal was never charming," Petra murmured.

"We all have our dark sides, I guess," Gabe said, taking a swig of his beer.

"Yeah. And sometimes, the darkness finds us."

The bartender moved away, humming something that sounded suspiciously like "The Devil Inside."

HE SUSPECTED.

But he needed to see it for himself.

Gabe drove Petra's Bronco across the field. A thaw had come early, making the field mushy and thick with slush. As it evaporated, a thick mist clung to the earth. He wheeled the truck through the bumps and ruts. His own inner compass showed him where he needed to go.

The Lunaria.

It was dangerous going back to Sal's land, he knew. Owen had not approached either him or Petra since they'd emerged from the backcountry. It had been six weeks, and no one had seen or heard much at all from the sheriff. Gabe was hoping he could drive in and drive out, beneath Owen's notice.

He stopped before the remains of the tree and shut off the engine. Popping open the truck door, he gingerly let himself out. He walked with a cane that was frustratingly slippery in the mush. The sight in his left eye was gone permanently, they'd told him. When he looked at the eye in the rearview mirror, it looked dead to him. But he was alive.

He stumped over to the site of the tree.

He didn't expect much. The burned-out hulk of it had grown soft and begun to rot, the flesh soft underneath his palm.

But it lived. The sapling tree, the one that had been given life, had grown. It had grown at least two feet since the last time Gabe had seen it. It was nearly as tall as he stood now, empty of leaves. But the wood was supple and smooth. It was growing.

And that was what he suspected had happened to him.

Gabe looked up. A white shadow dropped from the grey sky and landed on the dead tree.

A white eagle. It ruffled its feathers, gazing at Gabe with dark eyes.

He sucked in his breath. It was the bird from his dreams. In alchemy, it was paired with the lion, for transformation.

He held out his arm. It lit on it with massive talons that dug painfully through the leather skin of his coat.

"Hello, Gabriel."

Gabe turned, and the eagle took wing.

"Hello, Owen. It's good to see you."

The sheriff seemed as if he'd gotten his shit together. His hair was combed. He looked clean and reasonably present. Even his boot laces were tied. His right hand was wrapped in a leather glove with only two fingers. Looked custom-made.

"I was hoping to catch you here." Owen stood beside him to regard the tree. "Well, more than hoping. I've got a motion sensor back at the road that you tripped."

"Ah. So, you've moved in?"

"Seemed like the thing to do."

"I saw in the paper that Sal was buried."

"Yeah. Haven't seen so many flowers in one place since ever." Owen gave a small shudder. "I also wanted you to know, I reburied the rest of the men that we found here."

Gabe blew out his breath. "Thank you."

Owen gestured to a line of chunky, frost-heaved earth about fifty yards west. "Backhoe had a helluva time getting through there. But we got a sunny day, and that helped. Didn't know who was who, or what should be done about markers . . ."

"That's enough. I'm sure they'd appreciate the burial." Anything would be better than spending years in the back of a coroner's freezer, awaiting identification.

"I heard that you made a decent recovery."

"Can't complain. Wouldn't do any good, if I did."

"Glad to hear it." Silver metal flashed in Owen's hand, and a handcuff clicked in place around Gabe's wrist.

Gabe stared down at the bracelet. "What's this?"

"You're coming with me."

"I can't do that."

Fast as a snake, Gabe reached out for Owen's wrist and wrenched it down, hard. The bracelet of the handcuffs spun and glittered in the overcast light, popping free of Owen's grip.

Funny how all that old Pinkerton training came back. One of his instructors had been a magician, a man who went on later to train Houdini.

"Goddamn it," Owen swore, reaching for his gun. Gabe recognized it immediately—it was one of Sal's favorites, a Smith & Wesson .357 with ornamental silver stocks.

Gabe swung back with the hand encased with

the handcuff, hit Owen squarely across the jaw. A
bright line of red tore across Owen's face, and he
reeled back.

Gabe limped toward the truck, reaching under
his coat for his gun. He got exactly two yards
before he was tackled from behind and tasted dirt.
He struggled to get his gun free of the holster,
pressed between the ground and his ribs, the ache
in his lungs blossoming fire up his throat. Blood
speckled the cold slush.

"You aren't going anywhere," Owen panted,
working his arm around Gabe's neck. He shoved
his knee in Gabe's back and began to choke him.

Gabe's vision dimmed, but he smelled leather.
Fresh, new leather. He turned his head and bit down
on that soft kidskin, on Owen's wounded hand.

Owen howled, but Gabe didn't let go. Owen's
grip loosened enough for Gabe to strike him in the
nose with the back of his head. He crawled out from
under the sheriff, clawing forward on the ground.

His fingers knew this land, knew the trapdoor
in the dark. He grabbed the ring that opened the
door, hauled up with all his might. The door in the
sod opened.

Gabe launched himself into the darkness. Out
of habit, he expected the tree to catch him. But the
tree was dead, and he slammed into a static tangle
of frozen roots, clawing at them to keep from falling directly on his ass. The icy tendrils shattered

under his boots, sending him falling down to the bottom of the chamber in a hail of splinters. He landed on his wounded leg, pain jarring up and down his spine.

"You won't get away from me."

Owen's silhouette loomed in the opening of the trapdoor.

Gabe drew his pistol and fired. Owen ducked out of the way. Dirt spewed back at him, and muzzle-flash illuminated the chamber below the tree.

It had been hacked to pieces. With his good eye, he could see where the roots had been sawed away, where the Hanged Men had been taken from their slumber. There was no liquid sunshine here, just sawdust and a rusty stain on the floor where Sal's body had once been. He felt it in his aching bones. The tree was gone. But more than that . . . malevolent things had begun to creep into the space it occupied. Shadows slithered through the ruins of the tree, scuttling and chattering.

A lump rising in his throat, Gabe turned to stump off down the dark passageway. Once upon a time, this had been his world. No longer. This place, his kingdom, was dead. Something new was on its way to take his place.

The lurid red light of a signal flare caught and sizzled behind him, stirring shadows. Owen was coming.

Gabe fled into the dark beyond.

Acknowledgments

Many thanks to my amazing editor, Rebecca Lucash. I appreciate all the support and wonderful opportunities. Thank you for the chance to get Petra and Sig out for a romp in the snow!

Much gratitude to my wonderful agent, Becca Stumpf, for championing my work all throughout my career.

Thank you to Caro Perny, for all her magical publicity super powers.

Thanks to my dad for the long discussion about melting antimony. I knew you'd know, even though I had no idea what I didn't know.

Thank you to Marcella Burnard for the last minute reading and listening to my never-ending story angst.

Thanks to my brother, Matt, King of the Dungeon Masters, for rolling the twenty-sided die and giving me a fresh read.

And gratitude to Jason, who knows how to argue the finer points of frostbite and head trauma. You make sure that I don't beat my characters up beyond retrieval. Unless I meant to do that (which happens often enough).